LAST TRAIN

A novel by Perry Kincaid

Shadow Max
Publishing

For my grandfathers.

LAST TRAIN

1

The train rocked, waking him from a restless sleep.

He blinked several times, his vision adjusting to his surroundings. Children pressed their faced against windows, yanking at their mother's arms to point at the wonders outside. A gray, lifeless light filtered into the train car highlighting small molecules of dust slowly making their way through the air. He looked out to see the snow topped mountains. He rubbed his calloused hands together, his palms sounding like sandpaper. He brought his hands to his mouth and breathed warm air into them trying to keep warm. His joints ached. He snorted. Something always hurt these days.

"Sir? Do you need a blanket?"

He studied the attendant for a moment. Brunette hair fell over her slender shoulders, a smile beaming from her round face.

"No," he said, clearing his throat. "I'm fine."

The man rolled his flannel shirt over his weathered hands and leaned back. He pulled a letter from his pocket, tracing his fingers across Malissa's name. The letter had arrived two days ago. He had been chopping wood on his day off, and the letter carrier surprised him. Rarely did he receive mail. He had dropped the axe and tore into the envelope, expecting the worst.

After reading the letter, he sat on a tree stump in the cool mountain air for a long moment, the paper still in his hands as he pondered the logistics of making the trip back home. The next day at work, he told his boss, Chad Murdock, he'd have to take an extended vacation. Chad didn't mind.

He slid a wrinkled hand through his graying hair and leaned against the window, feeling the chill from outside. June and still cool. He shook his head, thinking of his youth spent in a hotter and more humid climate.

For the first time since he could remember, he had trouble sitting still.

If he had flown, he would have reached his destination a lot faster. He leaned his head back in the seat, thought, *Yeah, if I had flown.*

He hadn't flown in nearly forty years. And back then it wasn't for reasons he enjoyed.

He tried to nap but instead listened to the children point out everything the train passed. One boy continued to ask his mother if she could climb every rock, hill or mountain they passed. He grinned as his mother provided answers. Elk mingled near a cluster of trees, prompting excitement from the children. Passengers pointed and raised cameras in unison to snap a picture of the wildlife.

He closed his eyes and enjoyed the sound of their delight, the sound only the young could produce at the start of a fresh journey.

*****

The sun glistened. A light breeze brushed away the sticky Georgia humidity for a moment. It didn't last. The black robes magnified the heat, and students packing into the tight seats only made it worse. Samuel Wrightman felt each breath behind him, every laugh at his sides. He stared into the cloudless sky.

Spending the summer working at the Wrightman General Store—knowing it would not end with the first school bell in the fall—made his stomach turn.

"And now we are on the cusp of greatness. We are on the forefront of tomorrow. Greatness is waiting for us to grasp it. All we have to do is reach out. Perseverance will pay off."

Some of Joe Davis' speech made sense. After being named the valedictorian, Samuel's best friend seemed nervous about his speech, biting his nails beforehand and claiming to have stayed up all night. He even said he thought about winging it.

Samuel shook his head. Maybe he should have …

"And now, my classmates, my friends, we are taking the next step in our lives together," Joe smiled, raising his hands. "The world better watch out. The Class of forty-one is coming."

The crowd erupted into a chorus of cheers. Caps flew into the air. Samuel squinted, watching the caps spin and fall to the ground. A drop of sweat rolled down his cheek. He took a deep breath. Gary Burns embraced him, an unconvincing grin on his pudgy face. He spoke about their classes together, how he would miss chemistry and the chance to stare at Christy Whitlock during class. Samuel smiled and nodded. He hadn't spoken to Gary in months.

Samuel watched Gary weave through the crowd, embracing more familiar strangers, offering more weightless smiles. He shook his head. There is only one person I want to see, he thought, his heart beating a little faster.

"Remember today, son," his father had said that morning. "Other than a handful, you'll never see these people again."

Trying to enjoy the moment, he strolled through the cheering crowd of students. He laughed at the stories, and smiled at his classmates. But he was looking for her.

"Kept your cap, Sammy?"

Samuel turned around to see Annie Ruth Taylor, brown hair blowing into bouncing curls around her ears. She gazed at him, her eyes widening as they looked at each other. For a moment, they stared at one another, graduates crossing between and around them. Laughter boomed as more families entered the field to celebrate. There was so much he wanted to say to her, about how his life had forever changed when she stepped into it.

But the words didn't come.

"Oh," he finally said, blood rushing to his face as he touched his cap. Amazing, she still had the ability to make him blush. "It's good to see you."

She took the hat from him and kissed him on the cheek. "Happy graduation."

"You, too."

"Ready to get out of this gown."

She cocked her head. "My, my, Sammy," she whispered, glancing around. "That's not like you."

Samuel smirked. "Come on. Let's go find my parents. They'll want to take a picture."

"Sounds good." Her eyebrows raised. "We are hanging out later, right?"

"I wouldn't miss it."

He winked, and they walked away together, the rest of the crowd slipping by unnoticed, unheard.

*****

The car bounced. Samuel hit his forehead on the glass.

"I thought Jerry fixed this road." His father loomed over the steering wheel, his massive shoulders slumping as the car drifted to the left. Sweat lines soaked his shirt. "Remind me to talk to him."

"You didn't want to go with your friends today?" his mother asked. "I had assumed we would be making this ride home alone."

"I will later," he said. "I really wanted to change first."

"Well, I thought Joe's speech was marvelous …"

Samuel listened. Mother droned on about Joe's greatness, how good Mrs. Gardner's son looked—you know, after the accident last summer—and all the other gossips and happenings of the families in downtown Bloomsdale.

The car moved east away from the city. They turned down the familiar dirt road lined with tall trees. Fields stretched on either side. The car accelerated in tune with his father's frustration, leaving a cloud of dust swirling in the breeze. As they approached the house, his father didn't hit the brakes until they neared the oak tree and almost sent his mom through the windshield. She looked in his father's direction with disappointment and exited the car.

They entered the house through the kitchen. His mother walked towards the refrigerator and pulled out a pitcher of lemonade. She handed him a glass. The brilliant sunlight glared through the windows, revealing the garden beyond. Samuel set his cap on the kitchen table and fell into the old wooden chair. He exhaled and stared out the window, listening to the ticking of the grandfather clock. He tapped his fingers on the glass, relishing in the cool breeze moving in from the field and passing through the open windows.

"I thought Annie Ruth looked lovely today, Sammy," his mother said as she washed her hands in the sink. "You guys doing anything later?"

Samuel took a sip from his glass and licked his lips. "Yes, ma'am."

His mother sighed and walked to the kitchen table. She ran her hands through his hair. His father wandered across his field of view, searching for something in the yard.

"What's Pa doing?" he asked.

She stared out the window. "Said something's wrong with the car. You know him." She looked him in the eye. "Is there anything you wanted to talk about?"

He blinked. "What do you mean?"

She tilted her head, eyeing him.

He had seen the look before, the expression telling him she knew he had things on his mind.

Samuel swallowed, staring through the window. "I can't really explain it."

"Sure you can."

Samuel looked away from the window and into her eyes. He remembered when he was younger never being able to talk about anything serious with his mother. It wasn't that she was unavailable. He just struggled to talk openly about his feelings. He tried to avoid any topic more serious than dinner, baseball, and the movies.

"I just thought today would have been different."

"How so?" she asked, not allowing him to retreat away from the conversation.

He leaned back into the chair, hearing the wood creak as his full weight dipped against the back. "It's something we have all looked forward to for so long, something you always hear about. And now, it's over. I didn't think about what would happen after."

She tapped the top of his hand. "You can do whatever you want to do. I've always told you that."

The front door slammed shut, and his father's heavy steps echoed through the hall. A gust of wind followed him inside the house and sent tiny pebbles of dirt across the kitchen floor. His father stepped in front of the sink and washed his hands.

"Car's going to need a little work," he grumbled, exhaling and splashing water on his face. "Nothing serious. Hot out there today."

Samuel's mother squeezed his wrist once more before getting up to join his father at the sink. He listened to them talk about the car, groceries, what Mrs. Jenson had said before graduation. He left his parents and went upstairs to his bedroom. He set the lemonade on his bedside table and collapsed on the bed.

It felt right.

It felt like home.

He buried his face deeper into the pillow before staring outside to the oak tree in his front yard, the family car parked as it always had been. Music played from below and signaled his father getting lost in the afternoon baseball game.

Samuel let his shoes fall to the ground, and he rolled over on his back. The sunlight played across the ceiling from the sharp reflections of the car. He didn't think much about celebrating tonight, although he knew the usuals were meeting downtown. He would have much rather spent the evening with Annie, but Joe would never forgive him if he didn't show.

The reflecting light crossed the pennants lining his wall. He watched the wall for a while before changing his clothes. Samuel gave himself a quick look in the mirror.

He charged down the stairs.

His father sat in the living room, his eyes fixed on the radio.

"Sammy you gotta get in here. Bases loaded. Two outs. Bottom of the eighth. Dawson's up to bat and you know he's never been good at pressure," his father said, never looking toward Samuel.

"Pa, I've got to go meet everyone for dinner. Last night and all."

His father stared at the radio. "Go ahead, Sammy. Be home at a decent hour. We've got church in the morning."

"I know."

*****

"I can't believe you made it."

"Of course, I made it." Samuel frowned, staring at Joe. "You gave a fine speech."

Joe grinned. "You thought it was good, huh? What was it in particular that you though was so good? I mean I thought all of it was good—"

"All of it was good, Joe," Samuel interrupted, giving his friend a pat on the shoulder.

Joe shrugged and opened a beer, passing Samuel a bottle. "Where's Annie?"

Samuel snorted. "I'm not bringing her out here."

"You didn't even see her?"

Samuel thought of his time on Annie Ruth's porch before it got too late. He wished they didn't have to leave each other all the time. "Yeah, I saw her. I'm just not bringing her to this place."

Downtown Bloomsdale, Georgia smelled like a cocktail of garbage, alcohol, and burnt tires. The sticky humidity allowed the stench to enter the mouth and live there, making the beer somehow taste better. Samuel grimaced as he surveyed the trash-filled alley behind the *Corner Pocket* billiards hall. Dozens of beer bottles showed the party had started long before he had arrived. A dozen graduates ready to take on the world gathered together. Some were regulars. Benny. Jerry. Steve—the older guys from the plant. All were talking over a smoke in the corner. The fresh graduates stuck together, all of them adhering to the unspoken rule of safety in numbers in a place like the alley behind the *Corner Pocket*.

Samuel had heard of the young boy off Maple Street that stopped in for a beer and instead received a knife through his belly. No one ever knew the kid's name, what happened to him or if anyone pressed charges. It just became the story everyone, especially every parent, loved to spread as a cautionary tale to young people. But even the *Corner Pocket* had a last call, which usually led to the packed alley. Many of Samuel's classmates had spent the night between old crates and trashcans at least once.

Joe stumbled a bit, shaking Samuel's thoughts back to the present. Samuel sighed. "You're drunk, Joe. Maybe you should go home."

"Ah." Joe waved his hand and faced the rest of the graduates. "I want you all to take a good look. It'll be the last time you ever see me. I'm leavin' this town and never com'n back."

Some of the old timers from the plant chuckled.

Samuel stared at them. "Come on, Joe," he said, "enough of the speeches."

"I don't want to end up like any of those guys," Joe said while pointing at the plant workers.

The workers didn't laugh.

Samuel pulled Joe away. "Would you cool it?"

One of the larger men stepped forward. "What'd you say, boy?"

"He said nothing, Steve. Let it go," Samuel said, stepping in front of his friend.

"No one said anything to you, Sammie boy," Steve said, his voice deep as a bass.

Without warning, Joe moved forward and struck Steve's companion in the face, a slapping sound like meat striking meat filled the alley. The workers fought back with brute strength, launching wild uppercuts and hurling beer bottles. Most of the fresh graduates fled across the alley like insects disappearing into the night. The drunken workers fought with no skill; their eyes blurred with the drink. Samuel stepped back to avoid a massive fist, then struck the older man across the jaw. The man collapsed, splashing into a small mud puddle. Samuel waved his fists. Pain flared from his knuckles, splitting his skin across yellowed teeth.

Samuel turned around, saw Joe held by one man while another hit him.

Samuel lowered his shoulder into the worker's waist, crashing the two into the ground. The water in the alley splashed up and blinded him, stinging his eyes. A fist hit his face, hands squeezing his throat. His lungs burned, darkness surrounding him. Warm spit hit Samuel's face, the smell of alcohol burning his nose.

The hands released him. Samuel blinked, coughing and rolling over on his stomach.

"What's going on here?" a voice called through the haze.

Samuel saw Joe lying in the middle of the alley. Police officers placed handcuffs on the workers. One officer approached Samuel.

"Get up," he said. It was the same voice from before. "Come on, get up."

Samuel stood, wavering on unsure legs and swaying as he tried to stand. He licked his lips and tasted copper on his tongue. Somehow Samuel made it to a police car. The officer pushed him into the back seat, and he collapsed into the headrest.

*****

The sounds of the jail echoed across the cold room. Joe grumbled on the cot in a nearby cell.

Samuel cupped his swelling cheek, licked his split lip, and tasted blood seemingly unwilling to clot. The pain on his face flared. He leaned back, staring at his hand. His knuckles cracked on both hands, brown splotches of dried blood covering his skin.

When they were young, Joe had stolen chocolate from Samuel's family general store. Samuel covered for him, took the blame and punishment. He could still remember the disappointment in his mother's voice and the sound of his father's belt against his backside. Much later, Joe had the stupid idea of taking the Wrightman's car to Atlanta to see the premier of the *Gone with the Wind*. They made the trip successfully only to arrive without the tickets Joe had promised.

But this time was different. Samuel had never been in a real fight before, not like this. Not one that lasted longer than a shove or one good blow before adults intervened. He thought of the nearly unconscious plant workers in the alley. Joe was right about saying he didn't want to end up like them. Samuel didn't want to be their age, drinking and fighting in the alley either, but he didn't need to say it out loud.

"Son."

Samuel held his breath, clenching his fists as he stared at the concrete floor. He felt his father's eyes on him.

"Son," his father repeated. "It's time to go."

Samuel stood without making eye contact. The officer unlocked his cell with a smirk. Joe rolled over in his cot, still out.

"What about Joe?" Samuel asked.

"I would be more concerned with my own problems," his father said, placing his hand on Samuel's shoulder. His father pushed him toward the door.

They did not speak on the ride home. Samuel peered out the window and watched families clad in their Sunday best spill out onto their green manicured yards. He blinked, realizing for the first time he had spent the entire night in jail.

His father grumbled as he turned the wheel to steer the car onto Brumby Street and toward—

Samuel swallowed. "You wouldn't send me to church like this, would you?"

"Wouldn't I?"

*****

His face flashed with pain during prayer.

Samuel opened his eyes to gain his bearings. The pain nearly made him topple. He glanced around the chapel. Joe hadn't made it, but his mother stood in the third row with her head bowed. Annie Ruth stood with her aunt and uncle in the fourth row, her eyes closed tightly. The sunlight beamed through the windows inside the church, highlighting her beautiful curls. Samuel licked his fingers and matted down his greasy hair. He thrust his hands deep into his pockets and prayed he could make it back home unnoticed.

The prayer ended. Church was over. Women picked up their belongings while men waited on their families.

The gossip began before people even left the building.

Men discussed issues ranging from the harvest to sports. A few discussed events in Europe. Mr. Jefferies hobbled toward Samuel's father as he did every Sunday. They spoke of the general store while his mother stood in silence. Samuel slipped away from the pew and from his mother's judgmental eyes. Churchgoers took an extra look as he walked down the aisle with his head down. The swelling on his face had reached an end and had finally stopped throbbing. Now the pain was dull and constant. He kept his hands in his pockets, moved toward the church door, ignoring more inquisitive comments and stares.

"Leaving so soon?"

Samuel turned. "Annie."

Her eyes widened, and her jaw dropped. "What happened to you? Your face looks horrible."

Others turned at her words, more disapproving stares. As he felt more eyes on him, Samuel grabbed her wrist with a bloodied hand. "Yours looks beautiful." He tried to smile. "Can we go outside?"

She nodded, and he led her into the sunlight. They moved under the large oak tree.

Samuel took a deep breath, enjoying the fresh air. A hot breeze blew under the tree and touched his face.

She clasped his hand. "Tell me what happened."

He looked into her green eyes, paused. "God, I've missed you."

Annie shook her head and caused a wisp of hair to fall in front of her face. "Charmer. You just saw me last night. Seriously, what happened after you left?"

She never let anything go.

He sighed, relayed the entire tale of graduation night, from drinking at the *Corner Pocket* to the fight with the workers. She listened without wavering or flinching, staring at him without expression.

More families filed out of the church, telling stories and nosey gossip about neighbors, friends, and their own families. Annie Ruth's aunt and uncle stepped out into the sunlight. Samuel looked behind Annie, then back into her eyes.

"Say something," he said, wanting her to say she wasn't embarrassed by his appearance.

Annie Ruth smiled at last and squeezed his hand. "I love you," she said before leaving to meet with her family.

Samuel watched her. They had met two years ago when he first worked a full-time shift at the general store. She entered on a summer afternoon while running errands for her aunt. Samuel eagerly helped. His heart raced. He messed up half the order, giving the wrong amount of just about everything on her aunt's list. He would discover later Annie Ruth had moved to Bloomsdale from Boston.

Her parents had died in a house fire, and her only living relatives resided in Bloomsdale. Her aunt and uncle, Emily and Jacob Taylor, lived two blocks from the general store in Bloomsdale while Samuel's family lived on the outskirts. Samuel didn't know much about the Taylors before Annie Ruth came. Jacob Taylor owned the diner in nearby Terrytown and Emily sold sweaters around town for newborns. She made dozens every year. Samuel had a blue one his mother stored deep in the attic. As far as Samuel knew, the Taylors never had any children of their own.

Samuel's parents came out into the grassy parking lot and weaved through the cars. His mother placed a hand to her forehead to block the sun. His father stood at her side, his hands on his hips as his eyes bore into Samuel's.

Nodding and staring at the grass, Samuel walked to the car.

2

A small red car sped alongside the train. A younger fella with a cigarette hanging out of his mouth leaned back as he drove.

"Shame to see teenagers smoke like that."

He turned to the sharp dressed passenger next to him. "How's that?" He leaned closer to the man.

The passenger with greasy hair and an expensive-looking dark suit peered away from his magazine, nodding toward the car. "That kid over there with that cancer stick. It's a shame." The passenger blinked behind thick glasses. "Can you not hear me?"

"Hear you fine." He cleared his throat. "I smoked when I was his age."

The passenger adjusted his glasses, snorted and turned back to the magazine. "Least you quit."

He shook his head and turned away. The teenager flicked the cigarette out and turned the little red car onto a side road. The train veered away, the car disappearing in the distance. He closed his eyes for a moment. When he opened them, the late day sunlight flashed off a tiny pond a few hundred yards from the track.

*****

The water looked like glass. An insect buzzed across the surface while the blistering August heat seared down. The air felt thick, difficult to breathe and washed the world in a sticky, invisible muck. Samuel waved the morning's newspaper, trying to break up some of the still air. It didn't help as he watched his line in the water of Malcolm's Pond. Nothing had bitten in the last half hour except an old car tire.

Joe snored from the other side of the canoe. Samuel took one last look at the line, thought, It's too hot. They had come out too late. Joe showed up late as always, had spent the previous night hanging at the *Corner Pocket*, where he visited most weekends. Samuel didn't listen to the tales, had heard them all before.

His first day off in two months wasn't going as planned.

With his fishing partner now sleeping, Samuel turned to the newspaper. Headlines read the same as most days. The baseball scores didn't offer much entertainment. Samuel never cared until fall. The top stories heralded the gloom of Europe followed by quotes from several politicians. He scanned the comics and found little to offer a laugh. He crumpled the paper and tossed it on the floor of the canoe.

Samuel took off his hat to wipe his brow. At least, he wasn't working.

His father had been working him hard the entire summer. Students came into the store, preparing for school. For the first time, Samuel didn't have to join them. The store was all he had in his foreseeable future. No goals, no end point.

Samuel sighed and thought of Annie. Looking beautiful as always, she had come into the store yesterday for some groceries, nothing more. She had spent the summer so far sewing for her aunt, helping to double the number of sweaters Emily Taylor sold to other ladies. Most ladies bought them to be nice while talking behind her back about the quality. Typical, Samuel thought.

Joe snorted, and Samuel tapped his friend with the toe of his boot. "Wake up, bum."

Joe stirred, rocking back. The canoe swayed, sending ripples across the pond. A nearby snapping turtle split the water and disappeared. "Didn't mean to doze off."

"It's okay, buddy. I didn't have the night you did."

"You never do," Joe smiled, his eyes still closed. "Once in a while you should go out with me."

Samuel shook his head. "Dad's got to open the store at the crack of dawn. I know most of the time you're just coming in."

"Live a little."

"That's what I'm trying to do. I need my job."

Joe peered at him from under the wide brim of his hat. "You plottin' something?"

Samuel pulled on the line. "We should probably head back."

"No, seriously." Joe sat up in the canoe and yawned. "Why do you need that job? Can't be just loyalty to the family."

"It's not." Samuel wrapped the line around the pole and put the lid on his can of worms. "A woman wouldn't want to be with a man who doesn't have a job."

"Come work with me at the plant," Joe said. He stretched as if just waking. "Good job, good pay."

Samuel slid an oar from the side of the boat. "I'll think about it."

"Hours are long," Joe said as if Samuel hadn't spoke at all. "Boss is a jerk, but you do get some time off here and there."

Samuel shook his head and pulled deep on the paddle, the movement breaking the stillness of the pond. "I said I'll think about it. I need to at least finish out the year for Dad. We'll see."

"Suit yourself." Joe grabbed an oar.

Samuel smiled. "Yeah."

Something droned in the distance. Samuel glanced at the bright sky, searching for the source of the noise. And then he saw it.

The plane was just a spot, at first, far off in the horizon. Samuel had seen them fly over before, but it was usually too fast to get a good look. He wondered what the pilot looked like, where he was going. Probably somewhere much more exciting than Bloomsdale. Maybe he flew to New York City to catch a show every weekend. Or maybe he was a mail carrier. Or maybe he was transporting a famous politician or a baseball player.

Samuel imagined seeing the world from above. This pond was probably just a puddle to the pilot. How peaceful it must be. He read of pilots in the Great War falling in love with soaring amongst the clouds.

"The hell you looking at?"

Samuel blinked. "Just trying to see the plane."

Joe snorted. "Still wanna be a pilot, huh?"

"Suppose I do." He watched the plane drone off toward town until it disappeared behind the trees.

"Don't know how or why anyone would let us fly something like that. Probably cost a couple thousand dollars."

Samuel laughed. "Yeah, at least." The sound of the plane faded, replaced by insects. "I'll probably never get up there."

"Speaking of getting somewhere," Joe said as the boat hit the shore. As they jumped out of the canoe, their feet sunk into the soft mud underwater. The rusty metal boat slipped into the high, dry grass that crackled with their footsteps. "What's with you and Annie?"

"What's do ya mean?"

"You've been acting like sweethearts for going on a year now and…well?"

"Well, what?"

Joe bounced his eyebrows. *"Well?"*

Samuel shook his head. "I don't know."

"What do you mean?"

"I don't know."

Joe swung his pole around his back. He turned and started down the path toward town. Insects jumped from the grasses. A rare breeze broke the heat and sent plants waving as Samuel followed.

"Jacob's marrying Deborah this fall."

Samuel frowned. "So?"

"So, a lot of guys are marrying sweethearts. What? Are you not serious about her?"

Samuel ducked under a branch. "You know that's not the case."

"Then, what?"

"I don't want us to be stuck here forever," he said with a shrug.

They walked on in silence for a long while. Sweat made his hat itch, his shirt growing damp. His feet throbbed. Samuel grimaced. Too many hours spent helping his father in the store.

"What's wrong with Bloomsdale?" Joe asked when the forest parted to reveal the road.

"It's fine," he said. "Just don't want to work in the store the rest of my life."

"You tell your Dad that?"

Samuel bit his lip. "Hell, no. I don't think he'd ever take that." He stared down the street toward town. "What about you, Joe?"

Joe slowed to allow Samuel to walk beside him. "Met this girl down at the mill."

Samuel blinked. "She works there?"

Joe shrugged and looked off toward town. "Yep. She does some of the paperwork in the office or something." He paused. "We're going out this weekend."

"This girl have a name?"

"Margaret."

Samuel frowned. "Never heard of her."

"She's older." Joe smiled. "More mature."

Samuel stared at him. "You're serious? Where are you taking her?"

"Don't know, yet. You can be sure it'll be some place snazzy."

They parted on Main Street. Cars and horse-drawn carts moved through town as Samuel made his way to the store. He couldn't believe Joe had a date. He wasn't sure if he should believe it. Joe had lied about stupid things in the past.

He tossed his fishing pole next to the trashcans in the alley and sat down, leaning his head back against the store. The brick cooled his scalp. He looked up. A wisp of clouds streaked across the otherwise perfectly blue sky. He thought of the hours of mindless work ahead of him tomorrow, realizing his day off was over. Samuel tossed the can of worms, watching it crash against the wall of the nearby building.

"Not their fault." Luther Jackson stepped through the screen door of the back of the store. "You shouldn't take life's problems out on the weak." He laughed, creating a sound like bones scraping together in a stiff breeze.

Samuel shook his head and scooped up the worms. Luther had been working with his family since Samuel had been a boy. His main task was stocking shelves and helping Mr. Wrightman unload trucks. Samuel believed Luther saw it as part of his responsibility to watch over him.

"What's wrong, Sammy? Not a good day off?"

"Fine."

"Fine, eh? Never seen a fine man hurl worms." Luther placed a bag into the trash, his dark skin glistened in the afternoon sun. "You been sitting back here since you was a boy. You know that? Always back here when you was in trouble or not wanting to be talked to. And I always come back here, goin' in and out all day long. You don't want to be bothered; you should go somewhere else."

Samuel clenched his teeth. "It's nothing. Just life stuff."

Luther chuckled that same, grinding laugh. "It's a woman."

Samuel's face warmed. "It's not a woman."

"Yeah."

Samuel looked at his hands. "Joe's got a date this weekend. I didn't even know he had a girlfriend."

Luther placed another bag in the can. "And you've got your Annie. You're grow'n up. That's nothin to be sad about."

"I know." He stared at his hands a moment longer, then gazed back into the sky before looking back to Luther. "Bright and early tomorrow, right?"

Luther smiled, revealing a grin full of glowing white teeth. "You betcha, Sammy. Bright and early."

*****

Another crate of canned vegetables. Brooms came next, followed by yard tools. His muscles pumped and burned, sweat irritating his skin. Just when he thought the final box came off the truck, Luther produced another to be hauled into the general store.

At least three games of stickball had taken place down the alley since the truck had arrived. The sidewalk on the north side of the post office was always home plate. The pitcher stood down the alley at differing distances. Cheers and accusations of cheating echoed down the city streets despite the sound of midday traffic. Six boys now enjoyed ice cream from the curb.

"Boxes won't unload themselves."

Samuel shook his head. "You need some new lines, Mister Luther."

Luther chuckled and dropped another box. "Truth is truth no matter the line. You know that."

Samuel laughed and peered into the truck. Three more boxes. He glanced at the dead light blue of the fall evening. "Almost done anyhow. We need to get going."

Annie Ruth expected him at seven. Her post office job lets her go at four-thirty, so he was always working later. School life now seemed so far away, almost like it never happened. Samuel had trouble remembering classes he took last May. Most of the students on that bright summer day of graduation had spread out. Some went to Atlanta for better jobs. Others were bound for the coast, taking jobs they could on shrimp boats near Savannah. Johnny Tyson joined the Marines. Robert Thompson the Navy. Brian Weaver was somewhere in the Merchant Marine. Joe Miller was still at the mill on the other side of town. A few lucky ones were in college.

Samuel was one of the only guys from his class still in town. Annie had taken a job at the nearby post office in August, so he certainly wasn't alone. They met for lunch whenever they could. Sometimes Annie would bring Max, her black and white Rat Terrier, to work with her. Max would stay at the back of the post office. Annie and Samuel would take Max for long walks as the humid air finally lifted. It was a routine grown in the six months since graduation.

But today would be different.

The light at the post office had been turned off. Samuel took off his apron and helped Luther with the final three boxes. He stepped into the warmth of the store.

"You guys finished back there?" his father called from inside.

"Yes, sir," Samuel said. He reached deep into his coat pocket while it was still on the hangar. He wrapped his hands around the contents of his pocket. "Pa, I'm going to have to get going soon. All the work's done. Anything I missed, I'll do tomorrow."

The looming figure of his father stepped into the back room. "You didn't sweep out the front of the store. Mr. Clemens came in today straight from the field. Cow crap's all over."

"But, Pa, I really gotta to go."

"No." His father tossed a clipboard on the counter. Samuel's stomach turned as he heard the seriousness in his father's tone. "Not until I can shake your hand to wish you luck. My Daddy did the same for me."

Samuel's jaw dropped. "Pa, I …"

His father smiled. They shook hands, and something pressed into Samuel's palm. He turned over his hand to see a roll of cash. Samuel looked back to his father.

"Sammy." His father opened his mouth to speak but instead hugged his son.

"Truck's finished Mister ..." Luther walked into the store. "I'm sorry Mister Wrightman. Didn't know y'all were chatting."

Samuel parted from his father. "I probably should be going."

"Yes, you should." Their eyes met for a moment. "Your mother told me."

Samuel nodded smiling. "Should've known."

"I know. I'm proud of you, son."

*****

It took less than twenty minutes to wash the grime and smell of the store out of his skin. He tried to eat dinner, but just redistributed his mother's dinner around on the plate because his stomach rolled around. He drank three glasses of sweet tea, his face still hot and flush like a sunburn.

After dinner, he paced across the wooden floors of his upstairs bedroom. He recited his speech for the countless time, adjusting some of the words around once again. A cool breeze moved the curtains from his window, sending some of the baseball pennants and pictures on his wall moving in waves. Insects echoed outside in an otherwise silent night. His father laughed downstairs to something on the radio, the walls muffling most of the sound. Dishes clattered together softly as his mother washed and cleaned the kitchen.

He surveyed his clothes once more in the mirror he was too tall for, and frowned at his red face, thought, close your eyes, breathe and everything will be fine. He glanced at the clock and frowned. Fifteen minutes until he was supposed to pick up Annie. Annie Ruth's uncle would always look at him while asking a series of questions, then glaze over as Samuel answered. Neither her aunt nor uncle would ever listen, but he spent most of his time at their house gazing at Annie.

Ten minutes. Annie Ruth lived at least ten minutes away.

Here we go.

He galloped down the stairs, shaking the entire house. His mother muttered a quick goodbye, her attention on the dishes. The radio had swallowed his father's attention with the help of a drink. Outside the air had cooled. Mosquitoes and moths fluttered around the porch light as he stepped through the screened door. The floorboards of the porch groaned and popped.

"Be careful, Sammy," his father said without coming to the door. "Bring her back in one piece, will ya?"

"You got it, Pa. Thanks!" Samuel called back.

His beagle, Henry, ran in from the yard and nuzzled at his knees. He bent down and touched the floppy ears. Many years ago, his father used to take Henry hunting. The gray beard around Henry's face showed his hunting days had passed. Samuel scratched behind Henry's ears and watched his dog's lips curl back.

Giving Henry one last pat, Samuel rushed to the car. The engine cranked, and he drove in silence.

No radio to calm his nerves. He just rehearsed. Should he just blurt it out? Or should he ease into the big question?

He froze. Would she say yes? It hadn't occurred to him until this moment, but she might say no. Would she? His heart raced, a cold sweat covering his skin.

He nearly missed the turn.

The dark wooded road leading to the Taylors never revealed itself at night. The trees stretched over the path as if joining hands, the branches forming a tunnel at night, interlocking overhead to block out the stars. He slowed, tires grinding and popping into gravel. The headlights beamed down the red, sandy driveway that looked like rusted powder.

Annie Ruth sat in the white wooden swing on the porch, a sole light shining down on her curly brown hair. He swallowed, putting the car in park. The box had fit neatly into his pocket. He tapped his leg, ensuring it hadn't fallen out.

Get out of the car.

The door seemed heavy as it opened with a screech. The sound echoed across the old farm. He looked over the grass disappearing into blackness.

Get out of the car.

He stood a moment. Annie Ruth waved. He returned the gesture, touched his pant leg. Still there. He walked to the porch like concrete had been poured into his shoes.

"Evening, Sammy." She kicked her heel to send the wooden swing swaying once again. She held a tall glass in her hand, and another sat on the porch railing. "Was wondering when you'd get here."

"Lot to do at work." His voice sounded rough. He swallowed once again and stepped onto the porch. "How are you?"

"Swell." She stopped swinging. "Lemonade's for you."

Samuel grabbed the glass and fell hard into the swing. Annie Ruth's feet flew up into the air for a moment. She giggled. Samuel's face reddened.

He listened to Annie Ruth speak. She stared out into the darkness of the farm as she talked about her day. A curly strand of hair had fallen onto her smooth cheek before she brushed it away. She took a long drink.

"Annie," he said after a long pause.

She nodded. "Dinner is ready. I made sandwiches."

He bit his lip.

They moved onto a blanket in the front yard under the twisted oak. Stars poked through the shroud of leaves. The blanket felt cool under his legs. The turkey sandwich tasted dry, but it was probably his distracted mind. The small talk continued through sandwiches and extra lemonade. Mr. Taylor appeared at the window once, twice, and disappeared behind thin curtains.

"Do you think about the future?" he asked.

She glanced at him, half a bite of sandwich still in her mouth. "Future?"

"Yeah."

She stared back into the sky. "All the time."

"Do you want to stay here?" He placed a shaking, sweaty hand in his pocket. "Do you want to stay in McGovern County?"

She bit her lip. "You know, we never could see this much sky in Boston. Daddy used to talk about that all the time." She exhaled. "All the time. I never knew what he was talking about." She looked back at him and placed her sandwich on the blanket. "Never thought I'd find a home again, you know? Then I had to move here. I hated it. Absolutely hated it. No one liked me. And people talked funny."

Samuel frowned. "I don't talk funny."

She smiled. "You do, and I love it." She peered down at a half-eaten sandwich. "You treated me different, made me feel safe, welcome. I don't ever want to leave now. I can't imagine being anywhere else."

He slipped the box out of his pocket. "I've loved you since I met you. I've always known there was no one else, even if I haven't always showed it. I think it's time, Annie ... if you'll have me. If you ... would you marry me?"

She stared at the box, her red lips parting slightly.

"I can make a living for us," he said. "I can't promise you much, but you'll be happy. You might even not have to work at the post office. There are homes downtown for rent where we could start. I'm learning the business, and I think I could make you happy ... if you'd let me."

Samuel closed his eyes. The wind brushed through his hair. When he opened his eyes, Annie Ruth had moved closer across the blanket.

"You are amazing," she said slowly. Her warm breath touched his cheek. She slid her tongue across her lips and smiled. "I will. You do make me happy. Always."

She kissed him, and they embraced under the oak.

*****

Samuel folded the blanket and placed it into Annie's basket. He pulled the top down onto it and smiled. "You are still going to the game tomorrow?"

"Of course," she said, still grinning. "What are we going to tell everyone? When do you want to get married?"

Samuel grinned. "We can tell everyone whenever you want. My parents already know."

Annie froze. "They do?"

"Well, all except for your answer."

She still stared at him. "Did they...well, I mean, do they mind?"

He stared at her. "Why would you ask me that? Of course, they don't mind."

She smiled, her eyebrows wrinkling. "I'm not from here. They don't mind me being a Yankee?"

"Half-Yankee." He reached out and touched her chin, feeling the smoothness of her skin as he caressed her cheek. "You're aunt and uncle live down here, after all."

Annie pushed him on the shoulder. "I guess that counts. You think I'm all right, so I guess that's enough. Of course I will marry you!"

They walked up the porch and stopped at the door. Samuel passed over the basket. She stepped forward.

"Thank you for asking me," she said, her eyes lingering on his mouth.

He took a step toward her. She tilted her head back, her eyes taking in his face.

"Thank you for saying yes," he said.

They kissed and the night was over.

He drove home, the entire world looking different as he accelerated through the empty road. The most beautiful woman he had ever seen had just agreed to marry him. What a day. He wanted to yell out the window, tell the whole world. His heart pounded in his chest, but it was different than the nervousness he felt on the way to her house. Now, it was excitement. Amazing how fast your life can change, he thought.

Of course, his parents had waited up. Samuel and his father had a beer while his mother told stories about her wedding day. Her father had been so pleased—because Mr. Wrightman already had a job—and her mother was thrilled Dad came from a good family. They stayed up late on the porch.

Samuel stared out into the dark front yard, listening to his parents tell stories. He didn't want it to end as all things do. He finished a beer with his father as his mother smiled at him.

3

The mother at the front of the car wiped her child's face. Three children sipped on small milk cartons. One little girl stood on the seat, staring at him before slipping out of sight. He gazed out the window.

Night had fallen across the landscape. He gazed at the twinkling stars. He raised his arms high into the air to stretch. The train rocked as the mother herded the children back to their room for sleep. He watched the family leave. Silence fell over the car as the train prepared for the night.

A bright light swept across the land. He craned his neck for a better view. A town approached. He forced his eyes open. A baseball field illuminated the night sky at the edge of the darkened town. He pulled his flannel shirt closer, folding his arms over his chest. Families in the distance surrounded the field. He grinned as a little boy rounded first base.

*****

Bases loaded. Two outs. The crowd jeered. The runners cheered. Mr. Wrightman yelled something about keeping an eye on the ball, giving it a ride.

The ball climbed its high arc. He watched the bat connect. The stinging tingle of an inside pitch rattled his fingers. He darted toward first, watching the ball soar into Joe's glove at shortstop. The crowd inhaled at contact, sighing when Joe caught the ball. Joe's laugh broke the silence.

"Nice try." He trotted in from the field.

And the annual December softball game with the church had ended. The teams lined up to shake hands while mothers, old and young, lifted napkins off rows of food under the nearby oak tree. Samuel took off his sweaty hat and shook his friend's hand.

"Why ya always do that to me?" he asked.

Joe grinned. "You're my best friend. Whatta ya want me to do, drop the ball so you can be the big hero?"

Samuel had played the game since high school, as did every other boy within ten miles. And nearly every year Joe ended up on the opposite team. Annie Ruth had cheered this day from the stands while sitting with his mother and father. A cool wind blew, the sky a brilliant and cloudless blue. Napkins blew into the grass as players left the field. Small children ran around the bases pretending to be Joe DiMaggio and Hank Greenberg. A game of horseshoes broke out among a cluster of adolescent boys. Mothers shepherded children back to long tables while men spoke of trivial things seeming so important. Some spoke to Samuel about business, something that had never happened before.

Pastor Daniel prayed, silencing everyone in attendance. A dog barked in the distance. Following the prayer, everyone sat to eat. The table of vegetables, salad and meats could feed twice the number at the table. All the families would take home leftovers to eat until Christmas. Families gossiped under the guise of caring and religious fellowship, using the Lord's name to pry into the deepest darkest secrets of their neighbors. People feigned interest while others spoke of their business interests and happenings of those family members long since gone from Georgia. Some cared, some patiently waited for their turn to speak. Others simply listened.

Samuel heard nothing. He stared at Annie Ruth while she ate, remembering their kiss from the night before and his proposal. He watched her hair interfere in conversation, gusts of wind sending curls bouncing and cascading into her face. He smiled when their eyes met. Had he the chance, Samuel would have broken through the constant chatter and jumped on the table. He would have interrupted the idle talk and told his little world of his big news. Of course, to break through any tradition was taboo. The motions must continue as if an act of a play. It had been this way since he was a boy watching his father play. Now, his father had just sat out his first game, moving to umpire the game rather than take part.

When the moment finally arrived for Samuel to announce his news, somewhere between refills of sweet tea and slices of pecan pie left over from Thanksgiving. People applauded, hugging him after the announcement. Women gathered around Annie, smiling and asking questions about wedding plans. Most of the attention fell on Samuel's parents. The Taylors had not come to the event, but Samuel knew they would soon hear the news. Samuel and Annie found each other in the sea of the congregation, standing at the edge of the table as people congratulated them while carrying a piece of pie or a sparkling glass of tea.

Samuel watched Annie speak to everyone, deciding to be silent at her side while the spotlight fell on them. People launched a barrage of questions they had never planned on answering.

"When's the date?"

"When are y'all having the shower?"

"What church will the wedding be in?"

"How did he ask you?"

He shook hands as men warned he was getting into a mess. Some of them joked. He pretended to laugh when Pastor Daniel asked about his new "honey do" lists. None of it mattered to Samuel. He watched as his bride-to-be deflected intimate questions, wondering what she would look like in a wedding dress.

*****

The next day, the church service was a non-event. Samuel hadn't heard a word until the final "let us pray" signaling it was time to leave. A warm breeze greeted the Wrightmans as they left the church.

"Congratulations, son."

Samuel turned to Mr. Taylor, a tall, thin man in a blue suit with plump Mrs. Taylor nearby in a yellow Sunday dress. "Thank you, sir."

"We are completely thrilled," Mrs. Taylor said, her voice soft and kind. "You're a nice young man with a future. Her parents couldn't have dreamed of more."

Mr. Taylor smiled. "Yes. Annie's a fortunate young woman."

"Thank you, sir," Samuel said, shaking Mr. Taylor's hand. "I'll try not to disappoint you, sir."

"I know." The man cocked his head. "We'll have to talk about what sort of arrangements you would like to make. Church, reception, that sort of thing. Times have been good, but not that good. These things cost money, you know?"

Samuel nodded. "We haven't talked about it much, sir."

"You know what the date is?" Mrs. Taylor asked.

Samuel stared at Annie Ruth. "I'd like Annie to be ready. That's all. Whatever she decides."

"Women from our family always got married in the spring." Mrs. Taylor said, eyeing him. "Any reason we should have it sooner?"

"None that I know of," Samuel said. He suddenly frowned, bitting his lip. "Wait a…no. There is no reason we should have it sooner. Wait a year, I don't care."

Mrs. Taylor's jaw dropped, her hand falling to her chest. "Now I never meant—"

"What did ya mean, then?" Mr. Taylor asked with a laugh.

"Well I declare," she said, her face turning the shade of a ripe tomato. "I never thought anything of the sorts."

Samuel's father stepped up behind him. "You ready to go?" He nodded at the Taylors. "Unless there's something you were discussing."

"No, Pa, I think we're finished." He turned to the Taylors. "Thank you for your kind words."

Samuel waved to Annie Ruth as they entered his father's car.

"What was that about, son?" his father asked from the front seat. "Mrs. Taylor looked like she was about to faint."

"Oh, good Lord…it was nothing."

"Right. Speak up."

He sighed. "They were just getting touchy with wedding specifics."

Mrs. Wrightman turned around from the front seat. "Like what?"

"Reception, church, that sort of thing."

His father grunted.

Samuel pressed his head against the window. A squirrel ran along side the road, bouncing its way through the tangle of weeds.

"Where we going?" he asked.

"Thought we could get some ice cream," his mother said. "A treat for the big weekend."

Samuel smiled. "We ever going to stop celebrating?"

"Only if you do," his mother said. "And you should never stop celebrating this. Not as long as you live."

Samuel nodded. He leaned into the seat, closing his eyes. Annie Ruth loved him. He dreamed of their life together. The store, its cracked windowsills marking the years. Little Samuels and Annies running wild, his parents becoming loving grandparents. Joe bringing his children over to play on a Saturday afternoon while they talked of the past. Annie taking the children to school. They would be a part of the community, a happy part. Christmas dinners would be held at their store for the entire town. The mayor would speak at his table. The family business would succeed and thrive. And then he would pass it to his children.

The car rolled in front of the ice cream parlor where patrons sat still as statues. No one spoke. Several children were lapping up ice cream on brown cones, little white rivers rolling across their fingertips. Samuel opened the car door. His parents followed. All attention in the parlor focused on the small transistor radio announcing to the small town of Georgians what just happened, thousands of miles away, on that Sunday, December 7, 1941.

4

The bitter coffee burned his throat. "Excuse me, ma'am. Can I get some sugar?"

The attendant nodded.

The sun ascended over rolling hills. Cattle grazed on land that stretched into infinity. Mountains loomed in a distant haze like dark clouds over the plain.

The attendant, carrying a small white bowl full of different colored packets, weaved through the crowd.

"What's this?" he asked.

"It's the sugar you asked for."

"Mmm hmm." He took the bowl, looked at the blue, pink and yellow inside. "Thank you."

He chose a pink packet tore it open, dumped the contents into the murky coffee. Sugar came in big white bags or little bowls, he thought, not these little paper things.

*****

"I have to go," Samuel said with a grunt, lifting another crate of sugar bags.

Luther looked at them while he placed a crate in the alley. He said something about a floor needing sweeping before he shuffled into the back of the store, leaving Samuel and Annie Ruth alone.

"Just tell me why." She gazed at the ground, the rest of her body still. "I deserve that."

Samuel sighed. "Of course, you do. You know I love you. I always have. Somebody has to do this."

"What about our life together?"

"That has to be put on hold for now."

"So I've got no say in this? You're just going to ship yourself off to die?" She stepped closer. "Look at me. Why did you ask me to marry you?"

Samuel let go of a crate from the back of the truck. "You already know why," he said. "I can't imagine my life with you. You know that. But I can't help that this happened. I have to do something."

She grasped his hand. "Just tell me why."

Samuel turned to look at her. He stepped forward, lowering his voice.

"What would the rest of the town say?" he whispered. "What would they do if a young man didn't join up? How would we go on living here? Would people still do business with the store? Would they ever look at me the same again?"

"I don't care about any of that."

He squeezed her hand. "The life we wanted is going to have to wait. It will still come. I'll be gone a few months, maybe a year, and then I'll be back."

She shook her head slowly. "You're wrong. Nothing good will come of this. Nothing. And you won't listen to anything I say." She glanced at her watch. "I'd better get back to work."

Annie Ruth stormed back to the post office. Samuel watched the wind ruffle her blue dress.

She didn't turn back.

"Finish with those Christmas decorations?" Luther asked. He raised his hands. "Oh, Miss Annie gone already?"

He lowered his gaze. "Like you didn't know."

"I know she'd been here the whole lunch hour." Luther hauled the final two boxes off the back of the truck. "Smart girl, that one."

Samuel blinked. "What does that mean? You gonna tell me I shouldn't go now, too?"

"It's not a decision you make in a week. War's just started. They'll be plenty of time for this."

Samuel sat on the truck's bumper. "I feel I am supposed to do something."

Luther nodded. "That's called being a young man. Ask yourself why you want to do this? It better be more than what people think about you."

"I am scared what people will think," he said, "but I feel even more that I have to go."

Luther shrugged. "Then I guess you should go."

*****

Samuel peddled his bicycle home. The sun dipped low as he leaned into the driveway. The dry powdery dirt swallowed his front tire. He dropped one foot for balance. Mr. Wrightman clipped the bushes in the front yard. Wednesday and Thursdays were his father's new days off, leaving Samuel to handle the deliveries for the upcoming weekend's shoppers. His parents spent much of this time together doing odd jobs around the house and tackling another jigsaw puzzle on the back porch.

"Dinner's ready, son." His father clipped the last of the bushes and waved him over. "Set your bike down and help me, will ya?"

Samuel dropped the bike in the thin grass of the front yard. "What is it?"

His father shook his head. "Just need some help with the clippings."

The two of them worked until the sun disappeared and insects moaned without end. A coyote howled as they dumped clippings into the dark woods.

"Hadn't said much tonight."

Samuel shrugged. "You wanna talk?"

"Only if you do."

Samuel tipped the wheelbarrow and watched leaves fall into the darkness. "Nothing you want to know about."

His father snorted. "I know you got in a fight with Annie."

Samuel sighed. "Who told you that?"

"Wasn't born yesterday." He turned, heading back to the house where a sole light beamed across the otherwise dark yard. "What was it about?"

Samuel paused. "Don't think she likes the idea of me leaving."

"I don't think any of us do."

Samuel looked at his father.

His father held his gaze and then shook his head. "I reckon I would be signing up, too, if I was your age." He rotated his arm around like a sore baseball pitcher. "Those days are gone now."

His father sighed. He pushed his wheelbarrow to the side of the house. "You're looking for my blessing, but you don't need things like that anymore."

"I don't?"

"Hell, no." His father frowned and shook his head. "Why would you think that?"

"I just thought the store and—"

"Stop," his father said, jabbing a finger into Samuel's chest. "You don't ever make that store an excuse in your life. I started that store. It's not your burden. Don't you carry that on your shoulders. That's where regrets are born, son. Don't ever let other people's decisions control your life."

He watched the wind blow the tire swing as Henry chewed on a bone at the edge of the yard.

His father took a deep breath, exhaled slowly. "Feed Henry. After that, we'll tell your Mama."

Samuel nodded and moved off to fill the dog bowl.

5

Loud waves of rain slapped against the window. Rivers of clear veins stretched across the glass. He tilted back the seat, took a deep breath, and watched water beads race backward. Condensation clouded the bottom of his window. He wrapped the sleeve of his dark red flannel shirt around his fingertips and wiped.

The passengers sat in silence. Silverware clattered as the cars bounced over a swelled river. The world outside seemed to hide away from the storm. Little moved other than trees swaying in the wind.

He folded his arms across his chest, feeling a chill and stretching his legs. His muscles ached. He rubbed his thigh near the old scar. He stood and stretched, trying not to wake the napping passenger next to him. Leaning against the window, he watched the rain lessen, and gray clouds swirl.

*****

The sky was gray, the air cool. The wind blew ripples across the surface of the pond. The water lapped against the side of the canoe. Fish weren't biting.

"Little too cold, I think," Joe said, his hat pulled down over his face. A worm curled over his thumb as he pressed the hook through its flesh.

"Probably," Samuel said.

He smiled as a plane flew above. It looked like a toy from this distance. Could the plane see their little pond? What did the world look like from up there?

"You sure you want to do that," Joe mumbled.

Samuel half turned. "Fly?"

"Mmm, hmm."

Samuel pulled his rod back into the canoe. "I do."

Joe nodded, his hat still covering his face. "Why?"

"I don't know."

Joe paused and pulled his hat back. "You scared?"

"No," Samuel said quickly. "You?"

"A little." Joe sat up in the canoe. "You know, I never been out of Georgia. Is that weird?"

"I guess."

Joe cast his line. "What's your lady say?"

"She said she'd wait on me," he whispered.

Joe titled his head to look at Samuel. "You know that Tomlinson kid's been hanging around the post office lately."

"What? Matt?"

"That's the one. Seems interested."

Samuel snapped around, and the canoe rocked. Joe laughed.

"That's not funny." Samuel gazed out into the dark, dirty water. He shook his head. "You've got a good job waiting on you. Plant'll take you back in a heartbeat."

"I hope so." Joe pulled his pole back into the boat, staring into the darkening sky. "Hadn't caught anything and it's getting dark. You reckon it's time to call it a day?"

"Yeah," Samuel tossed down his pole and grabbed a paddle.

"We should try to do this more often."

He grinned. "Yeah."

They paddled in silence. The boat slipped into the muddy bank. The calm waters behind him, he watched the bluish tint of the sky give way to black. Two stars dared to blaze through the soft sky.

6

A mother at the front of the car grabbed a young girl by the arm as she tried to escape down the aisle. The woman pulled the little girl toward her and spoke in hushed tones through clenched teeth. The little girl's eyes welled up as she crawled back into the seat next to her mother. The two turned to the front of the train and sat in silence.

*****

Mrs. Wrightman made no eye contact when Samuel entered the room. It had been two days since Samuel told her he would soon be volunteering to go to war. Samuel bit his tongue whenever he was around her. He wasn't sure if he should act like nothing was wrong or bring up the obvious source of ill will.

"Do you think she'll ever get over this, Pa?" he asked as they prepared firewood for Christmas. "She's said nothing since I told her I was leaving."

"Sure she will," he said, snapping a branch. "When you come back home safe."

The firewood loomed high on the porch. Henry sniffed the wood carefully and hiked his leg on the closest log. He looked at Samuel and almost smiled as his long tongue hung from his mouth. Samuel watched the tire swing moved gently under the lone tall tree sheltering the house his grandfather had built.

Father and son stared into the darkness for a long moment. The clattering of dishes ceased.

"She's not the only one."

Samuel blinked, turning to his father. "What?"

His father's jaw muscles clenched. He bit his lip. "You can't know what this feels like, son."

"I know."

"You don't. You couldn't." He turned toward the door. "Someday, you might," his father said softly and slipped into the house.

Samuel sat alone and looked into the starless sky.

*****

"My train leaves before the sun comes up. Pa said he'd drive me to the station."

Annie Ruth nodded as a car drove in front of the outdoor post office bench. Her bloodshot eyes stared down at the dry brown leaves moving across the sidewalk.

"I might be able to come back right after training," Samuel said. "I don't really know how any of this works."

Annie Ruth sat in silence. She sniffed, and looked at the sky. She wrapped her arms around her shoulders. She brushed her left eye, and then stared across the street. Her red lips parted, closed, and then her chin quivered.

Samuel glanced down at his hands. "I hope you know how hard this is and how much I love you. This will only be for a little while. When I come back, we can get married like we wanted. We can have a family like you've talked about."

Annie shook her head.

"What is it?" He touched her cheek. "Say something."

She looked at him, her eyes moist, her expression muted. She touched his cheek, her warm hand lingered. Opening her mouth in silence, she squeaked the words, "Just come back."

Her hand shaking, she leaned forward and kissed his forehead. She stood up.

Samuel watched her slowly walk away, arms crossed over her stomach. The wind brushed her blue and white dress.

"Where is she going?" Marge, her older co-worker, asked as she opened post office door. "She coming back?"

He inhaled deeply, releasing the breath steadily. "Not today."

He walked across the street to the family store. Samuel still felt her lips on his forehead. He started questioning if he was doing the right thing. Would Annie forgive him?

*****

Joe walked into the store and slammed his hands on the counter in front of Samuel.

"You wanna have a drink with me?" Joe asked.

Samuel smiled and glanced back at the boxes on the shelf. Luther and his father could finish this in the morning. "Yeah."

They sat at the bar of the *Corner Pocket* billiards hall two minutes later and a beer in their hands thirty seconds after that. The place smelled of old liquor, men's feet, and toilets full of aged urine. The first pitcher was nearly empty before they spoke.

"You scared?" Joe asked.

"Not a lick." He looked at himself in the glass behind the bar and shook his head. "Course I am. You?"

He frowned. "Don't tell anyone."

They bumped their fresh mugs together with a clink.

Old timers sat in the corner playing cards. A pair of women sat at the bar and stared at the drunks playing pool in the back. The men threatened each other, but the game continued. Samuel had witnessed many swinging sticks and flying fists at the *Corner Pocket*. He thought about how he would miss it. He turned around, leaning on the bar. A light flickered above his head.

"We never did go again," Samuel said.

Joe frowned. "Go where?"

"Fishing."

"That was only a few weeks ago." Joe took a drink.

"I know." Samuel looked at his friend and grabbed his shoulder. His stomach turned as he thought of what lie ahead of him. "Let's have one more. I have an early day tomorrow, but it's my last night."

They bumped their glasses again. Joe smiled and ordered another.

*****

Strong fingers gripped his shoulder. Samuel wasn't sure where he was, and then saw the silhouette of his father.

"Get up, son," his father whispered. "We leave soon."

Samuel sat up, wiped his eyes and yawned. He turned to the window. The sun had not crept over the trees. Only the light from the house lit the front yard like an oasis in a sea black as pitch. Henry sat on his haunches near the oak. His head cocked to the side as if he heard something running through the fields. The floor creaked with Samuel's weight.

He cleared his throat and trudged downstairs, one slow step at a time. He turned to see eggs and toast waiting on the kitchen table, the back of his mother hovering over the sink already doing dishes from his father's breakfast. Dad, steaming mug of coffee in hand, had passed through the screen door to the porch.

"Morning, Mama." Samuel pulled out a chair. "Thanks for breakfast."

His mother turned around with a glass in her hand, her apron dampened from the dishes. "Coffee?" She didn't look at him.

"Please."

She poured a hot cup into a plain mug and handed it over. Samuel smiled and thought of sitting at this table the day of graduation when he watched his father scurrying through the front yard with Henry following. His mother finished the dishes and pulled a chair out from the table.

"How are the eggs?"

Samuel swallowed another bite. "Delicious as always. The best."

She nodded and locked her fingers together on the table. "Please be careful."

Samuel stopped chewing, his mouth still full. "I will, Mama."

She grabbed his hand. "You are my treasure. You always will be."

"Margaret, we've got to get going," his father called from the porch.

She stared at Samuel, and he felt his eyes blurring. She pulled his hand to her cheek.

"No matter what happens," she said softly, "don't take any chances. Take care of my sweetie."

"Honey," his father said when she didn't look away from Samuel. "I'm sorry, we really have to go. Sammy'll miss his train."

She let go of his hand, stood and stepped around the old wooden table. She brushed her hands on her apron, bent down, and embraced her son. "I will pray for you."

Samuel swallowed and clenched his teeth. He gripped her back before she released. His mother patted down a piece of hair above his ear and smiled.

And then she was gone, disappearing out of the kitchen and hurrying up the stairs.

Samuel and his father drove away from the house in silence. Henry ran along side the car as he always did. Samuel watched his dog's little legs move faster and disappear into the dust of the fields. Henry's mouth gaped open, his tongue flying wildly behind his face. And then Henry disappeared behind the pine trees near the main road leading into town. Samuel craned his neck for a better view of his four-legged childhood friend, but Samuel didn't see where Henry gave up the chase.

*****

The Wrightman's car sped down the main road.

Downtown seemed a vacant, dark mess. A windy night had knocked over trashcans. A swirl of discarded papers and rotten fruit littered sidewalks. The train station illuminated the sky in the distance. Samuel bit his lip. His father wheeled the car to the front of the station. One man, suitcase in hand, walked through the front door. Samuel looked out the window.

"Well?" His father slapped him on the back.

Samuel turned. "Thanks for the ride. I appreciate it."

"Wouldn't have had it any other way, son." He gripped Samuel's shoulder. "No matter what happens, you just do right. Understand?"

Samuel nodded. "Yes, sir."

"You've made us all proud … I am, uh, I am very proud."

"Thank you, Pa."

His father waved his hand. "Now shoo," he said with a smile. "You best get. Don't want you missing this trip."

Samuel clasped his father's hand, remembered how it once engulfed his own. He stepped out of the car, grabbed his suitcase, and did not look back as he heard the car switch gears. Samuel glanced back to see his father's eyes watching him in the rearview. He stopped, raised his suitcase slowly in a shallow wave. His father nodded.

Samuel sighed and entered the train station.

7

The passengers filed out of the train. Idle chat buzzed throughout the cabin. He leaned against the window and watched the people in the train station go about their lives. They hurried, dragging wheeled luggage to and from the platform. Some embraced long-lost lovers and family members. Others rushed to pay phones.

He sighed.

The station's cool air filled the car, the air conditioning blasting a frigid wind around him. He waved for the attendant, and asked for the blanket she had offered earlier. The blanket helped. He rubbed his hands together, fighting back the chill and he shivered.

*****

Only blood warmed the cold. James Wagner had said that once.

The cold seeped through his gloves, into his jacket, down into his underwear and his boots. The frigid air invaded his mask and hit his face like icy daggers. Samuel tried to ignore it, staring out the B-17.

Not much of a view.

Even on clear days without much chop, the plane rarely provided a clear look at the English Channel. He craned his neck trying to catch a glimpse of Holland in the distance. He knew they headed for Gilze-Rijen. It was supposed to be an easy day, but that just made Samuel nervous. He saw nothing but a white haze. He remembered telling Joe so long ago about wanting to fly. He chuckled at the thought.

It is nothing to write home about.

He hadn't written home since Wagner had his guts blown out two weeks ago. It had been a bombing run deep into France. Wagner's original crew was dead or out of action before he was reassigned to Samuel's on the *Lucky Girl*. Somehow, Wagner had survived the crash back in Molesworth, England. The incident gave him one hell of a story to share during those long periods they waited in their bunks or wasted time at the base. Samuel had heard the story several times.

"I never knew how hot blood would be," Wagner had said once. "It seems stupid it never occurred to me. I didn't know how much there would be."

Wagner always told Samuel it didn't bother him, but repeatedly saying such a thing only convinced Samuel it had bothered the poor Indiana boy. Wagner had been the only person Samuel had ever met from the state. He was shy, falsely projecting a transparent toughness.

And now he was gone, killed by a German fighter plane. Wagner's blood had been as hot as Healy and Chapman before him. Samuel had seen comrades killed behind him on the left side of the plane. He would never switch from his position as the right waist gunner. Everyone on his crew had their superstitions. The right waist gunner position had become his sole lucky charm. He begged Lieutenant Ray Fischer never to move him. The tall man from Mississippi had so far obliged.

Samuel glanced over his shoulder. The rookie replacing Wagner, Scott Adams, checked his machine gun once again. He rolled his eyes.

"Looks like fighters forming up to hit us," Fischer said, his voice crackling over the radio.

Samuel placed his hands on the gun.

"Where, sir?" Teddy Taylor, the spark plug from Massachusetts, said from the ball turret.

"10 o'clock," Fischer said after a pause.

Samuel turned back to Adams. "That's you, Scott. Drop what you can."

The fighters swept in like insects spitting fire. Bullets rattled the plane's shell. A mad chorus of radio chatter filled his earpiece in the midst of machine gun fire. German planes buzzed past the bombers on both sides, close enough to touch. Samuel fired into the tail of the closest fighter, couldn't tell if he'd hit the mark as the target dipped into a cloud.

"Never seen 'em so close," Adams said.

"Me, neither," Samuel admitted.

Samuel surveyed his field of view and saw no other fighters. He leaned against his gun, staring out into the clouds. The bomber formation was still intact and packed in tight.

"Is it always like that?" Adams asked.

"What's that?"

"Fighters coming in like that." He pointed toward the sky. "They move so fast."

"You expect 'em to slow down?" Samuel did not turn, staring toward the sky.

Adams stopped talking.

Time dragged. His skin felt rubbery, the hairs in his nose icing and hardening.

"Everyone wear your flak jackets," Fisher said. "Should be any minute."

The boom, pop of anti-aircraft fire rattled the bomber as it soared over Holland. Samuel closed his eyes. The plane shook, nearly knocking him to the floor. Outside the sky was pockmarked with black hazes of smoke. The bomber above banked left, splinters of debris twirling from the nose. Metal sparkled in the sunlight. The aircraft dipped lower, slipping behind the formation.

Tommy Folz said from the top gunner position. "Looks like *Stric Nine's* been hit."

"I see it," Fisher said.

Stric Nine fell back from the formation. Now even with the *Lucky Girl*, the damaged bomber caught fire. Samuel watched some of the crew fall into the clouds below as the plane fell. He hoped they had parachutes. The bomber shuttered. An engine popped and spewed pitch black smoke into the white clouds before she dipped out of Samuel's vision.

"What will happen to them?" Adams asked, his eyes focused on the clouds.

"Shut up." Samuel shook his head.

The *Lucky Girl* shook and dropped a hundred feet. Samuel hit his head on the end of his machine gun, blurring his vision. Blood pumped into his ears.

A lump formed in his throat. Thousands of pieces of metal rattled against the fuselage like hail on a tin roof. He clenched his teeth.

When Chapman died in his arms from shrapnel in the neck, the wound had drenched Samuel's pants. The German fighters never bothered Samuel, but the flak did. The endless flak. He couldn't fight off flak.

He closed his eyes to return home again under the big oak with Henry on his lap. His father worked on the car. His mother stood behind the sink of clattering dishes. The sun set behind massive pines in the distance. Annie approached, carrying lemonade.

The plane bounced.

"Oh my God!" Adams yelled.

"What?" Samuel asked, whipping around to see where the boy had been hit.

"Is this normal?"

Samuel shrugged and sighed. "Sometimes, it's worse." He winced at his lie.

It was *always* worse.

"All right boys, we're all set," Fischer said. "Dave, you got the control."

Samuel swallowed hard. Dave Wright took control from his bombardier position. Wright peered through the bombsight. "Got it, sir."

Adams stared at Samuel, his blue eyes wide, surrounded by redness.

"Bombs away," Wright said and pulled away from the bombsight. He wiped his eyes before leaning back. "Take over, sir."

Adams stood up. "That's it?"

"Don't jinx it," Samuel said. "We're about to go through it again."

Adams deflated, staring at the floor. The plane shook as if to underline Samuel's point.

The flak eventually lightened and then, finally, ceased. The entire formation gained altitude and moved into the clouds. Samuel scanned the sky, but it seemed the formation was alone. He smiled.

His thumping heart slowed, sweat droplets on his forehead disappeared. Cold air surrounded the exposed skin on his face. He prayed for a quiet flight back to the base, to England.

*****

Stric Nine hadn't made it home. The bomber was last seen disappearing into the white cotton clouds hovering above Europe. No one spoke of the loss as everyone exited the plane more than three hours after taking off. Instead, everyone was talking about the *Black Diamond Express*, a B-17 whose tail gunner had been hit by a twenty-millimeter shell in the right hip and arm. The B-17 was expected to return to Molesworth after stopping at the twelfth evacuation hospital. Just hearing about it all made Samuel feel lucky, too lucky.

"That wasn't so bad," Adams said while lifting his gear.

Samuel checked his gun and moved to the end of the plane. He jumped down to the landing field and walked fast to avoid any more of

Adams' talk. The barracks' door opened, and two chatting men walked inside. The rest of his crew must still be out on the landing field.

He sighed, sat back on his cot, crossed his feet and closed his eyes. His thoughts drifted to earlier as he wondered if the German fighter pilot survived the fire Samuel sent into the plane's tail. His thoughts turned to Joe. His old friend was fighting in the Pacific. They had spoken only once since their final drink together when they talked about fishing and Annie Ruth.

Annie.

He'd written her twice in the first week of the month, but today was August nineteenth, and he wished he had sent more, but he never felt like writing. It wasn't Annie or penning the letters. He hated dating them. He hated the reminder of how much time had passed.

All correspondence from home had been the same. Mr. Luther had a great Saturday. Pa fixed the old blue truck again. Church was thinking about adding a pavilion for the summer picnics.

Samuel pulled the most recent letter from beneath his cot. The letter had arrived three days before. He felt the corners of the envelope. With his index finger, he traced the curls and loops of his name. Across an entire ocean, Annie had held this envelope before sending it. She had written the words, probably during her lunch break. He pictured her at a desk in the back of the post office, hovering over the letter as she considered what to say. Max probably watched her, wondering if Samuel would show up so they would go on their walks once again.

"Wrightman."

A voice echoed across the bunks. Samuel folded the envelope back beneath his bed once again. "Yes, sir."

"Need to talk to you." Lieutenant Ray Fischer marched through the barracks. His pointy nose and thin bone structure reminded Samuel of a rat. The man's steel blue eyes remained trained on Samuel as he stepped closer.

The other men in the room stepped outside. Samuel remained at attention.

"Relax, Sergeant."

Samuel exhaled. "How'd we do today, sir?"

"Twelve confirmed. Ten probable. Damaged a handful, but we lost ... too many men." Fischer sighed before he continued. "Need to ask you a favor."

"Anything, sir."

Fischer peered back over each shoulder and took one step closer. "We need to look out for each other. You know that. That begins on the ground."

"Yes, sir," Samuel said and frowned, unsure where Fischer was going. The Lieutenant nodded. "I know you used to talk to Wagner."

Samuel chewed on his tongue for a moment.

"The man died in your arms after three missions," Fischer continued. "Don't think I don't know what you've been through, Wrightman. Wagner. Healy and Chapman before him. You've been through hell. And you and I have been together since the beginning."

"It's been an honor, sir."

Fischer's thin lips parted before revealing a crooked smile. "I want you to work with Adams. He needs your experience, your concentration. I know he talks too much. Seems too anxious. I want you to shut him up a little bit without making him feel he's not part of the crew. Give him some tips." He stared at the wall and sighed. "God only knows I don't have all the time in the world to help him." He looked back at Samuel. "Do you understand?"

"Yes, sir."

Fischer seemed to look off to another place for a moment. "That was a tough one today. Some milk run."

Samuel blinked. Fischer smiled, snapped around and marched back out of the room.

Samuel collapsed back down on the bed and pulled out Annie's letter. He held it to his lips, inhaled deeply, and left the envelope on his chest. He closed his eyes, allowed darkness to take him.

*****

"Wrightman."

He opened his eyes. The light hurt.

"Wrightman," a voice called. "I hate to wake you. Lieutenant said you wanted to see me."

Samuel opened his eyes. Adams youthful face stared down.

"Yeah." Samuel clenched his teeth and sat up. He slid his legs down, gesturing for Adams to take a seat on the cot in front of him. "You okay?"

"I'm okay, I guess."

Samuel sighed. "Scares me every time."

"What?"

Samuel pointed up. "Being up there. Bullets rattling around inside the plane. Fighters zipping past trying to get a clear shot."

Adams nodded. "I didn't know …"

"You thought it'd be like a shooting gallery, didn't you? Yeah, they don't slow down for you. Fighters don't bother me, though. It's the flak."

His eyes widened. "Does that get any better?"

"No," he answered without delay.

Adams leaned back. "I just wanted to fly." He smiled. "Never really gave much thought that somebody'd be trying to shoot me down."

"Smartest thing you've said all day."

"What's that?"

"You never gave it much thought." Samuel nodded. "You can't. Don't. Just keep pushing it all out of your mind. Sooner you do that, happier you'll be."

*****

55

The room filled. Men spoke about women, war, and buddies fighting in Africa and the Pacific.

One of the guys spoke of his older brother fighting somewhere on an island he couldn't pronounce.

Samuel and Adams went to eat. During the meal, Samuel endured endless questions. As they finished, Adams asked him about the women in England. Samuel grinned at the question because he had no idea of the answer. Adams had no wife or child waiting on him at home. Samuel discovered Adams had nothing but his parents waiting.

No friends.

No lovers.

8

The young man kissed her on the cheek. Her head swayed as he caressed her face. He said something. She nodded. The man ran away as an announcement echoed throughout the hallways of the train station.

He leaned his head against the window as the drama unfolded. The train rumbled, rattling the windows. The young woman stepped back from the train and propped herself against the wall. The train pulled him away from her, and she disappeared.

The view changed, the city revealing itself.

The young man walked into his train car and sat next to him.

*****

"We're going out again." Teddy Taylor's words seemed to hover in the air. "Tomorrow."

Samuel squinted in Teddy's direction, lifting his hand over his eyes to shade them from the sun. "France again?"

"That's the rumor." Taylor nodded, his chubby face full of stubble that never really seemed to go away. "I bet the officers are over there right now planning the next disaster."

Four days before, they had carried out a mission to Watten, France. One crew hadn't come back. Samuel thought of the them, trying to remember their faces.

Teddy walked away. Samuel's vision fixed on nothing. He kicked a stone into a pile of weeds next to the base of the building. Mechanics scurried like ants on a carcass over the line of bombers. Samuel watched them work, some laboring on the engines, others going in and out of the aircraft.

Adams walked up behind him.

"We're going back to France already?" he asked, licking some food off his lips.

Adams has been on four missions now. Still the endless questions persisted.

"Why would they do that? Those other guys didn't have a chance. What makes them think we'll be any better?" Adams asked, his voice cracking with the final word.

Samuel turned. Adams' wide eyes remained fixated on the bombers.

Samuel looked back at the planes. That familiar twist in his stomach tightened, his mouth drying up as he watched the crew prepare the planes.

"They send us where we need to go. It's not worth worrying about," Samuel said.

Staring once more into the overcast sky, he trudged back to the barracks. He made his way to his cot and grabbed a piece of paper. A tremendous weight pressed on his chest as he grabbed a pencil and started to write, unsure how he would convey what he wanted to communicate. He paused and started writing.

August 30, 1943

My Dear Sweet Annie,

I should have been writing more, but I think you would understand if you could see the sadness of this place. It ain't sad cause of the war. It's sad cause you're not here. I suppose a person doesn't know how strong their foundation is until they have to do without it for so long. You are and always will be my foundation, my one and only rock, forever.

If something should ever happen to me, know I will be watching over you. I promised you I'd come back, but in this place fate is out of my hands. I pray you find happiness and the means in your heart to forgive me for leaving you. If I can, I will let you know I am there through the gentle caress of a breeze on your face or the whispers of the wind swaying through the treetops. All will be right in the end; I promise you. I know now I should have left the decision to leave up to God.

But it's too late now. I'm here. I have to live with that.

More importantly, I should have stayed by your side and married you before I left.

I miss you. Tell Mama and Pa I miss them, too.

Love,
Your Sammy

*****

Waiting was the worst part of the war.

His vision blurred into the white of a cloud.

Instead of a wife waiting, he had a fiancé. Annie Ruth had never spoken out against waiting to marry. But he knew every sewing circle from Bloomsdale to Terrytown discussed bad ol' Sammy Wrightman leaving Annie when he went off to war.

She had only told him to come back.

And that's all he wanted to do. He wanted to hold her again, really hold her. It will mean so much more now. Throughout his last years in school, she had always been there for him. He knew now he took her for granted. As the bomber flew closer to enemy territory, he wondered once again if he would ever get the chance to tell her in person, confess he had been wrong to volunteer.

Samuel sighed as the frigid air caused his eyes to water.

"Check two o'clock, Sam," Folz said from the top. "You see anything?"

Sammy gripped his gun and searched the area. The *Lucky Girl* had been flying on the edge of the formation. Anything coming on the right would be his for sure. "Nothing. Don't see a thing."

Folz sighed into the radio. "Getting a little jumpy."

"Don't blame you," Samuel grumbled, tightening his gloves. He looked back to the same area of clouds. The clouds began to turn. The distant whiteness parted. "Wait."

All radio chatter ceased.

Only the constant drone of the bomber's engines and the rush of wind filled his ears. Samuel stared back into the cloud. There was something, wasn't there? Had it been a little lower, the sun wouldn't have been such a problem. There had to be something there, something dark in the clouds.

Wait. Wait.

Turbulence vibrated the bomber. His gloved fingers rested on metal. *Wait.*

A flash illuminated the clouds followed by another. Two German fighters zipped out of the white.

Samuel squinted. Another pair appeared nearby, flying in tight formation. "Fighters coming in," he said. "Four of them, one o'clock."

He fired into the closest fighter, tracer rounds flashing a radiant light as they shot through the sky. The enemy bore down on the lead bomber, machine gun fire blazing from its wings. Samuel led the dark gray fighter, noticing the black cross on its wings. Pulling the trigger, he fired lead into the air. Spent bullet casings ejected from the gun, clattering at his feet.

"Where are they?" Adams asked.

Samuel pulled back on the trigger, unleashing a steady stream of lead. Debris crumbled off the front of the fighter, smoke bellowing from the engine. The plane turned on its side. Samuel ceased fire, watching the fighter spin beneath the belly of the lead bomber, *Winning Run*, whose belly gunner continued to pelt the doomed German with bullets.

"Scratch one fighter," Samuel said.

"Those suckers move!" Adams fired behind other German fighters moving away from the bomber.

"Shut up and shoot!" Samuel yelled as he checked his gun.

"Fighters swinging around," Folz said. "One's coming your way, Sam."

"Got it."

The fighter swept through the clouds at an incredible speed. Samuel shook his head, took a breath. He watched the fighter level out and speed towards their bomber.

"Straight for us, guys."

Samuel didn't wait for the response. He unloaded into the fighter. Tracer rounds zipped brightly through the sky. The German had guts. Or he was stupid. Samuel knew he had riddled the fighter with holes, but the fighter kept coming. He fired until the gun smoked hot. The return fire rattled into the bomber.

The German fighter dove beneath *Lucky Girl*.

"Teddy?" Samuel asked.

"I think you took care of him," the turret gunner said. "Pilot's dead."

Samuel smiled beneath his mask and checked his gun once again. Adams fired behind him in quick bursts. Fainter, he heard the other gunners doing their work.

"Our friends are chasing away the other two," Fisher said. "Looks like we're clear. Report?"

Samuel watched the Allied fighters blaze after the Germans. "We took some hits. Nothing major, Lieutenant."

"*Winning Run* took some hits, but they're still in the lead," Fisher said before shutting off the radio.

"Stay ready, Scott," Samuel said.

"I will."

"No." He stepped closer to Adams. "Really, stay ready. This is what we've been talking about. Our fighters are heading back home. You shoot anything out there."

Adams nodded.

Samuel moved back to his gun and scanned the skies. The flak would soon start up. He clenched his teeth and searched for more fighters.

Minutes stretched. He stared until his eyes spilled tears. He rubbed his face, focusing back out of the plane. There had to be another wave. There had to be.

"I don't see anything," Adams said.

"I know." Samuel tracked his gun across the sky. Come on.

"Flak ahead," Fischer said. "Prepare for some chop."

Samuel took his hands off the gun. Adams remained at his post.

"Get ready, Scott."

The plane bounced before Adams finished with his flak jacket. An explosion jarred Samuel to the floor. Adams reached down to help, but another jolt to the aircraft forced them both to the floor in a graceless heap.

Samuel struggled to one knee, saw dark smoke billowing from one of the right engines.

"Great," he said.

"What?"

Samuel turned back to Adams, gesturing toward the smoke outside. Adams nodded, his mouth gaping open. Samuel placed one arm up to brace against another bounce.

"Little banged up back here, Lieutenant."

"Hold it," Fischer said, his voiced straining. "We took a hell of a hit. Sound off."

All the bomber positions acknowledged, all but Teddy in the turret.

"Teddy, come back," Fischer said. "Sammy, check it out."

"Yes, sir." Samuel moved toward the turret gunner's hatch. He knocked on the metal.

Nothing.

He pounded twice.

Nothing.

Adams stood with his back against his gun.

"Get over here," Samuel said. "We've got to get this thing open. You might have to help me pull him out."

Adams had been moving toward Samuel, but suddenly stopped. "Pull him out?"

"Just do it!"

The two men forced open the hatch. Teddy lay crumpled in the fetal position, a dark crimson pool filling up the clear bubble of the turret. Adams recoiled. Samuel motioned him away with a push on the shoulder.

"Lieutenant, Teddy's gone," Samuel said.

No one responded. Samuel studied Teddy once more. Two large holes in the glass and a puncture in Teddy's neck told the story. Samuel shook his head and closed the hatch.

"Everyone," Fischer said, "get ready for the worst of it."

Adams stared at the hatch. "What about him?"

"Nothing we can do for him right now," Samuel said, looking back at the smoking engine. "Get back to your position."

"We're just going to leave him there?" Adams asked, his eyes wide.

"Scott! Do as I say!" Samuel jerked a thumb toward Adams' gun. "Get back to your gun!"

"We're pulling out of formation," Fischer said, his voice cracking over the radio. "Drop the payload. We're turning around."

Samuel watched the rest of the bombers move away while *Lucky Girl* slowed and dropped in altitude. The formation disappeared in the clouds. The damaged engine sputtered and stopped, the propeller slowing and finally ceasing.

"We gonna make it?" Adams asked.

"Gonna try," Samuel said, his hand clasping his chin. "If we can avoid fighters … just start praying."

Adams swallowed. "Already started."

"Yeah."

The bomber shook, dropped and leveled again. Samuel watched Adams' eyes widen. The rookie bit his lip and peered down at clenched fists, his fingers interlocking tightly. The floor vibrated.

"Is that normal?" Adams asked, his voice shaking.

"Don't go wacky on me, Adams." He stared out at the wing, saw another engine poured smoke out the back. "Lieutenant, we have another engine smoking."

"All right." Fischer paused. "Altitude's dropping. Take off your masks."

Silence. Samuel slipped off his mask. The cold air smacked against his cheeks.

"Get ready to lighten up," Fischer said.

Samuel stood quickly. "We gotta drop some of this."

He grabbed extra ammo and equipment, dragging it near the window. The clouds thinned, revealing green country. Samuel swallowed, glancing back at Adams, who was staring at the floor.

Samuel leaned against the wall of the aircraft. The wing flashed again. "Lieutenant, we got a fire."

Fischer acknowledged.

Samuel watched the propeller slow.

"All right boys," the Lieutenant said, "start lightening up."

"Guns, too?" Adams asked, his voice laced with panic.

"Hang on to 'em a little longer," Fischer said. "Go for the channel before we ditch the weapons."

"Got it." Samuel turned to Adams. "All right, Scott, toss everything that ain't nailed down. Save your gun. We might need it."

The crew tossed their equipment out every opening of the aircraft. Samuel ripped off his masks and gloves, told Adams to do the same. The plane quickly emptied. Now on two engines, the plane whined, cracked and moaned, but still flew. Samuel went to the window, the air slightly warmer than before.

"We got a problem, guys," Vincent Mann, the tail gunner called from the back of the plane. "Looks like a pair of fighters."

"Everybody get to their stations," Fischer said. "Now!"

"Do you see the channel, yet?" Folz asked.

"Don't worry about that."

"Not sure they see us, yet," Mann said.

"They see us," Fischer said softly.

Samuel yanked back on the gun, preparing it to fire. Adams did the same. Folz moved back to his position. Wright stood in the middle of the plane like a man waiting for bad news, his job as Bombardier finished.

"You can't fit in the belly," Samuel said to Wright.

"I want to do something," he said.

Samuel stepped closer, lowering his voice. "There will be an open space soon enough."

Wright looked at him, his eyes moving around the crew.

"They're closing," Mann said.

The machine guns crackled, the engines sputtering. Mann's tail gun spit lead out the back of the plane. The bomber rattled.

"They're splitting up on each side," Mann called. "Eight or nine of them."

"Got it." Samuel scanned the skies. The fighter whisked into view. He centered the gun ahead of the fighter, squeezing the trigger. The gun expelled hell into the sky. Tracer rounds flashed into the fighter before it passed out of sight.

Samuel breathed heavily, blood pumping into his ears. "Score a hit?"

"I don't know," Adams said. "I couldn't tell."

"Doesn't matter."

"They're coming around again," Folz said. "Coming right for the nose."

"Everybody hang on," Fischer said.

Samuel clenched his fists around the gun. Metal smashed into the front of the plane, glass sparkling onto the floor.

"Lieutenant's hit!"

"What?"

Bullets pounded into the plane. Metal shredded. Samuel hugged the gun. The barrage exploded the world around him, debris hitting his face, arms, and legs. Adams writhed on the floor, round after round piercing into his body. Blood splattered the wall. Adams kicked twice, his hands gripping his throat. Blood poured through his fingers, his eyes wide. The bomber lurched. Samuel moved away from his gun. The inside of the plane was ravaged. Holes revealed the sky. Wind gusts blew navigation charts and paper fragments into a swirl. Samuel steadied himself with one hand. The plane engines groaned as the aircraft pitched forward.

"Bail!" someone screamed. "Everybody bail!"

Adams' body slid to the front of the plane, leaving a crimson trail behind him. All the spent casings rattled behind Adams, who gurgled, reaching out a hand. His fingers shook, his eyes widened. Samuel grabbed Adams' hand, and saw the life of his eyes fade. The bomber pitched forward.

Samuel moved to the escape hatch. "Everybody out!" he yelled, checking the straps on his chute.

Wright tumbled out of his bombardier post, three holes in his back. Samuel slipped, steadied himself with his right hand, and moved to the exit. The door blew open, and a rush of wind bashed him in the face. The bomber tipped forward. He swallowed.

Samuel threw himself out into open space. The bomber disappeared. The world twisted, the wind rushing into his ears. His eyes burned, filling with tears. Samuel reached for the ripcord. His hands flailed. He turned over again. His stomach turned. He closed his eyes. The world spun round. He clenched his teeth, thought, Mama and Pa will receive their telegram. Annie will hear the news from the rest of the town, from gossiping women who enjoyed the sound of a tragic story coming from their lips to virgin ears. The joy of shattering someone else's world because they so hated their own. Worse, he wouldn't come back as he said he would do.

His fingers found the ripcord.

Samuel yanked, the chute unfolding from its pouch.

The spinning world stopped. His body jerked. He felt as if he had hit the ground. His head pounded, his feet swinging in the open space. A soft wind touched his cheek, a welcomed feeling after the chaos. He exhaled, allowing his head to fall back. His mouth gaped. He took several rapid breaths, his heart racing as he realized he didn't know where he was.

Samuel opened his eyes to see a chute above and another chute farther away. Someone else had escaped *Lucky Girl*. The sun gleamed through the parachute's canvas. Samuel blinked.

The German fighters turned around, bearing down on the other parachute dangling helplessly above him.

"Oh, Jesus," Samuel said through clenched teeth as he gripped his harness hard enough to whiten his knuckles. "Please no!"

The fighters fired into the parachute. The bullets hit the man. Was it Fischer? Maybe Mann?

He couldn't tell.

Two other fighters passed in front of the other parachute, firing into the poor soul hanging in space. Samuel watched and finally looked away as the Germans soared off into the distance. He knew whoever had escaped the *Lucky Girl* with him was dead, the body slowly falling down to France. He frantically looked around. No other chutes. No one else had made it out alive.

He was alone.

Thunder crashed. He looked into the horizon, saw smoke rising from the forest in the distance.

Fire engulfed the trees.

His B-17. The *Lucky Girl*.

He shook his head, trying to clear the fog. Warmth slid down the side of his face. He touched his cheek, saw blood dripping down his fingers. He reached for his knife and gazed at the endless miles of green and brown fields rushing toward him. He scanned the sky once more and saw no chutes. He tried to decipher the location of the channel. The clouds masked the sun, and he couldn't tell what direction was west, toward the channel and England.

The horizon fell and decreased his visibility. The dark green tree canopy revealed a small pond. He smelled rotting logs and damp leaves, just like the pond back home. Something split through the air, zipping by his head. A realization shot through his body.

Bullets.

Germans from below were shooting at him. He didn't have much time. The parachute's canvas tore into two holes, and then three, four. Someone shouted in the forest, followed by more voices.

Samuel grabbed his knife and sawed through the harness. Another bullet tore into his chute. The wind rushed into his face. His muscles clenched.

He was falling.

He cut through one harness and turned to the other.

A bullet struck his calf. Samuel cried out, clenching his teeth. Sweat beads formed on his forehead. He fought back the urge to scream, sawing through the remaining strap.

And he was free.

He tumbled through leaves. His arm snagged a branch before he submerged into cold water. Samuel spun round under murky water, grabbing his calf muscle and screaming. Bubbles fluttered around his face. His boots sunk deep into slush. He pushed up gently, ignoring the flash of pain.

Water split over his head. The air felt frigid on his wet face. He took a deep breath, and ducked beneath the surface, kicking hard for the shoreline. He swam until his muscles burned and his lungs caught fire. The ringing in his ears increased. His hands dipped into the soggy mud at pond's edge. Samuel rose above the water. The weeds provided some cover. He stayed low and surveyed his surroundings, his hands and lips trembling.

The pond did indeed appear like McPherson's Pond back home. Instead of pine trees, thick hardwoods with lush green leaves encircled the water. The ripples and waves from his landing subsided. The parachute blew from treetops on the other side of the pond. Voices shouted through the forest. Another voice answered back, much closer. Samuel swore and glanced at his leg. A neat hole started on his inner calf and ended on the other side.

He pulled his pistol from inside his uniform, prayed the bullets still fired. He ripped a strip of fabric from his shirt, ignoring the pain and placed the makeshift bandage onto the wound. A small stick caught his eye and he placed it between his teeth, bit down, and yanked the knot tight. Pain flashed, and he closed his eyes. Samuel fought the urge to throw-up. He leaned back into the shore's mush, feeling cold water surround his head. It seeped into his scalp as he gazed into the darkening, gray sky.

9

The young man asked about the trip and where he traveled. The old man obliged the apparently wealthy youngster. Shortly after, the young man fell asleep. He glanced at the colorful photos inside the glossy pages, wondering at the images of faraway places and rich people. All of the places in the photographs had to be reached by air, something he didn't want to do again. The drizzle continued outside his window, droplets streaking in long, horizontal lines.

*****

A cold mist sprinkled across his face. A cut on his forehead burned. Samuel opened his eyes to a dark sky. He blinked twice, shivered, and folded his arms over his chest. A breeze sent ripples across the pond. The voices had ceased, and Samuel wondered dimly how long he had been asleep. The shoreline sludge slurped as he sat up on his hands. He rolled his neck around. His stomach grumbled. Insects buzzed around his face. He couldn't see much.

A small wooden barn stood at the edge of one end of the pond, a pair of cows dipping their long tongues into the water. At the other end, stretched a line of thick trees. The pond parted into a creek behind him, twisting and turning away from the main body of water. He took a step toward the creek, but pain flashed through his leg. Samuel placed one hand on the creek bed to steady himself. The mist turned to full rain. Samuel shivered.

He shuffled across the creek bed to the other side. He inched through the trees, crouching low behind the shrubs. At the edge of the forest, the trees ended at a green field stretching off into the horizon. Massive craters pockmarked the entire area from a string of bombs dropped long ago. Samuel leaned against a thick tree and peered at the landscape.

Broken farm equipment littered one end of the field. To his left stood the barn with the two drinking cows. The wind shifted, and rain fell sideways across the land. The smell of cow manure swept into his nostrils. It reminded Samuel of his grandfather's farm. Thunder rumbled. The sky flashed with lightning. The rain intensified. Large, fat raindrops splattered onto his head from the treetops.

Samuel crept along the tree line toward the barn. The cows had moved toward the trees by the time he reached the fence. He gripped his pistol and pointed at the barn door. He cocked it with his free hand.

Samuel stared back across the field. When lightning flashed, he saw a small farmhouse stood a half mile away at the top of a short rolling hill. One lone light burned on the porch. He squinted. No movement.

He stepped into the barn and pulled the doors closed. Rain dripped through the roof. He moved some hay into a dry area and fell in a heap. Samuel rested his head on a patch of hay and curled into the fetal position.

The shivering wouldn't stop.

Samuel felt around in the dark, searching blindly. He found no tools to make a fire. A blanket hung on the wall. He grabbed it and wrapped himself before he burrowed into the hay.

The storm worsened, thunder rumbling for hours. The rain poured outside like waves crashing onto a beach. Samuel closed his eyes tightly, trying to will himself somewhere—anywhere—but this barn in what could have been any country in Europe for all he knew. He didn't think the Lieutenant had veered off course during the mission. If he hadn't, then this barn was in France. He had slept the previous night in a bunk in England. Now, he was under a stack of hay.

Two years ago he would have been sleeping in his bed at his parents' home. He would have awoken to his mother's breakfast or his father scurrying around outside. Maybe his day would have included fishing with Joe or working the afternoon at the general store. Or he and Annie Ruth would have met for lunch or dinner.

But now he was in this barn surrounded by the smell of cow manure and hay. And he had no one to blame but himself. Thunder continued as he pushed away the voices of his parents and Annie echoing in his mind, asking him not to leave.

*****

Sunbeams cut through the barn doors. Dust slowly travelled within the light making the room look peaceful. Samuel blinked trying to remember what had happened and where he was. The barn was hot, yet, he continued shivering. His clothes had gone from drenched to an uncomfortable dampness. Samuel sat forward. Hay fell out of his hair and into his face. He pulled up his pant leg to see the bandages had turned a dark red. The pain in his leg and forehead intensified when he moved.

Some tools, a pitchfork, and other smaller items, hung on the walls and the fabric he had found to wrap himself in looked like a horse blanket. The cows grunted, and he heard them move around outside of the barn.

Samuel froze. Someone walked in the field near the barn.

He crawled to the back of the barn and created a pile of hay in a corner. He crawled around behind the hay, his leg flashing in pain with movement. The pounding in his head continued, and the cut above his eye throbbed.

Two pairs of footsteps, a grunt, and the barn doors flew open, sunlight bursting through the space. Samuel peered through the hay and watched a man walk through the doors. He was tall with broad shoulders, a hint of gray touched his sideburns under a black hat. Stubble spotted his face like pepper. His clothing was plain and brown. The man grabbed a pitchfork and loaded a wheelbarrow with hay. He passed back through the doors. Another younger man, probably recently a teenager, stepped inside with an empty wheelbarrow. He had brown hair. Peach fuzz peppered his cheeks and arms. He wore brighter clothes than his father, blue shirt, and dark pants, but still plain.

Samuel held his breath. He clenched his chattering teeth. The boy took his time placing hay into the wheelbarrow. The boy whistled softly, peering out over the pond, and grew still. Samuel gripped the butt of his pistol tightly, finger resting on the trigger.

"Papa!" the boy called and ran away from the barn.

The boy and man ran toward the pond and spoke in a hushed tone. The adult spoke to his son, grabbing the boy's shoulder. Together, they rushed back and closed the barn doors. They moved away from the barn, and Samuel stood by bracing himself with one hand against the wall. He limped over to the door. More cows gathered around the father and son as the two worked. The early morning sunlight bathed the field in a golden hue. The sky had cleared from last night's storm.

In the distance, Samuel saw a small farmhouse. Fields and dense, dark green patches of plant growth made up the rest of the countryside other than a compact dirt road stretching past the farmhouse and over a rolling hill into the distance to the east. Samuel wrapped his arms around his chest. A chill ran through his body. He sat and sliced through the blanket. Samuel tore several pieces, forced them into a crumpled ball, and stuffed the remainder in his pocket. He tied a new, fresh piece of fabric as a bandage for his calf.

Something droned in the distance and broke the otherwise silence of the morning. Through the cracks in the barn, Samuel looked to the sky. The sound grew louder, and he searched the sky for bombers, but couldn't find them. He knew they were there. The constant pain, cold sweat, and hunger pains distracted him, twisting his stomach into a pretzel. He frowned, staring out into the fields and watching the sky reflect in the ripples of the pond.

The afternoon passed without incident. The father and son had gone inside around midday, probably for lunch. His mouth foamed at the thought, his stomach rumbling. Two vehicles had traveled down the dirt road, but Samuel never got a clear look at them through the barn walls.

He passed out in the hay.

When he awoke, drenched in sweat and his mouth dry, the sun had fallen behind the tree line on the other side of the pond, painting orange and light blue hues across the water. Samuel stepped toward the barn doors, stretching his mouth and rubbing his jaw. His tongue felt like sandpaper. His hands shook as he pushed one door open far enough to slip through. His eyes watered, the blood surging in his ears drowned out the sound of insects. A dog barked somewhere in the distance. Samuel surveyed the landscape, studied the trees around the pond. He glanced back behind him to the farmhouse. The lone porch light burned once again, illuminating the small shack near it.

Samuel rushed to the edge of the pond. He thrust his face deep into the water and took long mouthfuls. After several minutes, Samuel rolled over with a deep sigh and stared into the sky. He saw a couple of stars peeking through before the sun had finished its day. The cool of the grass at the edge of the pond eased into the back of his shirt. He exhaled slowly, sliding a wet hand through his hair. Annie Ruth loved looking at the stars. It was something she always enjoyed, gazing into the quiet beauty. She always discovered the gold nugget of the day; the one item others would have overlooked. The one flower rising in a sea of weeds. The soft, cool breeze touching your face after a hard day of work. The way the grass felt more inviting and pleasant under a picnic blanket.

He sat up on the edge of the pond, staring at the mirror-like stillness. The smell of fish moved over the water, mixing with that of wet grass. Darkness fell, the sunlight replaced by the faint light of a crescent moon. He stood on aching feet and picked out a nearby hedge. He crouched low, ignored his leg, and limped across the ground. Samuel tumbled into the hedge and listened.

Silence.

Even the dog had shut up. Samuel took a deep breath, looking toward the farmhouse and the closer outbuilding. He stood and moved slowly towards it. There had to be food, clean water, maybe even medicine. Slow and steady. Sweat dripped into his eyes and rolled off the end of his nose. His shirt stuck to his back, the humid air surrounding his skin like a wet glove. He reached the door and glanced back to the darkened house. He paused, catching his breath. He watched the dark house for a moment before he shoved against the door. Inside he found shelves full of tools and jars. Samuel yanked on a lid. The stubborn top released. He plunged his hand in, pulling out something that felt like a cucumber.

The building spun and tilted. He pressed his hand on a nearby shelf to steady himself, but the wood toppled and sent the entire shelf to the ground. Jars shattered and splattered across the floor. Samuel collapsed, falling into a heap of glass and pickled items. The crash echoed in his ringing ears. He fought to keep his eyes open.

Voices cried out. A door slammed. He closed his eyes, bringing his arms around his chest. His body shook, his teeth chattering like a jackhammer. A man with a deep voice spoke in what sounded like French and asked a question. A woman responded followed by a young man. He forced open his eyes. Three blurry figures in silhouette stared down at him. One carried a lantern. The light behind them kept their faces hidden.

He tried to respond, to get up, and run. But his body refused.

Darkness seeped into his vision until there was nothing.

10

"You okay, sir?"

He jumped at the voice, glancing around the train car. The young man stared at him, his brow wrinkling in concern.

"You were having a bad dream," he said. "You need some water or something?"

He shook his head. "Don't worry about it."

They sat in silence. The water beads continued across the window. He tightened the blanket around his shoulders.

*****

A heavy blanket pressed down on him. He tried briefly to lift up, but an overwhelming pain surged through his body sending him backward. He looked around, fighting heavy eyelids. He was in a basic room with a tiny dresser and a brown rocking chair near the window. It smelled faintly of mothballs, wood, and manure. The bedside table held a bowl of water and a wet cloth. He pushed up the blanket and slowly tried to sit up again. He turned to hang his feet off the edge of the bed before trying to stand. He looked down to see dark pajamas and wool socks. His wounds had been dressed.

The room spun and Samuel leaned back into the bed. He didn't know if he'd leaned back for five minutes or five hours. The light outside his window had turned from bright white to a soft, dark blue. He pulled the blanket around his shoulders and drifted.

*****

A cool sensation covered him. His body shivered. He couldn't stop the images from flowing through his mind. The pond. The parachute. Bullets zipping past his ear. The chute tearing. The plane tumbling through the black sky. Adams reaching for him. The boy disappearing through a window. Samuel calling for him.

A woman's voice entered his mind. A voice unfamiliar to him. He allowed the warm words to replace the chill that had surrounded him.

*****

A stiff wind howled. The panes rattled. Samuel stared at the wood ceiling. Footsteps echoed outside the room. He closed his eyes.

The doorknob moved, and the door creaked open. Samuel opened one eye enough to see a young, attractive woman carrying a tray into the room. She stepped softly, carefully as if she knew the squeaky boards on the floor. Long dark hair tumbled around her shoulders over the plain blue dress. She slid the tray onto the side table and twisted the cloth over the white bowl. Water dripped into the bowl and onto the table as she worked. She touched the cloth to his forehead with hands soft as silk. Her hair fell onto his face, tickling his skin.

Samuel flinched, and she recoiled.

"It's okay." Samuel opened his eyes. The woman dropped the cloth and put her hands over her mouth.

She spun around and ran through the door. Samuel heard her run down the hall. A door slammed. He threw back the blanket, ignoring the pounding in his skull, and swung his feet around. He slid out of the bed and stepped on the floor. His leg muscles trembled. He stabled himself against the side table. Samuel took one step, then another, slowly, towards the door. The floor creaked. His body felt as if it had been in that room for months.

The hallway outside his bedroom had no light. The front door at the end of the hall remained open, light shining through from the outside. He passed a living room and an eating area, both with very simple wood furniture and decorations. Samuel leaned against the wall. He nearly fell into the living room.

The front door crashed open. Samuel turned and stared down the barrels of a shotgun.

The man said something in French.

Samuel threw his hands in the air. "I'm not going to hurt you."

The man repeated his previous statement, his eyes boring into Samuel.

"Look, I don't understand what you are saying. Please—"

The man gestured with the shotgun.

Samuel nodded. "Just calm down." He stepped back down the hall without turning. "I'm going back to the bed, okay?"

The man followed Samuel down the hall, keeping distance between them. He stared at Samuel with piercing, black eyes.

Samuel backed into the room and sat on the bed. "I don't want to hurt anyone," he said.

The man and younger woman stood in the doorway for a moment before the door slammed shut. The doorknob rattled and locked.

*****

Days passed when Samuel saw only the young woman, Maria—he had heard her name during conversations throughout the house. The boy's name remained a mystery. Samuel had not seen him since the first encounter.

Maria showed up twice a day to bring him food, water and check his wounds. She never spoke, and since the incident when he first woke, Samuel had decided it best to keep quiet. The man stood in the doorway whenever Maria entered the room. He glared at Samuel every time. When she was finished, the pair would exit and lock the door.

Samuel spent his days enjoying the limited view of the bedroom window. A thin tree blocked most of what he could see, but he looked into the sky through the leaves and saw the grass in the field. The first few days he didn't move much. Instead, he slept away fever and chills. Samuel fought back his fears of the Germans arriving to take him away.

But the Germans never came.

There were only four books in the room, which didn't help pass the time since they were in French. However, he was amazed how much of one book he could understand, thanks to the pictures throughout. It was the story of some fairy tale, possibly King Arthur, complete with knights and damsels in distress. One of the women in the book could have been Annie Ruth if he squinted just right … and imagined she had red hair.

A few weeks passed. Samuel had lost track of the days. The nights had grown cold, and he asked Maria for an extra blanket, but she cowered away and left the room. He heard bombs dropping in the distance nearly every night and watched the sky flicker with light.

One morning he woke to a frigid room. His window was frosted over with tiny white veins leading out from the corners of the pane. His legs protested as he walked over to the doorway. The mirror caught his eye and he stopped. A complete stranger gazed back. The weeks had brought about a dark bushy beard, and his brown hair was much longer, a few hairs stretching over his ears.

He stopped.

His plane had gone down. Had Bloomsdale been notified? Had anyone told his parents? Or had they given up hope already? Surely the news couldn't have traveled that quickly. What would Annie say?

Samuel opened the door carefully.

"Hello?" he called down the hall.

When no one answered, he called again. A dull, bluish light filtered in through the windows. Maybe no one was awake, yet, he thought.

He moved down the hallway to a closet door. He opened to find no extra blankets inside. He wrapped his arms around his chest and worked his way to the kitchen, ignoring the cold wood floor on his bare feet.

Maria stood in the kitchen, her back toward him as she worked.

"I'm sorry," he said.

She spun around.

He held his hands up.

"Brrrr," he said rubbing his hands together. "It is cold. Do you know cold?"

Maria stared for a long moment, her dark eyes darting around the room and back to him. After a long moment, she nodded. "Yes."

Samuel smiled. "Can I have some thicker pajamas or a blanket? Something a little warmer."

For the first time, she smiled and turned around to the kitchen counter. She poured a cup of coffee and placed it on the table.

"Coffee," she said quickly.

Samuel bowed slightly. He pulled back the wooden chair and sat. Steam swirled off the top of the plain brown mug. He sipped and enjoyed the bitter heat as it slid down his throat.

"Good," he said and nodded at the mug. "Good."

She turned around and smiled again.

"Good."

"Good." Grinning, Samuel leaned back in the chair and held the warm mug in his hand. The kitchen reminded him of his mother. The window revealed the farm outside. The sunlight played on the floor. Cooking pots and pans lined the countertop. If it weren't for the language barrier, he might be able to convince himself he wasn't so far away.

The front door opened. The man stepped through, his hat soaked with sweat. His dark eyes widened when he saw Samuel at the kitchen table. Maria and the man argued in front of him. The younger boy stepped up and stood behind the man, watching every point in the argument with his mouth open. Samuel tried to stand but was ordered to sit by the man who did not cease to stare at Maria.

Samuel heard a few familiar words, but couldn't make out any of it. After a few minutes, he sighed and stood up in the middle of the kitchen.

"Look!" Samuel raised his hands. "I don't want to cause any trouble. I thank you kind folks for boarding me here, cleaning up my wounds and all. But I don't think I can stay. I don't really want to go to a Nazi camp, and I don't want to get you folks in trouble, either. So it might be best if I just go on my way."

A silence hung in the air.

Samuel considered trying to run out the door but saw the double-barreled shotgun looming over the front door and thought better of it. The man stepped forward, his hand held out. He motioned to sit.

Samuel took a deep breath and sat at the kitchen table once again. The man allowed a brief smile before he murmured something to Maria and the boy. The two abruptly walked out the front door and left Samuel with the man. Samuel inhaled sharply, wondering if the man was going to kill him.

Instead, the man placed one hand on the table and the other on his leg. He stared at Samuel. The only sound in the house was the ticking of a clock. Samuel studied the kitchen a little longer to avoid the intense black eyes of his host.

"My name is Gerard Durant." The man's voice sounded deep as a church organ. "I am glad you are feeling better."

Samuel swallowed. "You gonna turn me in?"

Gerard said nothing. Instead, he concentrated on a pipe he produced from the dark jacket. He moved the tobacco around inside the pipe for a moment. "No."

The tension in Samuel's chest eased a bit. "Then what am I doing here? I'm not here to harm you. If you want me to head off, just say the word."

"You do any such thing, and you will certainly die." Gerard stared at him with his dark eyes. "The patrols have made their way off by now. I don't know what you did, but you seemed to have avoided them. Chances are they won't come back here anytime soon." He lit the pipe carefully. "I couldn't take that chance."

Samuel fingered the bandages. "Am I going to be okay?"

"Maria cleaned your wounds when we first found you. There was a fierce fever in you at first, and the wounds did not look good. You slept for two days, babbling on about this and that."

He puffed on the pipe twice.

"You nearly died. Then—" he snapped his finger, "you woke and the fever had left you."

Samuel stared out the kitchen window and exhaled slowly. "Thank you."

Gerard nodded slowly and closed his eyes to the point Samuel thought the man had fallen asleep. "You should thank the patrols. We heard your plane come down a few miles from here. It happens a lot, but never so close. Soon after, we saw your … your … how you say?" He held his hands over his shoulders.

"Parachute?"

Gerard smiled. "We saw your parachute in the tree and thought you were dead. The patrols searched my buildings and the pond after." He eyed Samuel. "Tell me how you did it?"

Samuel blinked. "Did what?"

"Eluded them so…completely."

He thought a moment. The past days were still a haze. "I think I passed out in the pond for a time after landing. My leg felt like hell ... pardon the expression. I hid in your smaller hay barn near the pond after that and slowly made my way to where you found me. Nothing special." He shrugged. "Lucky would be the word."

Gerard seemed to take it all in, occasionally nodding at the story. He leaned forward with an outstretched hand. "I am happy you are better."

"Name's Samuel." The men shook hands. "Look Mister Gerard, I know I can't stay here forever. I think I've imposed enough."

Gerard waved his hand. "That is stupid talk. You would be picked up in a day out there. I assume you are American?"

"Yes."

"Where are you from?"

"Georgia."

"Ah."

Samuel studied the man. "How do you know English?"

Gerard tilted his head, his eyes boring into Samuel. "I spent a lot of time in London years ago. Taught the children a little."

Samuel shook his head, wanting to get to the point. "That's great, but I can't just stay here. What would you tell people?"

Gerard laughed. "We never get visitors out here." He looked around the house. "I don't know why my brother ever moved out from the city."

"It's not your place?"

"No." He nodded outside. "My brother's children. Their mother died when they were very young. Charles thought a new start out here in the countryside would be good for them. Then the Germans came. I spent my time fighting until I heard he was dead. That was the end of my fighting days."

Samuel bit his lip. "How did he die?"

Gerard stared off into some far away place before looking back at Samuel. "A story for another day, perhaps. I think, for now, you should try getting out and about. I feel safe enough about you now, I think."

After finishing his cup of coffee and the remainder of Gerard's interrogation, Samuel toured the land and officially met Maria and Charles, Jr. It wasn't until later Samuel realized Gerard had truly been testing the waters with him, determining if the strange American was safe enough to be allowed on the land where cows filled the luscious green grass.

By the end of the day, as the cool air touched his cheeks and he sat near a trickling creek leading to the pond, he had nearly forgotten what had brought him to this precious piece of green.

A cluster of planes, mere dots in the clear sky, served as his reminder. He watched Maria and her brother smile as they spoke. For more than two years, Gerard had provided them the father they needed. He had forsaken duty for family, honor for the simple pleasure of caring for one's blood. And it seemed the two wanted for nothing. Out of all the places Samuel could have landed on this war-torn continent, he could not imagine a more perfect landing zone.

11

The train passed a large pond. He smiled.

"You ever fish?" the young man asked.

He turned. "You like to talk."

The young man shrugged. "Trying to keep my mind off things."

He watched the younger man. "She will wait for you, son. She will."

"How do you know?"

He sighed. "I just do."

The younger man allowed a crooked smile. He turned back to the window and watched the pond pass the train …

*****

"Annie liked to fish. We didn't do it often, though."

Samuel stared out over the still pond smooth as ice except for little ripples moving away from the line. Charles nodded and watched his fishing line. A cold wind blew across the pond, causing both of them to pull their coats around them tighter. The gray sky made it impossible to gauge how long they had been fishing. It had been a while since he'd seen the bright blue sky he had fallen from in the summer.

The leaves surrounding the pond had mostly fallen except for a few stubborn holdouts. He glanced up the tree to where the remainders of his parachute hung weeks before. Gerard had decided to cut it down one night in fear of the patrols returning. He had tied large rocks to the chute and tossed it into the blackness of the pond where Samuel's uniform also rested.

No patrols came back. No soldiers ventured down the thin dirt road. Only other farmers ever passed by the farm these days, and even then rarely. The first time had caused Samuel to panic. He didn't know what to say, but Gerard stepped in nicely at the time, saying Samuel was his second cousin, Jean, from a fishing village near Normandy. His family had been killed in action and Samuel hadn't spoken since. This story seemed to appease the first couple that came by so it stuck. Samuel, or Jean, was a mute.

Gerard told him his cover story and what to say if any of the other locals came by after the couple left. Samuel knew all too well the imposing nature of country folk, but this incident had started him on the path to learning the French language out of necessity. Gerard had been a ruthless teacher in those first months, refusing to answer even the most basic of questions in English. His children loved trying out their English when Gerard was working in the field. As a result, Samuel learned quickly.

"Smells like snow," Charles said, glancing at the swirling sea of clouds.

Samuel looked. "Does it happen here every year?"

Charles nodded. "Yes." He gazed into the water. "Jean?"

"Yes, Charles."

"Do you miss your father?"

Samuel swallowed hard, knowing the young boy had lost his father to the horrors of war. "I miss them all."

"When do you think you will see them all again?"

Samuel bit his lip. "I guess when the war is over, whenever that'll be. Thanks to your family, I don't have to worry until then."

"And then you'll leave us?" Charles cocked his head to the left and kept his eyes on the water.

"That's a long time from now." Samuel placed his hand on the boy's shoulder. "Come on, it's getting colder now. We should go in."

They gathered their fish baskets. It appeared they had enough for a small meal.

"Why the interest in my family today?"

Charles kicked a hardened cow pie as they walked across the field. "I want to know where you come from."

"Really?"

"That and ..."

Samuel stopped. "And what?"

Charles shrugged. "Maria wanted me to ask you."

Samuel sighed and resumed walking. Maria started hanging around more often. Gerard had noticed, too, with sharp judging eyes. He did not try hard to hide his disproval. Samuel had tried not to stir the waters.

"Well, you should have asked me earlier. I don't think I can tell you what you want to know before we reach the house," Samuel finally said as they neared the shack. "We should do this again sometime after our chores and then we can talk about my family."

*****

Dinner was a silent affair. The ground rumbled, and the sky flashed as it did every night. The family did not look out the window anymore. Maria stared at Samuel during dinner, studying his every move. Gerard looked between the two of them, shook his head, and turned back to his meal.

They cleared the table, and Charles went to bed. Maria cleaned the kitchen while Gerard motioned for Samuel to step out onto the porch. There was something different about Gerard's face, something filled with caution. Gerard lit his pipe after closing the front door behind him. Stars had already poked through the giant sea of a dark blue, contrasting with the fading orange in the west.

"You have been a great help here, Samuel," he said in English.

Samuel blinked. "Thank you, sir."

"It's been three months."

"Yes, sir."

Gerard puffed on the pipe. "How long till your countrymen come?"

Samuel frowned and gazed back into the sky. "I really don't know."

Gerard turned to face him. "Can you wait?" he asked in French.

When Samuel didn't answer, Gerard nodded toward the house.

"You mean for Annie?" Samuel smiled and let out a silent laugh. "Of course. I miss her. I think of her and beat myself for not marrying before I left. Besides, I wouldn't do anything to jeopardize your home. If it weren't for you, I would probably be inside a camp somewhere."

Gerard sighed. "She is not my daughter. You are the first man she has been around for a long time. I don't want her to get hurt." He tapped Samuel on the shoulder. "But you are a good man, Samuel. All I ask is that you talk to me if you change your mind."

Samuel smiled. "I will, but don't worry. There is a girl over there waiting for me. I wouldn't let her down for anything."

"Really? You are sure?"

"Yes. And I would never be able to look her in the eye again if I betrayed her. I've never been perfect, but I've never and will never stray."

He nodded, took a few puffs, and watched the light orange fade to black. Samuel stood in silence and listened to the insects begin their nightly song. A cool breeze moved over the land. The trees near the pond swayed.

1 2

The passing landscape was bleak, barren. Mobile homes dotted dead grasslands separated only by the occasional irrigation ditch. Colorful plastic toys littered brown grass in front of each home. Inflatable pools overflowed with green water.

"Where are you going?" the young man asked.

He sighed and stared out the window. "Home."

*****

Snow covered the branches, powdering the fences and barns across the countryside in a frosted white. It reminded Samuel of being inside a cloud.

The ax handle jarred his hands each time it collided with the frozen trunk. The work was slow, the wind cutting into his skin with each passing minute. But the snow had lessened compared to the days just after Christmas when the howling gusts nearly blew him into the ground. Maria and Charles had tumbled down the stairs Christmas morning when they realized snow had fallen the night before.

Samuel had crafted his wooden presents for the three of them. He gave an army soldier to Charles, a simple jewelry box to Maria, and a pipe to Gerard. He had hidden the three presents at the fireplace in the middle of the night. With no stockings to spare, Samuel had created some by folding over his shirts. Somehow, it had managed to feel like Christmas.

He chopped the trunk twice more and wiped his mouth. A white cloud of vapor encased his head for a moment, and he peered out over the horizon. Nothing moved. Only the wind made a sound.

The gray sky had darkened slightly and prodded Samuel to finish the firewood. After taking a breath, he continued without stopping, falling into a trance. He slashed down with the ax until his arms burned and fire seared his veins. The tree tilted and toppled into the snow. Puffs of the fresh white powder lifted into the air.

"Almost finished?"

Samuel spun around, eyes wide. Maria stood in the snow, only her reddened face visible under the winter hat.

"You scared me," he said in English.

Maria frowned. "What did you say?" she asked in French.

"Scared," Samuel said, now in French. "That's all. I'm almost finished here."

"Your French is improving." She smiled and held up ice skates. "I thought you might want to skate before dark?"

Samuel grinned and sat on the tree stump. "I thought Charles had had enough of me yesterday."

Maria shook her head and looked toward the pond. "Charles is with Gerard. I thought we could go."

Samuel stared at her as he breathed. Snow flurries fell between them. She pushed a strand of dark hair from her eye that had managed to escape the thick winter hat.

"I have to finish this," he said after a long pause. "But…"

Maria's brown eyes widened. "Yes?"

"Maybe we could do it another time."

She nodded. "I will not forget."

She turned and strolled through the trees back toward the house. Samuel watched her leave as he rubbed his hands together. She walked through the snow and disappeared into the trees. He hacked the wood into smaller pieces for the fireplace. The work didn't seem as difficult as before, and he was able to mangle the remainder of the tree long before dark.

*****

"I wish I knew what was going on," Samuel said as he looked out over white landscape in the predawn light. A cloud of vapor surrounded his mouth before it swirled out away from the porch. He cradled the hot cup of coffee.

Gerard leaned against the side of the house, a cup of steaming coffee in hand. "You mean the war?"

Samuel shook his head. "Home."

"Ah," Gerard sipped the coffee and stood in silence. A stiff wind howled from the fields and sent the trees swaying. "Maria told me you were going skating soon."

Samuel bit his lip. "Charles might come, too."

Gerard sighed. "Be careful. Maria has been through so much. And she's not your Annie."

Samuel turned and rubbed his dark beard. "What was that?"

Gerard stared at him. "Maria would be fortunate to have you. But not this way, not when your love is so far from here."

"I don't know what—"

"Don't insult me." Gerard looked back over his shoulder and stepped away from the house. "I have seen the way you look at each other."

Samuel nodded. The man had given him everything. He had answered the questions from inquisitive neighbors, created an entire story about Samuel's presence here, put the lives of his remaining family at risk—all for a man who fell out of the sky.

"Why did you do it, Gerard?"

"Do what?"

"Why did you take me in?"

Gerard snorted. "Because you needed us. Because I have heard too many stories of your comrades being captured by the Germans."

"That's it?"

Gerard sighed and looked at Samuel. "I really don't know why. You've been a great help. You have been kind to our family. I worry about you. I know you try to hide it, but you are sad."

"I … never mind." Samuel held his gaze as he thought of Annie, wondering if she still waited for him to return. He glanced up at the brightening sky. "Guess I'd better get to the firewood."

"Yes." Gerard tossed the small amount of coffee left in his mug out into the yard. "I have work to do as well."

Samuel turned to the front steps while he slid on his gloves. He turned back. "I would never disrespect you or our friendship."

Gerard smiled. "I know."

*****

The sun held high in the sky by the time Samuel had finished a wheelbarrow of firewood. The undershirt stuck to his skin, and the air felt cold when he removed his hat. His beard itched. He noticed ice crystals hanging off his fingertips after scratching his chin. The cold was different here, harder. It reminded him of being back in the B-17, feeling the frigid wind slicing through to his insides. He stared into the sky and then to the lifeless forest.

Maria appeared from behind a pair of trees that led back to the house. She carried a small plate and a glass. Samuel wiped his mouth and took off his gloves.

"What are you doing out here?" he asked with a grin.

"Bringing you food," she said.

Samuel blinked. The French was coming easier now. It was midday, and he hadn't spoken a word in English. "Thank you."

Maria shrugged. "There is only so much tending to chickens and housework one can do, no?"

94

Samuel nodded and sat on a tree stump. He devoured the lunch. It wasn't as good as mother used to make, but it tasted good after a breakfast of coffee. He washed it down with the cold water.

"Good?"

"Yes. Thank you," he said, returning the plate to her. "You did not have to come out here."

Maria tilted her head forward. She sat next to him on the tree stump. Their hips touched. "It was no trouble."

Samuel watched her speak. Her lips had grown a deep red from the cold air, just like her cheeks. Her eyes stared at his mouth, and Samuel turned to gaze into the forest.

"What is it?" Maria asked.

He shook his head. "It's nothing."

"Is it your woman back home?"

"Yes."

Maria turned and placed a hand on his knee. "You shouldn't think of her. You are here. You should always be here and never leave. Someday, this war will be over, and that place will be something you don't even remember. *Please*. Stay here with me."

Samuel stood and took a few steps away. "Maria—"

Maria stepped behind him. Her feet crunched on the snow. "If you had been mine, I never would have let you leave. I would have done anything to make you stay."

He shook his head, frowning. "You don't know her."

"I know she has been told of your death by now. She has moved on from you, found someone else. I do not understand why you cannot do the same. You know she has gone on with her life, married the mail boy you told me about." She sighed. "Look at me." He did not turn. "Look at me."

Slowly, Samuel turned while he kept his eyes on the sky. He glanced at her, then to a tree, then the snow. "What?"

"I want you to tell me the truth," she said, her tongue sliding across her lips. "If you tell me the truth, I will leave. I will not bring this up again, and I will be happy with your friendship. Do you care for me?"

He bit his lip and stepped forward. "Of course I care for you, but—"

"Then we should be together."

Maria took a step and put her hands on his shoulders. She stared up, tilting her head back. Their lips met.

Samuel gently pushed her away. "Maria, I cannot do this."

She moved toward him again, but he held her away.

"Maria," he said, "I won't do this to Annie. I can't." He shook his head. "I won't."

Her brow lowered. "But it is impossible to think she waits for you."

"Then I'll believe in the impossible." He glanced up at the sky. "It's impossible to think I could have survived the plane crash, right? Annie has never given up on me. I'm not going to give her a reason to."

"I can be good for you," she said, her eyes falling to the forest floor. "I can be what you want."

"Then be my friend," he whispered. "It's all that I ask."

She nodded slowly, resting her head on his shoulder. They embraced in the middle of the forest.

Samuel backed away, catching his breath and exhaling. "I must finish my work. We can talk more later."

She smiled. "You do care for me?"

He nodded. "Of course."

Maria picked up the glass and plate. "I will see you when you are finished then."

Samuel watched her leave and stood in the forest. The wind touched his wet hair, and he shivered. He reached down to put on his gloves, winter hat, and coat. The cold gnawed at his bones. He picked up the ax and hurled it into the wheelbarrow. The ax twirled, tumbled into the snow, kicking up white plumes of powder. Samuel fell to his knees.

He saw Annie's face, the perfect soft skin and her curly brown hair twisting in the wind. The way she walked across the street in their hometown. Her dress wrapped around her in the doorway of his family's store. And the way she crossed her arms, hugging herself as she shuffled down the sidewalk the last time he had ever seen her.

Samuel pressed his hands into his face. His throat tightened, and warm tears rolled across his nose.

13

"I don't know if she'll wait on me," the young man said. "I won't see her for a long time."

He leaned back. "She'll wait if that's the way it's supposed to be."

The young man locked his fingers together and bit down on his bottom lip. "How do you know?"

He turned away from the young man and stared back out the window. "I don't."

*****

The sun dipped low behind the trees. The air smelled of winter and tickled the inside of his nose. Several stacks of freshly cut firewood surrounded him. He had cut the wood into perfect sizes and stacked them into the wheelbarrow. What couldn't fit, he placed near trees. He would come back in the morning. It was getting dark. The family was probably sitting down to dinner, wondering where he was. Samuel stared at the darkening sky and considered wandering off into the woods to try his luck at making it to the English Channel. It wasn't the first time he had considered it. But somehow he always stayed another day, another week, another month.

He rubbed his beard. A chill shot through his body. He started on his way back to the house.

The trail meandered through the woods on the side of the pond. He heard something rumble in the distance. Samuel stopped. His eyes widened.

It sounded as if a car had stopped somewhere near the house. Samuel placed his knapsack on the ground. He pulled out his gun. He stepped away from the wheelbarrow and walked through the woods, far from the trail. He continued on a direct route to the house.

It was probably nothing, he thought. He passed through thick shrubs and tried not to disrupt the branches. The light from the house filtered through the trees and scattered across the landscape in the fading light. Samuel stepped softly. He heard voices, none familiar. He knelt to crawl under a few branches and stopped.

A car had parked just past the house's front porch. One man in a gray uniform stood by the car smoking a cigarette in the cold and holding a submachine gun with his free hand. The soldier stared off down the road and into the sky as he puffed on the cigarette.

The light from the house flickered. Shadowy figures moved past the windows. Gerard yelled from inside. Charles screamed. Other voices barked orders. Samuel clenched his teeth, watching the soldier by the car.

Samuel looked at the shack. Nothing.

The soldier stamped out his cigarette, strolled back to the porch, stretched and sat down on the front step. Samuel stood and stepped out of the cover of the woods, approaching the house from the side. He stared at the windows and the back of the soldier still at least a stone's throw from him. Samuel walked across the field through the ankle deep snow. The ground crunched beneath him, but the soldier never turned.

Samuel quietly walked onto the deck of the shack.

Maria screamed.

"No!" Gerard yelled, his voice booming outside of the house.

The gun felt heavy in his hand. Samuel leaned against the house. Maria shrieked again. He moved faster and made it to the corner of the home. Peering around, he saw the soldier on the porch had placed the submachine gun next to him on the stairs and lit another cigarette.

Samuel lifted his foot and held it over the side of the porch. He held his breath, his heart thumping. His boot lightly touched the porch.

Samuel added more weight and closed his eyes.

No sound.

He brought the other boot up and took another step. The soldier continued smoking and staring off into the star-filled sky.

Samuel held the pistol in his left hand and pulled Gerard's hunting knife out with his right hand. Five steps away.

Four.

Three.

The wood creaked. The soldier spun around, his blue eyes glaring wildly.

"Stop!" Samuel shouted.

The soldier reached for his submachine gun.

Samuel dove into the soldier with the knife forward. The two men tumbled into the front yard, kicking powdery snow around them. Samuel thrust downward with the butt of the pistol, shattering the soldier's front teeth.

The soldier slugged Samuel in the kidney and they rolled over.

"Stop!" Samuel said again. "Please!"

The soldier punched him in the face. Samuel's vision flashed. He smashed the pistol in the soldier's head, and plunged the knife through flesh until it halted abruptly against bone. The soldier gurgled, spitting blood and gasping for air. Samuel stared into his gray-blue eyes. The man fell still and Samuel, trembling, yanked the knife out. Blood trickled from the man and turned the surrounding snow red.

Maria screamed from the home again. Samuel wiped the knife on his pant leg and ran to the door. He gasped for air, inhaled deeply, and opened the front door.

The living room was empty. He heard Maria cry from the back bedroom. The bed rattled again and again. Samuel inched down the hallway.

"No!" Gerard yelled.

A soldier stood in the doorway of Gerard's room and laughed. Samuel stepped closer to the soldier and saw he was massive, standing nearly a full six inches taller than him. If he could get a little closer …

He gripped the knife, lifted it over his head and plunged the blade deep into the soldier's back. The German grunted, turned around, rifle in hand with the knife sticking out of his back. The soldier fired, and the bullet tore into Samuel's shoulder, spinning him around as he fell on his back.

The crying ceased from the back room, replaced by rustling.

Samuel raised the pistol, ignoring the pain from his shoulder. A third soldier appeared at the end of the hallway, his shirt wrinkled and hung down past his naked waist. He grabbed his pistol and fired. The bullet shattered the window at the end of the hallway. The soldier backed into Samuel's bedroom while the larger one had disappeared into Gerard's room.

Maria screamed again.

Samuel stood and ran to Gerard's room. He paused.

Gerard lay on the floor, blood on his face as the giant soldier held his rifle high. Samuel fired three times. Blood splattered on the bed. The soldier fell into the wall and turned around, his rifle in hand. Samuel fired and hit the soldier in the forehead. The man cocked his head to the right, and fell over like a downed tree, nearly crashing onto Gerard.

Samuel ran down the hallway to his room. Maria lay naked on the bed, her dress torn. The sheets dripped with sweat and blood. The window had been shattered, the German gone. Samuel swore and ran back through the front door.

The other soldier, still half naked, jumped into the car. Samuel unloaded his pistol, shattering metal and glass. He tossed the weapon and picked up the first soldier's submachine gun. The German car's engine rumbled to life and the lights illuminated the front porch, blinding Samuel.

He blinked and took a step to the left. He aimed the gun at the front of the vehicle and squeezed the trigger, pouring lead into the car. Bullets tore holes into the windshield. The car backed up and smashed into a tree. Samuel fired into the driver side, punching holes in the door until the gun clicked empty. He gasped and stared at the car.

Nothing stirred.

Samuel fell to one knee. Blood pumped into his ears like a drum. He gasped for breath.

Silence.

The gunshots still thundered in his ears, but slowly faded to the soft sound of snow flurries falling into the headlight's beams. He watched the snowflakes descend in neat lines. No wind changed their course as they appeared from blackness and disappeared into the fluffy cotton-like ground.

Someone stepped behind him.

Samuel spun around, weapon pointing toward the sound. Charles, still wearing his pajamas, recoiled into the doorway. Samuel dropped the gun, holding out his arms. The boy embraced him tightly. Samuel stood and carried Charles into his bedroom.

"It's cold out here," Samuel said, his voice wavered. He tucked Charles under the blanket. "You stay here until I tell you come out."

Charles nodded, and Samuel wiped away the tear lines on the boy's face.

Samuel closed the bedroom door. Maria cried in the back bedroom. He exhaled and grabbed a quilt from the living room. Maria, still naked, had curled into the fetal position on the bed, wrapping some of the damp, bloody sheets around her body. He moved toward the bed and gently placed the quilt over her.

He backed out of the room and moved to the other room to check on Gerard.

Samuel sighed. A dark pool had formed around Gerard's head. His face swelled. His hair matted against his skull. He knelt next to him. "Can you get to the bed?"

Gerard closed his eyes. "Maria? Charles?"

"They're alive."

Gerard stared blankly, one eyeball submerged in blood. "I cannot…feel anything, Sam."

He clenched his teeth. "We should get you in the bed."

Gerard stared.

"Do you want to get to a bed? Do you want your pipe?" Samuel touched Gerard's hand. His friend looked into the ceiling, unblinking.

"Gerard?"

Nothing.

"Gerard?" he whispered.

Samuel bit back tears. He pulled the blanket from the bed and placed it gently over Gerard. Blood soaked through the fabric. Samuel's breathing slowed. The German's body on the other side of the room twisted into an unnatural form, arms and legs reaching out in different directions.

Samuel kept his eyes on the bodies as he closed the door. He looked across the hallway to see Maria still on the bed, her back to him. Her shoulders convulsed.

Spent bullet casings covered the front porch. He would have to take care of that later. But the German car in the front yard was much more noticeable. Samuel wished he could ask Gerard what had happened. Why were they here? Was it a scout? Were more Germans on the way? What did they want?

But he couldn't ask Gerard.

And he couldn't ask Maria, either.

It took some time to push the body from the driver's seat. Several bullets had hit the German in the neck and head. Blood filled the floor of the car. Samuel drove the car to the pond and barn where he had spent his first nights in France. He shut the car off and sat in silence, his breath forming clouds in front of him.

Large snowflakes fell like cotton balls and the wind picked up. Flakes fluttered into his eyelashes as he jogged back to the house. Charles sat shivering in the living room.

"I told you to stay in your room," Samuel said.

"I want Gerard," Charles said with his arm wrapped around him.

Samuel shook his head. "Just go back to your room."

Charles dragged his feet back to the bedroom.

It took Samuel the better part of the night to remove the two other Germans to the car near the field. When he was sure the bodies were secure, he started the car once again and backed it up to the front of the house.

Hoping his plan would work, Samuel took a deep breath and rolled down the window. He hit the gas.

The car rumbled across the uneven surface. The bodies fell on one another in the back seat as the engine whined. He clenched his teeth. The front wheels hit the edge of the pond and the car tilted backward. The vehicle lifted into the air for a second before it crashed down into the water.

Freezing water gushed in through the open windows. It felt like a thousand needles stabbing into his skin. The car hit bottom quickly after it pierced the surface. Samuel knew he didn't have much time. Water surrounded his ears. He sucked in a chest full of air before the water covered his head.

He kicked out into cold blackness. Bubbles filled the space around him. His boots found the roof of the car and Samuel pushed hard for the surface.

The water broke over his head, and he was free. Snow fell into the freezing, bubbling water.

"Jesus," Samuel said aloud, gasping for air. "Jesus. Lord. Help me."

He pushed hard for the shoreline, concentrating on the light from the house. His fingers sank into the slushy bottom of the pond. Samuel ignored the protests from his body. The wound flashed. His muscles burned acid, his joints and bones rubbing together. He climbed out of the frigid bog.

Collapsing into the weeds at the edge of the pond, he felt the wind whipping over his body. He grunted and stood. His clothing suctioned to his skin, and his boots were filled with water. The muscles in his throat constricted. He increased the pace to a jog. The house seemed so far. He imagined the fire blazing in the living room, a hot cup of anything in his hand, and the large quilts of Gerard's family covering him. The wind cut through his body, cold slicing into his bones.

Samuel pushed open the door and fell in front of the fire. He stuck his shaking fingers close to the flame, pulling a quilt around him. The fire popped and crackled, the flames blurring together. His trembling slowed, and, finally, Samuel's eyes closed.

*****

Sunlight warmed his eyelids. The fire had long since died. Two swirls of smoke rose from the ashes. The clock chimed from the mantle, signaling it was eight in the morning. He stretched as he sat up. The quilt fell around him. A chill shot through his spine, and he pulled the fabric back around his shoulders. He stood and slowly walked back to Gerard's room.

The bloody blanket remained near the bed. Samuel stared, wondering if Gerard would sit up to tell him everything was going to be fine. Maria and Charles needed him.

But he was gone.

Samuel shook his head and dropped the quilt. With Maria still sleeping in his room, he needed fresh clothes. He pulled off his clothes and stood naked in front of Gerard's dresser. The air already felt better than his freezing, damp clothes. He slipped on a pair of Gerard's pants.

"What?"

Samuel spun around still shirtless, one of Gerard's sweaters in his hands.

"What are you doing?" Maria stood in the doorway. Her face was bruised, and a short trickle of blood started from her nose, spilling onto her upper lip. Tangles of black hair fell onto her shoulders.

"Maria," he sighed.

She stepped into the room. She walked to him placing her hands on his bare chest. He stared at the wall, avoiding her eyes. She pulled him closer and nestled her head on his chest, gripping him tightly. He put his arms around her back, rubbing her head. She exhaled, and they stood in silence. A bright sunlight filtered in through the windows. She sniffled.

"Is that him?" she finally asked, her head still on his chest.

He nodded. "We have to take care of him."

"What about the soldiers?"

"That's done."

She raised her head and recoiled, staring at his shoulder. "You are hurt?"

"I was hit."

"We need to clean this."

"It'll be okay." He nodded, wincing at the pain on his shoulder. "We will clean it after."

She sighed again. "I am thankful you are here."

He clenched his teeth. "You need to take care of Charles. I will take care of Gerard."

*****

The sun hung low in the cloudless winter sky. Samuel, Maria, and Charles stood in the family burial plot located in dense woods half a mile from the house. A soft wind moved through the trees, the branches touching with clicking sounds. The rest of the forest was lifeless. They stared at the shallow grave Samuel had carved out of the frozen ground. Gerard had been wrapped in his family's quilt. Charles had asked questions of Gerard. Where was he? Why didn't he want to play?

Maria put her arm around Charles as they stood in silence. Samuel knelt down and placed his hand on his friend.

"Thank you," he said softly, whispering so the others couldn't hear him. "Thank you for showing me the kind of man I need to be. If not for you…"

He glanced over his shoulder at Maria and Charles. He turned back to Gerard's body. "I will take care of them. I owe you that much."

Samuel stood, blinking hard to fight back tears. He placed his hand on the handle of the shovel. "Goodbye."

Maria left with Charles and walked back. Samuel finished covering Gerard just as the sun dipped behind the trees. The darkening sky dimly illuminated his trek back to the house.

*****

Winter soon gave way to a cool and rainy spring. Soon, his shoulder had healed, and the pain had lessened. Without Gerard, Samuel found it difficult to keep enough food on the table. The stores had run low at the end of February, and Samuel secretly ate very little, preferring to give the majority of the food to Charles and Maria. He noticed his face had thinned. His beard had grown in dark brown, and his once closely cropped hair now fell over his ears. His clothing sagged, and he added two notches to his belt by March when the world started to feel warm again.

Maria did not speak of her feelings toward him since Gerard's death. Samuel caught her eyes darting toward him at times, but they were few. She had changed and was now focused on Charles. Daily chores supplanted all other desires. He hunted daily to make up for the slow production of the garden, glad for the distraction. When necessary, he slaughtered one of Gerard's animals.

Days passed into weeks. No one came looking for the missing soldiers. Samuel would check the pond weekly to ensure the top of the car could not be seen from the shore. No civilians ventured down the dirt road anymore, either. The farmhouse appeared very much alone in the countryside. As a result, they received no news.

Waves of bombers and buzzing fighters still flew overhead on a regular basis. Whether he was hunting or chopping firewood, he couldn't help but watch them every time. He wondered where they were going or what the target had been.

He prayed daily for hope and the chance to get home. He wanted to send word but knew that was impossible. Although he wanted to make a run for the English Channel, he couldn't leave the farm now.

Two years it had been since he left Georgia. He constantly thought of his father's store, his mother's cooking, and Annie's beautiful face. It bothered him when he had trouble remembering details. They all blurred into a haze. But he always remembered Annie's laugh, her smile, her gentle hand when it graced his leg while they drove through the countryside of McGovern County. At times, he had to remind himself she was real and not a dream.

March passed into April. Samuel, Maria, and Charles had fallen into a routine. Life seemed, at times, even normal for Samuel. If he could push back thoughts of Georgia, he sometimes pretended life had always been in France. It made it easier, forgetting. Hope started to fade, and he adjusted to being a Frenchman. Samuel slowly accepted he would never return home again.

*****

The sun had not yet risen on a June morning. The grim weather loomed like a dark photograph, pestering clouds hanging low and storms battering the farmhouse. Samuel couldn't sleep, and stood at the edge of the pond with a long, crooked stick. He took a deep breath of the damp night air, his ribs protesting. His muscles ached. He considered taking a swim but decided against it.

He set his head back on a soft pillow of grass and stared into the sky. The ground felt crisp against his head. Clouds hid the stars from his view. He closed his eyes. Nothing stirred near the pond save singing insects and a cool breeze. He smelled the dampness of the grass. Joe had always loved McPherson's Pond. Samuel missed the canoe and the sounds of the water lapping against its metal hull.

Thunder rumbled in the distance. The ground vibrated. Samuel opened his eyes.

The blue-black sky had grown dark as pitch. Had he fallen asleep?

Thunder again, a storm on the way.

Wait …

That was not thunder. He propped up on his elbows. Light flickered off clouds in the west. Something was happening. The noise continued. Samuel sat forward.

"Samuel? Samuel, are you out here?"

"Over here." He stood and brushed himself off.

Maria stood several feet away with the lantern sending rays of light rippling across the pond. She sighed when she stepped closer.

"I was worried," she whispered. "What are you doing out here? Have you been out here all night?"

Samuel shook his head and shrugged. "I'm sorry. I was fishing. I guess I fell asleep."

The explosions in the distance continued.

"What is that?" Maria asked.

Samuel rubbed his beard. "An attack."

"An attack? By whom?"

Samuel smiled. "Americans."

He turned back to Maria. Her dark eyes blinked as she stared west. Her forehead furrowed.

"Let's get you back inside," he said.

Maria nodded. As they returned to the house, she turned several times to look back to the flashing horizon. Samuel put his arm around her to guide her, but she still turned back.

Samuel spent the early morning watching shapes on the ceiling created by the outside lights before the sun finally came up.

Thunder continued to rumble in the distance. He moved back to the living room as the floor bucked and creaked. Samuel slipped a light sweater over his head. The soft orange light flickered from the dying fire. He poked at the fire for a while. Sparks twirled and twinkled in their swirl up the chimney. Samuel sat back on the couch and wrapped a blanket around his shoulders.

*****

Warmth touched his face. Samuel opened his eyes and stretched. His back ached and neck popped. He walked to the kitchen.

He stopped.

Through the kitchen window Samuel saw a line of troops filled the small dirt road in front of their land. Some sat in the back of trucks. Others marched in ankle deep mud on the side of the road. All of the soldiers looked haggard, eye sockets dark and swollen. The force moved west. Samuel instinctively ducked behind the sink. He peered through the window and watched. No tanks, just infantry.

"Samuel?"

He spun around. "Charles, you scared me."

"What's going on?" The boy turned to run toward the front door.

Samuel grabbed his shoulder. "No." He picked him up and sat him on the counter. "Watch from here."

Charles watched in silence for a long moment. "What are they?"

"German troops."

"Where are they going?" Samuel swallowed. "Not sure. Maybe the front."

"What's the front?"

"It's where the good guys are."

"What are they doing?" Maria called.

Samuel turned around. "Nothing to do with us." He looked at Charles. "Why not sit down and get ready for breakfast? Maria, come with me."

The two of them sat Charles down and quietly walked outside. Samuel and Maria moved around the porch and headed for the shack.

"What do we do?" Maria asked when they entered the building. "They are so close."

"Leave them be. Act as if they aren't there."

Maria stepped up on the tips of her toes and craned her neck for a better view. "What about Charles?"

"Maria, look at me." Samuel placed his hands on her shoulders. She trembled. "Nothing will happen. If they approach, we will answer their questions." He glanced up at the collage of canned food. "Grab some food for breakfast and make your way into the house."

She stared at him, her eyes wide. "What if what happened last time—"

"It won't." He gestured with a nod. "Go."

She grabbed a few cans and rushed back out the door. Once she left, he calmed himself. The soldiers continued marching past the house. Most took no notice of the house or the land. The cows remained near the pond far from the road. After a while, the end of the line of soldiers crept over the hill to the west.

The soldiers would be back. They would return, and bring hell with them.

*****

A week passed since the company of soldiers moved past the farm. Samuel later found out Charles had watched most of the event from the living room window, despite Maria's attempts to attract his curiosity elsewhere. Other than the distant rumble of artillery, Samuel pretended the soldiers were long gone. He kept to his chores.

The sun soon broke through the days of rain and the sky was a brilliant blue. Samuel ate breakfast and left to feed the cows. The cows once preferred Gerard's hand. Now, they gathered around when he approached. He welcomed the smells, the dank dew mixed with manure and wet grass. The animals chewed, chomped and slurped. Samuel leaned on the fence and stared into the sky. Nearly no clouds at all, similar to graduation day three years ago …

Graduation day.

He looked at the midday sun. Three years ago he sat in his kitchen at home, speaking to his mother about the day. His father piddled in the yard. His dog sniffed at the door to come in.

"All right, guys and gals, eat up," he said to the cows, his voice sounding strange in the relative silence of the farm.

He lingered a moment longer before he turned to walk back to the house. A nice midday snack would do him well. Maria might even—

Engines droned and broke his thoughts. He immediately glanced up for fighters or bombers but saw nothing. The engines mixed in with metal squeaks.

Pop.

The shot echoed faintly across the land.

Pop-pop.

Samuel clenched his teeth and turned around. The cows had raised their heads, jaws still chewing slowly. The wind tossed the reeds by the pond. The tree leaves fluttered. He held his breath and listened.

Movement from the far side of the road caught his eye. Four soldiers, Germans by the looks of them, broke through the forest and plopped down behind a thicket. They worked like insects around the brush before they settled. Other soldiers followed, pouring out of the woods and taking positions on both sides of the road. Gunfire rattled again, closer, the echoes bouncing off the sides of the house.

Samuel dropped the bucket and ran from the field. Some of the cows dispersed into the road. Others moved to the far side of the pond away from the soldiers in the distance. Maria stood on the front porch before stepping inside.

Samuel burst through the door. Gerard's shotgun hung over the fireplace. Maria and Charles stood in the hallway at the back of the house, their eyes wide. Charles bit his bottom lip. Maria placed both hands around the boy's shoulders and pulled him closer. Her eyebrows rose, and the corner of her mouth cocked into a crooked, faint smile.

Samuel nodded, grabbing the shotgun.

Maria disappeared into the back bedroom with Charles. The bedroom window opened, and the two hurried toward the cellar door. Samuel knelt in front of the fireplace, the smell of burnt wood and ash still surrounded the hearth. He checked the shotgun and grabbed extra shells from the flour jar. He thrust the box deep into his pockets and stared outside. The sunlight blinded him. He squinted.

The German soldiers had disappeared. It was as if the ground had swallowed the entire force.

Nothing moved.

The cellar door near the outbuilding crashed shut.

"I did what I could Gerard," he said aloud, staring at the ceiling.

Samuel set the shotgun down on the counter and waited. For what, he did not know. But he crossed his arms and peered out the kitchen window.

The wind brushed across the scene before him and sent the trees dancing. One bush near the pond flashed, the silence shattered by fire and smoke. He flinched and ducked halfway down behind the countertop. The entire forest popped, sparked and moved. Explosions tossed the ground into the air and sent it back down from the sky in large clumps. The cows still near the forest scattered. An explosion sent one down in a heap of flesh, its hind legs missing. He winced.

He saw no soldiers but heard screams in German. His teeth clenched until his jaw muscles hurt. Sweat dripped into his eyes. He wiped his brow with a dish rag.

The ground shook. A small sapling crackled and fell across the road. Samuel watched Germans spit death into the unseen attackers ahead.

He wiped his brow again and leaned against the cabinet. The fighting slackened, replaced by silence.

Hours passed before he collapsed onto the kitchen floor. No soldiers retreated from the forest.

The sun dipped low in the western sky when the gunfire erupted once again. Samuel leaped to his feet and stared back out the window. The treetops flashed like fireworks as the shadows grew long. Explosions rattled the windows, and the machine gun fire ceased. Three figures moved away from the forest and crossed the dirt road. Gunshots zipped around the soldiers as they ran. Samuel slid the shotgun out the window, but they were too far away. The soldiers disappeared into the hay barn where he spent his first night in France.

More movement covered the forest like waves crashing onto a beach. The sunlight disappeared. Clouds drifted in and covered the sky with darkness. He exhaled slowly and slid down to the floor with the shotgun pointed toward the front door. It was the only door to the house, the only way inside

He slid back across the living room and waited. The insects buzzed and sang outside the windows. The wind tossed twigs across the porch.

A gunshot crackled. Another shot fired, much closer this time. Samuel kept the shotgun trained on the door.

A board outside squeaked, another popped. A man outside cleared his throat. Samuel held his breath and raised the shotgun, aiming both barrels at the midsection of the door. Blood pumped into his ears, and the room rang. He swallowed.

Don't open the door. Don't open the door.

The door knob moved slightly. The door rattled against the lock.

Silence.

A gun fired. Samuel jumped behind the couch, keeping the shotgun trained on the door. Bullets shattered windows, splitting wood. Some ricocheted throughout the house. Germans screamed and returned fire from the front of the house. The front door thrust open, and two Germans stepped through, one clutching his leg. Samuel remained hidden.

The wounded man fell to the living room floor. Samuel raised his head. The second man moved back to the front door and fired twice before moving out onto the porch. More gunfire hit the house. Something exploded near the barn.

Samuel slammed his fist into the palm of his hand. He slipped the shotgun over the couch and aimed outside. At least two Germans stood on the porch. They fired into the darkness. Return fire tore the windows apart and sent glass across the floor. The family dishes and glassware shattered to pieces. Samuel stood to see the German on the floor holding a pistol aimed at the door.

Suddenly, the wounded German spun round and fired. Samuel's upper thigh flashed with pain, and he fell back into the corner. The German unleashed a fury of single shots into the wall.

Samuel spun the shotgun around and fired back, the shot booming like a cannon and tearing apart the man's bicep.

The man shrieked and reloaded.

Samuel managed to sit up, his thigh flashing with pain. The German's head spun and Samuel unleashed his final shell. The shot hit the German in the face.

His head came apart. The soldier's body slid to the front door and came to a stop in the doorway.

Another soldier stepped in front of a window, firing a submachine gun into the living room. Bullets sent debris flying.

Samuel rolled behind the couch, reloading two more shells. He rose to one knee and fired, shattering the glass and dropping his target.

He held the shotgun toward the front door riddled with bullets. Submachine gunfire peppered through the front doorway. It felt like a fishhook penetrated his shoulder and ripped him around. He fell on the floor, the shotgun spinning away. He yelled as he landed on the wounded shoulder. The floor filled with dark blood around him.

The dead German lay a few feet away in the doorway. Samuel inched across the floor as the entire house disintegrated around him. Pieces of glass fell like tiny diamonds across the floor. Splinters of wood pierced his palms like sharpened toothpicks.

The dead German still gripped the pistol tight in his fingers. Samuel ripped the man's fingers apart and grabbed it before he fell on his back. He reached back with his good arm and propped against the fireplace. Gunshots flashed through the front door, bullets tearing apart the couch, kitchen and Gerard's bookshelf.

And then the world exploded.

The light blinded him, the sound wave threatening to cave his chest cavity. All the remaining windows shattered. Wood fell from the ceiling hitting Samuel's head. Another shock wave and Samuel's mind slipped into nothingness, comprehending only the ringing in his ears. A third concussion formed a fireball near the house, the heat searing against his skin. He covered his face and smelled burnt hair. Blood flowed from his ears and down the sides of his face.

A German tumbled into the living room with a submachine gun in hand. The man covered his bloodied ears.

"Hey!" Samuel yelled, his voice sounding as if it were underwater. He raised the pistol. The soldier stared with bloodshot blue eyes illuminated in the firelight. The man pressed his lips together.

Samuel hesitated and then fired. The bullet struck the soldier in the head. He tumbled to the burning floor.

Heat engulfed him. He pressed his eyes shut. The whole world burned. He fell over with his face pressed to the floor. Pieces of wood fell onto his back. Samuel heard, somewhere in the distance, screaming voices mixed with popping machine gun fire.

14

He traced the scar on his thigh and sighed.

The young man flipped through the colorful pages of a sports magazine, his thoughts apparently of the girl he left behind. He watched the young man turn the pages, his life ahead full of possibility.

The rain had stopped outside the window. The sun had burned away the clouds to reveal a brilliant blue. A small dog played with a boy outside a broken down mobile home flanked by three rusted out cars with blocks for wheels. The boy hurled a faded tennis ball across the field, and the dog gave chase. The animal ran and bounded through the grass.

*****

The dog licked his fingers until they were covered in slime. Samuel pulled his hand back slightly, but the dog kept licking.

"Not ready to get up, yet," Samuel said with a scratchy voice. "Henry, stop."

Henry never let him sleep past seven on Saturdays. It didn't bother Samuel. He'd loved the dog since he was born eight years ago. The dog had seen him through everything from school to tough baseball games to being nervous after meeting Annie Ruth. He had even been there when Samuel left for the war.

He paused. Henry had raced down his family's road early on the morning he left. The dog's tongue had flown out the side of his mouth, and his tail wagged in that furious way saved only for late night dinner table scraps or tug of war with an old sock.

Something pressed against Samuel's back, face and legs. His eyes opened to a strange face, a stray mutt's mug he didn't recognize in the early morning light. Samuel wasn't home. Rather, he wasn't in the home in Georgia.

He was still in France.

Smoke rose around him as he pushed off the blackened pieces of wood and ignored the pain. The dog whimpered but sounded muffled. Samuel raised his head, but his body wouldn't move.

He rolled over to stare into the sky. His leg flashed with pain when he moved, and his shoulder did the same when he tried to move some of the wood off his arm. Two blackened walls of Gerard's house still stood, that much he could see. Two boots from one of the Germans he had killed protruded from a pile of debris in the center of the living room. Several craters had destroyed the land around the house, and the outbuilding was completely gone.

His eyes darted in all directions. Had the Germans gone?

Samuel used his good arm and sat up to look at the remains of the home. He tried to call for Maria, but his voice wouldn't rise above a whisper. With a grunt, his body collapsed back into the debris. The stray dog sprinted off into the woods at the sudden movement.

He had to find Maria and Charles. The outbuilding's cellar would have been fine. Wouldn't it? His eyelids grew heavy, but he fought the urge to sleep. If he could muster the strength, he could get to the cellar door. But the darkness took him, and he was soon back in downtown Bloomsdale, watching Annie Ruth walk from the post office.

The customers stepped through the isles of his father's store. His Pa was busy. Samuel wanted to help, but couldn't. The scene played out before him as if it were at the end of a long tunnel. Every step he took toward the action did nothing. His father needed him. The lines were getting longer. Where was his help? Was he by himself?

"Easy there."

The voice was faint. Samuel tried to answer, but his parched throat rattled like rocks in a bag full of dry dirt.

"It'll be all right," the same voice said. It was a language he hadn't heard in a long time, and it took a moment for the words to register.

"Americans?" Samuel whispered and managed to open his eyes in the bright sunlight.

A young clean shaven face looked down at him with gray eyes. He wore a green helmet.

"That's right," the boy said. "Just rest." The soldier turned away. "Medic! We need a medic over here. Vinnie, get Nick over here quick. This guy's not looking too good."

The soldier bent down closer to Samuel. "If you say that kind of thing, they'll come quicker, you know? Truth is I think you'll be fine. The leg looks bad. I've seen worse. I don't even think it's more than a scratch on your shoulder."

"The girl."

The soldier leaned forward. "How's that?"

"Girl. Boy." Samuel managed to point despite the spinning ground around him. "Cellar door."

The soldier turned to the man behind him. "Vinnie, check out what he's talking about." He turned back. "You speak English?"

Samuel nodded and forced himself to swallow through his gravel-like throat. "Yes."

The medic patched up Samuel's leg.

He must have passed out at one point after closing his eyes. The sky had darkened to a reddish blue. The soldiers' faces had been

120

replaced. Grass tickled his fingertips, and he raised his head. Someone had brought him from the remains of the house out to the front of the yard. Wounded men groaned on either side of him. No civilians.

A man with a red cross on his sleeve tended a patient a few feet away. Samuel opened his mouth to speak, but only a hissing sound came out. He swallowed for no relief. Frowning, he stared at the gutted house that had been his home.

Soldiers rested on the blackened porch and smoked cigarettes. They laughed and talked about women and booze. The road in front of the house filled with men marching this way and that, some east toward the rumbling of artillery fire, some west toward the setting sun.

"How about you?"

Samuel turned to see the medic standing over him blocking the remainder of the sun. He raised his hand for a better view, but his shoulder ached. "Can't see you."

The medic knelt down. "Heard you spoke English. How'd you manage that? You a spy?"

Samuel glared at him until he saw the smile. "I'm American," he whispered, his throat throbbing with the action. But he didn't think the man was listening to the way he stared at the soldiers smoking on the porch.

"Don't talk," the medic said. "I was kidding. Do you feel tired? Dizzy? Just nod."

Samuel nodded.

"I think the previous medic gave you some morphine. Some Private told me they found you in this house surrounded by dead Germans. This your house? Nod."

Samuel responded again.

The meaningless interrogations continued for what seemed to Samuel like several hours. Apparently the initial soldiers he had seen earlier in the day headed east towards trouble. The night before had seen fierce fighting for miles around the farm, north and south.

Artillery had hit around the farm during a skirmish and took the buildings with it.

But that wasn't what Samuel cared about at the moment.

"There was a girl. And a boy." He coughed.

The medic paused. "Don't know anything about that, sir." He fiddled with the bandage on Samuel's leg and glanced at the shoulder.

"In the outbuilding," he said. "The cellar."

"Outbuilding's gone. From what I've heard about how they found you under debris from the house, anybody in there either didn't see you or left you for dead. You're really fortunate to be alive."

Samuel fought back the urge to yell, knowing full well it would only cause pain.

Maria. Charles. *Where had they gone?*

His stomach twisted at the image of the two of them emerging from the cellar to see the outbuilding and their home burning. The thought of them walking off into the dark made him nauseous. Where would they go?

The medic had turned away to treat other patients. Samuel leaned forward and ignored his pounding head. A rifle muzzle was suddenly shoved into his face.

"Don't go too far," a voice said. "We're still not sure about you."

Samuel pushed the rifle out of his face. Another young Private stood over him.

"I'm American."

"And I'm Mickey Mouse." The Private smiled and lit a cigarette. "If that's the case, where's your ID? Got any tags?"

Samuel took a long, deep breath. His lungs burned. The palms of his hands were blackened. Everything hurt.

"It's all in the pond."

The Private laughed like a hyena. "The pond, yeah, that's rich. The pond, he says."

"What's going on?" he asked.

The Private shrugged. "Not sure."

Samuel punched the ground with all the strength he had and collapsed back into the grass. Flies buzzed around some of the wounded men to either side of him. The place smelled of rotten flesh. He dimly realized none of his cows grazed anywhere nearby. He wondered where they had gone.

The Private wasn't entirely worthless. Samuel discovered the Allies had landed in France June 6 and had been battling since. Bombers still hit Germany regularly, or at least, that's what the Private told him.

And, of course, the soldier hadn't seen a girl or a young boy.

Night fell amid the sounds of men screaming for the mothers and sweethearts, sometimes both. One soldier came back from the front with the left side of his face missing. Samuel swallowed as he looked into the swirl of flesh and wondered how it ever resembled someone. Among all the activity moving up and down this road, no one had seen Maria or Charles anywhere.

Samuel managed to doze off in the grass after yet another Private left him. A truck had arrived to carry the wounded back … to somewhere else.

He didn't ask any questions and struggled to stay awake as two men helped him into the back of the truck. Other soldiers on stretchers loaded into the vehicle before it turned around in the field, swinging wide around the wood pile. It drove back to the road heading east.

He watched the pond reflecting the stars and moon, the pond he had landed in so long ago. Soldiers lined both sides of the road leading up to the house. The road bounced the truck around, and the scene soon faded into the blackness.

He stared down at his calloused hands. A soldier groaned next to him. He placed his hand on the soldiers' shoulder. He leaned against the back of the truck, rubbing his crusty beard with the good arm that didn't hurt, and closed his eyes.

* * * * *

Skin pulled against the adhesive bandage. Samuel recoiled.

The brunette nurse was here today, the one with the brown eyes like chocolate. He stared at them often, wondering where she came from. However, the first week at the hospital in England had been far from hospitable. The endless questions by men in uniform, asking him where he was from and the names of his parents repeatedly until he, too, wondered about the truth.

"Morning," he whispered.

The nurse smiled back to reveal her bright teeth in the sunlight glaring through the circular windows behind his bed. She placed the bandage back on his arm with a gentle pat of her hand.

"No signs of infection." She nodded. "You must have prayed hard. Fever's gone, too."

Samuel frowned. "I had a fever?"

"Yes," she said. "It broke yesterday. You have been in and out, probably due to the morphine they gave you in the field. You're coming off of it now."

As if to answer her, his arm and leg flashed with pain. He winced.

"Seen much worse come through here," she said while checking the bandage on his leg. "But not many with a story like yours."

"Like mine?" He stared at the ceiling, trying to ignore what the nurse was doing.

"They say you were found under a house…or what was left of a house—you're leg looks good, too—and they weren't even sure you were American."

He sighed. "Did they find Maria—the girl that was with me—did they find her? What about Charles?"

The nurse moved up to his face and placed her hand on his forehead. "I don't know."

He swallowed. Maria had been so afraid, her eyes flashing outside toward the German soldiers as she stood in the hallway, Charles in her arms. Her skin glowed with sweat. Her fingers wrapped around Charles so tight her knuckles turned white. The boy stared off into nothing as if he were already dead. Samuel had thought to join them in the cellar. Now, he wondered if he would have died with them.

But he didn't know they were dead, did he?

"You say they found me in a house?"

The nurse smiled. "They say you were under the burnt out beams from the house. You did have many burns all over your body. It was artillery, they said, that destroyed the building."

"And no one was found with me." His eyes blurred. He looked away, forcing himself to swallow.

"My name is Jessica." The nurse sat down next to the bed. "I'm from Missouri."

Samuel nodded, unable to look at her.

"If you need anything," she said after a pause when he didn't answer, "let me know."

She reached out and squeezed his hand. Her skin was soft to the touch. Samuel closed his eyes, felt a tear stream down his cheek. Jessica stood and walked away, speaking softly to other patients.

Gerard would have cursed him. He had let the entire family down. The family that had saved him, that took him in when others wouldn't have risked it.

And now they were gone.

Samuel fought back the sobs and lost. The groans of other wounded men fell away, and he heard only the sounds of his weeping.

A doctor came by hours later. His blue eyes were cold, his face expressionless. Samuel watched the ceiling as the man looked him over like he was inspecting a slab of meat. The doctor yanked back the bandages on his arm, and leg then grunted. He made marks on his clipboard and, finally, made eye contact with Samuel.

"Mr. Wrightman, your wounds have healed nicely. Your hearing might be permanently damaged. You'll be stiff and in some pain in your arm and leg for a while, but you should be ready to leave here tomorrow."

"Leave?" He raised his head from the pillow. "What do you mean?"

The doctor frowned and glanced at the clock. "This time tomorrow, you'll be gone."

"Where do I go?" he asked.

"I believe they're sending you home, but that'll be up to your command." He stared back at his clipboard. "Best of luck to you, Mr. Wrightman."

The doctor spun round and marched off between the rows of hospital beds, nearly bumping into a nearby nurse. Samuel leaned back into the pillow and listened to the man next to him breathe deeply as he slept. He tried to think of home, but suddenly nothing came to mind.

15

The attendants cracked open a few windows, allowing fresh air to circulate throughout the cabin.

"Feels great," the younger man said and leaned back. He turned. "You said you're going home. How long did you live in Georgia?"

He sighed. "A long time."

The young man rubbed his hands together. "How hot does it get there?"

The warm air touched his face and twirled his hair around. "Pretty warm. Pretty warm."

He closed his eyes, rolled up his flannel sleeves and allowed the wind to touch his skin.

*****

The wind tossed his hair around. The sun forced him to squint.

The truck bounced, rocking him to the side. Samuel had to place his hand on the dull, red metal of the pickup truck. The steel burned to the touch thanks to the hot Georgia sun. The road had not improved in the past two and half years. A young boy, who probably shouldn't be driving judging by the golden peach fuzz on his cheeks, had picked him up at the station with an offer to drive him near his family's property. The boy said he was one of the Franklins, but Samuel didn't know they even had a young one that age when he left.

His wounds still ached, but he had more or less healed. Driving in the back of this truck for twenty minutes didn't help. Every time the boy slammed on the brakes, Samuel sighed and braced himself.

When the tree line on the side of the road broke, he saw the familiar shape of Hawkridge Mountain glistening in the noonday sun. The logging hadn't erased all the green from the mountain. No, not yet.

His family's property revealed itself as the boy, Trevor, took the turn onto Wrightman Road. The long stretches of green grasses spotted by chicken coops and the family barn looked the same. Nothing had changed.

A small dog with a white-gray face walked to the edge of his parents' road.

Samuel froze.

The trot was slower, the legs had lost some spring, but it was Henry. Samuel pounded the roof of the truck's cab, and the vehicle slowed in a tan cloud of powder-like dirt.

"You wanna go to the house, Mister?"

Samuel stood, grabbed his bag, and jumped to the ground. "This'll do."

He paused and allowed the wind to touch his face. Gritty sand touched his mouth and moved between his teeth. The humidity pressed against his skin, a feeling he didn't quite want to remember but one that felt like home all the same.

He gazed down at Henry. The dog took a few steps and lowered his head, ears flattening back against his head. Samuel dropped his bag as the truck pulled away and rumbled down the dirt road. After a moment, all was still.

Henry cocked his head to the left. Samuel knelt down and held out his hand.

"Hey, buddy." Henry's tail moved left and right slowly. "Oh, God, Henry. Whatcha doin' out here buddy? You waiting on me? Come here. It's okay. Come here."

The dog moved slowly from the edge of the road toward Samuel. His old friend moved as if stuck in mud. His paws touched the ground deliberately, softly. Henry was trying to move toward him. Samuel took the last couple steps on his knees. They embraced. Henry attacked Samuel with licks, "doggie kisses" his mother used to call them. He rubbed Henry behind the ears.

"God," he whispered, fighting back the lump forming in his throat. "I missed you, boy. Missed you bad."

He held his dog tightly around the neck and stared into his whitening fur. Had Henry come out here every time a car drove by since Samuel left? Every, single time in nearly three years?

Samuel stared into his friend's cloudy eyes and noticed his black nose had turned a rubbery brown like someone had peeled off the darker layer. Tenderly, he set Henry back on the ground. The dog's backside waved as much as his tail.

The two walked down the long dirt road as they had countless times before. Samuel found himself leading Henry by a few steps, so he slowed down to let the guy catch up. He would stroll along the dirt road at whatever speed Henry could manage.

The lawn in front of the house had no car. His father's truck was parked in the barn away from the house. He stopped.

The house.

It somehow looked smaller.

The paint had faded in the harsh Georgia summers. His swing still moved in the breeze under the oak tree. The fields surrounding the house looked the same. Some of the trees in the distance had started changing color. Fall would soon be here and, with it, the festivals, pumpkins, and downtown dances.

Like a dream.

"Mama?" he called. "Pa?"

A wind chime jingled on the front porch as he stepped onto the grass. He leaned back into the swing and allowed his bag to plop into the powdery dirt. The rope complained under his weight. Henry placed his paws on his knee, but couldn't make the jump into the swing. Samuel lifted him onto his lap. They sat in silence for a long moment, the only sound Henry's deep panting. A merciful wind whisked across the front yard. He closed his eyes.

Home.

Henry jumped down and ran clumsily toward the road. Samuel watched him. A black car turned down his family's driveway, leaving a cloud of dust behind it. Henry ran beside the road until the car passed him. He then turned to chase after it with his tongue hanging out the side of his mouth and his eyes wide.

The car stopped about fifty yards from the tree. The glare on the front windshield prevented Samuel from seeing inside. He placed his hand over his eyes but failed to get a better view. After a moment, the car's engine died. Samuel stood from the swing and walked up beside the tree's trunk, hand on its rough bark.

The car door cracked open, and a woman stood, her hand over her gaping mouth. The hair was a little grayer, a little thinner.

Mama.

Samuel took two quick steps on weak legs and then slowed. His mother shut the car door and ran toward him.

She threw her arms around his waist.

"Sammy, Sammy, Sammy," she breathed. "Thank God. Thank God!"

Her body shook through her sobbing. She squeezed him so tight it hurt. He glanced back to the car to see she was alone. They parted, and their eyes met. Hers were bloodshot and teary.

She touched his cheek. "I don't know how you're here. I don't know...I just don't know." She squinted, and her face contorted as if she tried to hold it back, but the sobs continued as Samuel held her for a moment.

"Everything's okay, Mama. Everything's fine," he said with a confidence he didn't feel. He glanced back to the car and, when they parted, held his mother's gaze. "Where's Pa?"

*****

The headstones stretched like a stone field ready for harvest on the outskirts of the community. It was where Samuel's entire family had been buried for generations since they moved down from New England years before. Visits to this graveyard had always been reserved for people he expected to pass. He had come to the pastor's funeral when he was a child but remembered nothing but black dresses, veils, and one casket.

None of that was here now. Forgotten flowers dotted the landscape to give a little color to the colorless.

Somewhere in this field of stone, he would find his father.

The headstones marked countless lives, some of whom he remembered. His mother clasped onto his elbow as if she would fall any moment, her fingers feeling thin and soft touching his skin.

A bright United States Flag waved above one nearby tombstone. As they stepped closer, he saw the name:

Gary Burns, 1923-1942

Samuel stopped.

Gary was a goofy kid from his class, the kind that always wanted to get involved in everything, but never really got along with anybody. Samuel remembered the last time he saw Gary at graduation, the fake smile on his face and the memories he had tried to conjure up during their years in school. Most were stories Samuel had forgotten. Others seemed to have existed somewhere in the fantasies of a lonely boy without friends. The memory stung his heart. He winced, his gaze lingering on the tombstone.

"Gary went missing at Guadalcanal," his mother said just about a whisper. Her eyes never fell to the ground or Gary's grave. "After a year, the congregation had a service for his mother. Do you remember his father left them just after Gary started school?"

Samuel blinked. He paused at the grave and shook his head. The gentle touch of his mother's fingers pulled him back down the row between the monuments to so many different lives. They did not speak again until Samuel stood above his father's grave.

Pa near the end of 1943. Mother had already told him briefly of the heart attack Pa had one hot afternoon at the store. Luther had called the police when he couldn't wake him. Pa died by the time the doctor had arrived.

Samuel thought of his father's strong hand gripping his own outside the train station. His father had only wanted him to come back.

"He never really gave up hope you'd return." His mother looked away from the grave to the west as the sun had started its descent. "He always told me, 'They didn't find him, dear.' I have to say …" She wiped at her nose with a handkerchief. "I'm sorry, Sammy. I had given up hope."

Samuel stared back down at the gravestone. He should have been here. *The War. The War he "had" to fight.*

"When he died, I had to let you go, too," his mother said. "I wasn't going to wallow around. That store was his dream, Sammy. His dream and his only. I didn't ever want to do that. I thought … I thought it would destroy his spirit if I … I just let the place go."

She hugged him from behind. Samuel did not turn. He continued to stare down at all that he would ever have of his father. The only tangible evidence his Pa had ever been on this Earth was now at his feet. Samuel had no wake, no funeral, just this piece of rock in a field within sight of the city.

"I should have been here," Samuel said after a moment.

His mother's grip around his shoulders tightened as if a gust of wind would take him away at any moment. "Don't say that. You didn't know."

"But he did. Pa didn't want me to go. I knew it at the train station. I knew it before. He tried to tell me." He pulled his gaze away from the stone, turning to face his mother. "He knew all of it. He was right. Mama, he was right about everything."

She touched his face. "You did what you thought was right. That's all we ever wanted for you. For you to know when to do what you had to."

He looked over her head toward the mountain. "You don't know…you don't know what I saw. I shouldn't have gone. Nothing good came of this. Annie said that would happen. I should have stayed, Mama. Nothing good … nothing at all … came of it."

"No." She touched his cheek with her other hand. "Don't you ever say that. I don't want to hear that. You are here now. That's what's important."

"I miss…"

Samuel cleared his throat. He looked to the sky, to the ground and the city's buildings in the distance. "I want him back."

His mother pulled him close and he buried his face into her shoulder.

"I went for him," he said, crying into her shoulder. "For the store. For what people would have said. I went through all of it for him. And for what? So he could die without me here? I should have been here."

Closing his eyes, he saw his father's hand grasping his own inside the family car outside the train station. That morning, now a dozen lifetimes past, Samuel left his world.

He looked into his father's eyes, only a memory now and forever.

His father's half smile, only a memory.

The sandpaper-like stubble he rubbed his hands against as a boy, only a memory.

*****

The sizzle sounded like home.

His mother flipped pancakes at the stove. The scene outside the window appeared so strangely familiar yet foreign at the same time. Henry wandered around trying to chase a squirrel in the grass. The leaves had started to carpet the front of the yard. Some had formed a multicolored blanket on the front of his father's work truck, still tucked neatly into the barn.

"Whole town was asking 'bout you yesterday when I went into the store," his mother said without turning. "Wanted to know when you were coming back in. Know Luther would love to see you."

He grunted and sipped on the same glass of water he had held since the sun first came up. The town would certainly like to see him. He was, after all, the latest gossip with his recent return. People would soon be coming out to the barn if he didn't make an appearance. They could all go to hell as far as he was concerned.

Samuel thought of Luther. "How has Luther done this without…Pa."

His mother paused and seemed to flip the final pancake slower than the rest. "He's done the best he could. We've had some help. Annie's come by now and then to work after she was done at the post office." She set the plate full of pancakes down in front of him. "I had been saving all this for a special occasion. With the rationing going on, well, you wouldn't know anything about that, would you? Anyway, these kinds of things won't be happening all the time, big breakfasts and all. Sure, drove your father crazy."

She turned away and stared out at the truck. He looked at the deepening lines around her eyes, the thinning skin revealing more of her body's inner workings than he remembered seeing before he left. Silver streaked her once dark hair. She had grown old in two years.

"I'm sorry I left you, Mama." He grabbed a fork and started eating. "I'll come to work with you tomorrow. Give me one more day to fix some things around here. Luther needs my help. I'll help him."

His mother smiled faintly and sat down across from him. "We haven't talked about it. You know, Annie Ruth would like to see you."

He stopped in the middle of chewing. His mouth was still full of pancake. He shrugged. "Figured she'd run off by now, anyhow. Figured some 4-F bastard—"

His mother's eyes grew wide. Samuel finished the food in his mouth and set his fork down. He reached out and touched her hand. "I'm sorry, Mama." He paused and stared at the tablecloth. The blue and white square pattern interlocked like the fields he once flew over in Europe. "I picked up some bad habits. I have to work through this."

She nodded. When he felt enough profanity-free silence had fallen between them, he continued.

"I would, of course, love to see her," he said without looking at his mother. He swallowed, hesitating. "She hadn't found herself another man?"

His mother swallowed. "No." She took a drink of water. "When we heard you were missing in action, most in town told us to keep hoping. Then, less and less people told us that. The town seemed to move on. As more word came back of other boys being killed or wounded, it seemed everyone had forgotten about it. Some boys came by the post office to talk with Annie, but I don't think anything ever came of it. She just didn't seem interested."

She stared back out the window, her fingers touching her chin. "She came to your father's funeral and hardly said anything. I don't remember the last time we had a long conversation, matter of fact. Time kind of stood still. I just tried to keep things going, you know? So I ain't hardly had the time to think about Annie. Honestly, I feel you've been gone longer than you have been."

Samuel nodded. "Well, I'll tidy up things here today. You tell Mr. Luther I'll be there tomorrow."

"Sammy." She peered at him, her eyes focusing. "I'm your mother. If there's anything you ever want to talk about from when you were over there, I'm here. Don't forget that. It's the only time I'll say it. I don't want to bother you."

Samuel stared back at her. For some reason, he thought of Scott Adams and the other boys on his B-17, how they had all longed to be where he was at this moment; sitting at a kitchen table somewhere back home, chatting with their mother.

But most of them hadn't come back. Most of them had their guts spilled somewhere over Europe. He heard their screams—heard them every morning when awoke from the nightmares. Their shrieks morphed into those of the Germans he killed in the house. The chaos, hell and heat of the burning house he had made a home. Maria's cries from the rear of the house moments before the night had turned to fire, Charles somewhere weeping his name.

"Samuel?"

He blinked. "I'm fine, Mama. Let's just take things one hour at a time. How 'bout that?"

Following a kiss on his head, she was gone, leaving him alone in the house his family built. The memories echoed around him as if the radio had been left on. His father's voice, so deep he once thought it was God's, providing the advice he'd always needed although he didn't always want it. The time he and Joe had fought in downtown Bloomsdale, the same time he spent an eternity in jail that only lasted a night, and his father had made him go to church the next day.

He shook his head.

Church. How could he ever show his face there again? The countless questioning, judging eyes—all wondering what he had done "over there." Inquiries would shower across him like enemy machine gun fire as they tried to find out enough to keep the sewing circles active for the following week. Soon, they would all be wondering about Annie Ruth. Would he marry her? When would they have kids?

He shifted in his seat and gazed at the sunlight beaming through the kitchen windows. Through the screen door, Henry wandered around the base of the oak tree. The dog sniffed at the grass, dug with his left paw, and sniffed again. The edge of the screen had torn a bit and peeled back from the doorframe. Something to fix during this day of silence.

Had Joe made it home, Samuel might think about going fishing today. A soft breeze reminiscent of the fall air in France came through the kitchen. But Joe was not home, neither were many other of the boys from McGovern County. His mother said Joe was fighting in the Pacific, killing Japs and jumping from island-to-island. Not much had been said of his letters home, so Samuel knew very little other than his best friend was still alive.

The floor creaked as he walked to the sink and washed his hands. Some weeds had crept up around the barn near his father's truck. That's where he would start.

*****

By midday, Samuel had cleared the barn and the yard around the house of all the weeds. His thigh hurt from his old wound. His shoulder felt gritty and irritated as if sandpaper rubbed the skin. The doctors had said he might feel some soreness with physical activity, but he didn't care. He hadn't told his mother much of his injuries, despite her incessant questioning, and especially hadn't told her he had lost a significant portion of his hearing in his right ear.

His body didn't slow him down. The sunshine bore down on his sweat-soaked back. He hammered boards back into the barn, mended fences near the pigs, fed Henry, cleaned out his father's truck, and reattached chicken wire to the chicken coop.

At any moment, he expected Maria to come out of the house carrying a cold drink as Charles played somewhere in the background, probably too close to the cows near the pond. He worked as if the labor would push away these memories. Maria still floated around his mind. He saw her walking into the house with Charles trailing close behind. He wiped the sweat from his brow. They were gone.

The sun dipped low far before he was ready to quit. He packed up the tools and took them back to the barn. His father's work gloves still lay on the nails on the wall. He touched the workbench, sliding his fingers across the rough surface and remembering all the hours he watched his father work.

"I cleaned up the place, Pa," he whispered. "I don't know if you hear me, but I'll take care of it. Tomorrow, I'll take care of your store. I won't let you down. If you can, let me know you're all right." He shook his head. "Anyhow, good night."

He turned to stroll back to the house. Henry stood in the barn's doorway with his head cocked to the right. Samuel grinned and picked up a short stick, waving it around and tossing it into the yard. Henry rustled after it before something else caught his interest.

The car had pulled up and parked near the house. His mother exited the vehicle and walked toward him. "Samuel, I've been calling you, son. Couldn't you hear me?"

Samuel hesitated. "I was saying goodnight to Pa."

His mother stopped. "I'm sure he'd like that." She rubbed her hands together. "Well, I'll make dinner if you'd like some."

Samuel nodded as Henry plopped down in the cool grass, stick between his teeth. "That sounds good, Mama."

16

He rolled his neck to one side, pressing his hands into the muscle to relieve the weird feeling in his neck. The train was quiet, silence falling over the car as the sun went down. He leaned his head back, closing his eyes and trying to allow sleep to take him.

*****

The plane melted around him like butter. Holes ripped through the walls. Lightning crashed. Scott Adams' face, eyes wide with dread, shattered before him. He felt the heat of blood splatter across his skin. Adams called out to him, but Samuel couldn't hear what he said as if he were underwater. The plane dissipated away like a morning fog, and Samuel hovered over the pond. Dead cows littered the landscape. One figure stood in the middle of the smoldering crater. Samuel floated down so fast, like standing on an elevator that has lost its precious grip on the building. He clenched his teeth.

The pockmarked ground stopped before him. He had stopped falling. The lone figure standing in the crater was a child, a young boy with burnt clothing. The child faced away from him, somewhere in the distance. The fog burned away from the ground. The child took a step. Slowly. Samuel's heart bombarded his eardrum.

The child's skin had burnt away to reveal flesh, bone, and lines of tissue. Pockets of pus leaked down the exposed face.

"Samuel!"

Eyes opened. Patterns of shadows danced across his ceiling. He licked his lips and exhaled for what seemed like a long, dragging moment. When his heartbeat slowed, he sat up and swung his feet over the edge of his bed. The wind brushed against the window's shutters outside his bedroom.

The image had burned into his mind like a fresh branding on cattle. The boy's skin was rotting away, but there was no doubt it was Charles alone in that field. His clothing burnt, the ground around his home battered and bruised.

The leaves of the oak tree flickered light across his room with each gust of wind. Samuel stepped over to the window and took a deep breath. Henry's nose stuck outside the doghouse near the barn. Leaves swirled across the front yard like a dream. He turned and made his way downstairs, careful to avoid the creaking sound in the third step.

His mother's tea remained where it had been since he was a boy. He poured a glass in the near darkness of his family's kitchen. The clock ticked above the stove. Four o'clock. He sipped the tea and stared at the cabinets. The wood grains swirled underneath the tan paint. Samuel rapped his fingers on the table softly. He rotated his shoulder and ignored the reminder of his wound.

Yesterday's local paper lay on the table, a coffee stain ringing the left corner. His mother must have brought it back from downtown Bloomsdale. The headlines read of the war. Seemed things were going well. Most thought the war would be over by Christmas. The paper included a list of all the new local recruits from the area. Mr. Mallory, his history teacher, had been wounded in the Pacific. The paper said he would be coming home. The Hendricks' had a fire in the barn two nights before. A small ad from Wrightman's General Store caught his eye. He frowned.

"Started advertising soon after the war started."

Samuel turned halfway to see his mother had come down the stairs. "Why?"

His mother smiled and slipped into the kitchen seat across from him. "Your father thought it would help in these times. With all the rationing, salvage drives … I don't know. It didn't really make a difference. He just wanted to help the war effort. I think he wanted to do his part for you."

Samuel snorted and took another drink. He pushed the paper toward his mother. "I think he wouldn't mind if we stopped the ad." He drained the glass.

He sat in silence and tried to listen to the clock tick. Once such a staple in his memory of his parent's kitchen, he had to strain to hear it. Sounds were more difficult to hear. His mother called him yesterday, and he couldn't hear her. The doctor in Europe had been right about his hearing.

"Sammy, everything okay?"

"Yeah."

A pause. "How about breakfast."

It wasn't a question.

She stood and within minutes had eggs and bacon sizzling. The smell filled the room, mixing with bold, hot coffee better than anything he'd ever had in England. All of this she did without saying a word.

As he tried to force the nightmarish images from his mind, Samuel nibbled on the eggs as she watched with a smile. After several moments, she spread some butter on a piece of toast and looked at the paper, holding it in front of her. A half-finished crossword filled out the backside obviously with a dull pencil. He looked at some of the words.

"When did you start buying the paper?" He asked as he bit into a juicy piece of bacon, grease slathering the inside of his mouth.

"When you left," she said without looking. "Your father brought it home every day from the store. Everyone said he'd get there before the store opened, go to the drug store and have a cup of coffee over the paper. He read everything about it. Really learned about things he'd never known anything about before. He'd come home at night talking about raids he'd read about, wondering if you'd been involved." She slowly placed the paper on the table. "He was so proud ... so proud."

She cleared her throat and stepped away from the table. Without turning from the stove, she ate a piece of bacon. "Anyhow, that's how the whole advertising thing came about. So...you coming in with me today?"

"No." He finished the tea and wiped his mouth, smiling. He stood and stepped in front of his mother. "I'm going in by myself. You stay here. Things are going to be okay. We're going to get back to normal. You're going to enjoy this house again, and I'll get things back together at the store." He leaned forward and kissed his mother's damp cheek. "Thanks for breakfast, Mama. I love you."

He grabbed his father's keys and walked out of the kitchen, leaving his mother grinning.

The old truck rumbled to life and sputtered a cloud of black smoke in the predawn blue. He waved at Henry as the truck rolled by the doghouse. The white-faced dog tried to give chase but flapped his ears instead.

He passed the house, leaving the farm to begin his life again. His mother stood in the kitchen window, smiling as she waved.

*****

Turpentine.

The smell had been the same since he was a boy, signifying the time to work and sweat while taking endless orders from his father. But now the odor reminded him of home as he turned his father's truck off and sat in the back alley in silence. The sun had hardly crept over

142

the side street of downtown Bloomsdale. The street's buildings were still dark as the birds sang their morning chorus.

The truck's door opening seemed to crack open the silence, and he felt the need to close it back softly. The back door where he and Mr. Luther spent so much time unloading trucks full of dry goods, paints and anything else the people of Bloomsdale didn't want to drive all the way to Atlanta to buy. Somehow, his father always knew what the small number of the community wanted. Now, it was his job.

He sighed and fiddled with the keys. The door opened, and he was transported back years. The aisles of the store had not changed. Paints in the back. Hardware next to that. Even a few shirts and hats lined the next aisle. Two aisles of produce, tomatoes from Mr. Smallwood's farm. Four stacks of firewood sat near the front door. The same white sign with black lettering still hung above the front door.

Thanks! Come Again!

He smiled.

The lights turned on, all except one. He grabbed the ladder and changed the bulb while ignoring the brief pain in his shoulder. He opened the safe with the combination—his birthday—and loaded the register with all the change. The process was the same as it had been before he signed up and left for war more than two years before.

When everything was finished, he flipped the sign to "open" on the door and continued cleaning up. The small community of Bloomsdale slowly woke up for the idle Thursday morning. *Tony's*, a new mechanic garage that had not been there before he left, opened its two garage doors. A short, portly fellow stepped out into the early sunlight, stretched and rested his hands on his round belly. The man, obviously Tony, grinned a toothless grin before he turned back into the building. The small boutique, *Charlotte's*, also flipped its sign. Two women spoke outside the front door for a moment. One held a paper under her arm while the other carried a brown bag, their flowery dresses flapping in the fall breeze.

And then the post office doors opened.

Samuel couldn't move. His heart raced, and he leaned against the counter behind the register. An older woman stepped out of the front door and spoke back toward the building. He slowly stepped around the counter to his front door. He pressed against the glass. He continued to watch the rest of the town go through their morning routines. His lips and mouth felt dry. He inhaled, and then exhaled.

In.

Out.

He surveyed the street, his eyes darting across up and down the road. As his pulse raced, he realized Annie wasn't there. Today wasn't the day.

As he turned away from the door, she stepped around the corner. He froze. Her walk was confident. Her long dark hair curled around her shoulders, appearing lighter, almost golden, as the glorious sunshine formed a halo around her. She wore a dark blue dress accentuating her figure. Her slender fingers curled around the leash leading her dog, Max, down the sidewalk. The two women in front of *Charlotte's* smiled, and she returned the gesture, revealing bright white teeth that made her lips seem even more red, more full.

Annie Ruth.

Samuel instinctively lowered behind the glass, not knowing why. Should he walk out there and explain...what? What could he possibly say? Would she even want him back? Had she gone on with her life? What could he possibly offer her?

There was so much he wanted to tell her, so much he wanted to confess. He had waited for this moment, thought of Annie every day while he was in France. Now the moment had arrived, and he hesitated, unsure of what to tell her. It was like the words had left him. He felt broken, damaged.

Annie led Max into the post office and disappeared. "Morning, stranger."

"Damn it!" Samuel spun round. "Oh, goodness, Mr. Luther." He bit his lip and looked down at the floor.

"Oh, you okay?"

"You scared me; that's all. I'm sorry for the language."

Luther laughed quietly. "Didn't just fall off the turnip truck. Heard much worse in my day. Come here, my boy." Samuel made his way to the man and hugged him. Luther smelled of pipe smoke and gasoline as he always had. "So glad you're home, Sammy."

He clenched his teeth. "Yeah. Missed you."

"We all thought you were gone when they said you were missin'."

Samuel nodded.

"Knew you'd be back," Luther said, his eyes taking in Sammy. "Just knew it."

"Yeah."

"So, your Mama tells me you got back this week?"

"Just this week. Yeah. That's right, sir."

Luther nodded. "You plan on taking over some of the work 'round here?"

"If you'd like, Mr. Luther. I can start filling for what Pa…"

"Yeah," Luther said, his face crumpling. "Could use the help, too. It's been hard work, hard work. Sure would like to have you 'round here."

"Mama's going to stay home a little more from now on. I'm going to try and get things back to normal a bit."

Luther grinned. "Well, first off, I ain't no 'Mr. Luther' to you anymore, ya hear? You call me just plain 'Luther' from now on."

"That'll take some getting used to, Mr. Luther."

Luther laughed. "Well, I suppose so, Sammy." He glanced around the store. "Looks like you got everything off to a good start. We got a truck coming in about an hour. I'll clean out the back and get ready while you man the front. Sound good?"

"Sure thing."

With Luther gone, Samuel turned back to the street. He swallowed and stepped toward the door. The door pulled back, and he slipped the stop under it. Cool air breezed into the store. He stepped onto the sidewalk and into the sunshine. He took in a deep breath and felt the slight chill of fall air inside his lungs. He kept his eyes on the post office doors.

Go to her, he thought. You're a coward. Go to her and never look back.

He stopped and shielded the sun from his eyes with his left hand, squinting. A black car passed between the two stores. He watched the car drive away onto the dirt roads toward the fields around Bloomsdale. He turned back to the post office.

Annie stepped out of the building. Her hair wrapped around her neck. Some curls stuck to her trembling lips. He raised his hand slowly, his jaw dropping open. She stepped to the edge of the road, her eyes on him. A tear rolled down her cheek.

The fear disappeared. He smiled and ran across the street, sprinting toward her. She spread her arms wide and embraced him. Her arms squeezed his neck tight.

She shook him as she sobbed. "Oh, God. God. God. Thank you. Thank you. Thank you."

Samuel let out a slow breath. "Hi, Annie."

The two held their embrace as eyes peered out from windows across Bloomsdale. Residents hesitated on sidewalks, staring with cautious smiles and soft whispers toward the reunion on the otherwise normal Thursday morning.

17

"Write her."

The young man looked up from his magazine. "Write her?"

He nodded. "That little gal back at the station. Go ahead and write her."

"Yeah. I will when I get to school."

"No." He shook his head. "Don't wait. Write her now."

The young man held his hands up. "I don't know what to say."

"Yes, you do."

As the young man started his letter to the train station girl, he turned back to the window. A truck pulled an old silver boat on a trailer in the traffic alongside the train. He looked closer.

*****

The metal had faded over the last two years. Once a solid silver, the old fishing canoe on the edge of McPherson's Pond had faded in the Georgia sun. Weeds covered the boat, which Joe and Samuel had turned over nearly three years before during their final fishing day.

"You've never taken me here, Sam," Annie said as she stared down at the old canoe. "You both always talked of fishing out here. Is that why you wanted to bring me out here? To fish?"

Samuel stared in silence for a long moment as he watched the breeze ruffle the surface of the pond. A pair of ducks paddled away from the far shore. He shifted the picnic basket to his free hand. "Not today, Annie."

Samuel gestured toward the large oak at the north end of the pond.

They maneuvered along the banks of the pond just a few hundred yards from the river. He helped her cross some of the wet spots from the recent November storm. They held hands as they strolled along the edge of the water. Her blue and white dress was the same one she wore the day Samuel said goodbye.

When they reached the base of the oak tree, Samuel spread the blanket across the cool grass. They sat facing one another as Annie pulled lunch from the basket.

"Great way to spend a Saturday. Thank you."

"Sure." He watched her smooth hands unwrap his sandwich. She grinned as she passed it over to him. "Thank you."

They ate in silence. A duck sounded from the center of the pond. An insect buzzed between them.

Annie's head cocked to the side as she chewed. "Something on your mind today?"

He shook his head slightly. "Not really."

"You seem like there is."

Taking another bite of his sandwich, Samuel leaned back on his elbow and looked into the blue sky. Fluffy clouds peppered his view. The air was cool, but not too much for November.

"Sam, I've been wanting to tell you something since you got back." Annie wiped her mouth with a napkin. "When we got word you were missing, some of the people in town had thought you...they thought you had died over there. Had a few people even write me a letter saying they were sorry for my situation."

Samuel propped himself on both elbows and stared at her. He braced himself, not understanding why.

Annie took a deep breath. "A few other men kept coming around the post office in the following months. They seemed interested." She looked at him, a small smile appearing at the corner of her mouth. "But they weren't you."

She looked away. "They just weren't you. I was going to wait. I didn't care. As more and more boys weren't coming back ... their families received definite word, you know. Well, we didn't. I ate dinner with your parents every other Sunday until your father passed. Nothing had changed except the fact you were still gone. Those guys came by the office less and eventually stopped. One of them took a job down in Mobile. I think one of the others moved to Atlanta and took a job. They aren't around anymore."

Samuel nodded.

"Anyway," she said and brushed her hands together. "Nothing ever happened, but I thought you should know. Anyhow, you know how this town can be. People talk, rumors start." She laughed. "Sewing circles sew. Bible study turns to gossip. You've always known that better than anyone else, working at the general store and all."

Her smile faded away like a dimming light.

"You now know everything, Sam. You know what happened while you were gone. I worked. I went home. I woke up to work again. Every day. I put my life on hold for you. I was not going to do anything until I heard what happened to you over there." She turned toward him, her brown eyes meeting his. "Now you know it all. I'm here. I'm here for you if you want to talk. Always."

Samuel exhaled. "Marry me."

Annie's eyes widened, and her chin trembled. "With all my heart, yes. I'll marry you."

She leaned forward, and their lips touched. Samuel backed away and looked into her eyes. They smiled and kissed, embracing under the radiant sky.

*****

Word of the renewed engagement spread across Bloomsdale. Cards arrived at the house. People stopped by to congratulate the first local soldier back from the war and his upcoming marriage. Even the local McGovern County newspaper wrote about it. The pastor congratulated Samuel and Annie Ruth during church on Christmas Eve, which was promptly followed by applause.

So when New Year's Eve 1944 arrived, Samuel opted for a quiet evening at the house. Annie Ruth worked all afternoon to prepare dinner while Samuel and his mother watched night fall across the family land. Stars twinkled in the dark blue sky as they rocked on his father's rocking chairs. His mother wore a light sweater in the cool evening. Henry slowly fetched his scarred baseball that Samuel had tossed across the yard for years.

"Food's ready, y'all," Annie called from inside the kitchen.

He smiled and opened the door for his mother. "Happy New Year's, Mama."

She nodded and grinned as they made their way into the dining room. Three candles flickered a warm light across the room. Annie had delicately prepared the fresh chicken he had purchased from downtown Bloomsdale for the event. Even though his mother initially protested, they had opened a bottle of wine from his father's small collection.

They sat and prayed. Food was passed around the table, and they exchanged small talk about the recent events. Samuel had listened to the developments of the German advance and responding Allied counterattack. Everyone he had known in the European Theater had been killed. He tried to ignore the news, but it was everywhere.

"Heard Joe's parents received a letter from him yesterday," his mother said while cutting her chicken.

"And?" Samuel asked with a mouth full of mashed taters.

"Same as always. 'Everything's fine. Everything's good. Hope all is well at home.' The usual stuff. Kind of like the letters you used to send."

Samuel stopped chewing when Annie nodded. "What was wrong with my letters?"

"Oh, Sammy," Annie said with a grin. "Your letters were just fine."

"Don't lie," his mother said, turning toward him as if she were going to start a fresh lecture. "Why didn't you ever tell us what was really happening over there? All we ever got was what you had to eat. What the weather was like."

Samuel turned back to his food. "Wasn't much to talk about."

"Well," his mother took a sip of her wine, "it drove your father crazy."

They ate in silence with only the rattling of silverware against the dishes filling the room. Although the air had grown cooler, winter had been relatively warm thus far. Still, a fire crackled and popped from the living room.

Annie Ruth offered to clear the table when Samuel's mother moved to the living room. She cuddled up under a thicker blanket from the living room sofa while she held a framed photo of her husband. He looked at his mother as she stared down at the photo.

"She hasn't touched that photo since I've been back," he said, carrying two dirty plates into the kitchen. "Must be New Year's."

"She did the same last year," Annie said without hesitating.

Samuel blinked. "You spent New Year's with Mama last year?"

She turned. "Sure I did."

He touched the back of her head and stroked down. He leaned forward and kissed her on the cheek. "You are something else. You know that?"

"It was the only way I could be close to you." She nodded as if she had just made an important statement. "Besides, we had lots to talk about."

He glanced at his mother in the window's reflection. She had curled up on the sofa and sat motionless, eyes fixated on the crackling fire. His father had passed away last fall, leaving his mother to run the store on her own. They hadn't spoken much of that time after his father's death, but dealing with the first New Year's without him must have been…difficult.

"Thank you," he said as he stared back at Annie. "Thanks for being there for her. Thanks for being you."

She placed a freshly washed dish into the sink and turned around to face him. "Did you expect anything else?"

He grinned and pulled her close. They kissed softly, and he lingered for a moment before parting. "I guess I didn't." He turned toward the living room. "Mama, you need more wine?"

After a pause, she declined a refill. Annie Ruth and Samuel made their way into the living room, touching their glasses together as they sat down. All three sipped in silence. The fire slowly died. Midnight came and went, and the family quietly celebrated the coming of 1945.

Samuel stared into the fire and watched its fiery fingers twirl up into the chimney. Sparks popped like fireflies and zipped around like insects on the surface of McPherson's Pond. His mind wandered as Mama and Annie drifted off into sleep. The last fire he sat and viewed had been in France. He celebrated New Year's and Christmas in Gerard's family home last year along with Maria and Charles. The wine glass felt cool against his smooth cheek where a beard had been the year before.

He glanced around the fireplace in the home he never believed he would see again. The same painting of Hawkridge Mountain hung over the fire. He shook his head, and his thoughts drifted back to Charles and Maria.

The night had simply exploded. There was nothing he could have done. Death had descended upon the farm. He should have been dead. There was no reason to have survived. Many Germans had died inside that burning home, but he made it.

And why? What had it all been about? He survived to come back to run the shop his father had started years before. Was that really what this life was about? He had often dreamt of doing something special, something to make his father proud. And now Pa was gone forever. He would never get to see Samuel become a husband, a provider or a father.

He blinked his watery eyes. "Sam?"

He turned to Annie. "Oh, hey."

"What is it?"

Releasing a long sigh, he draped his arm around Annie and pulled her closer. "I hope 1945 is better than the last."

She stretched and placed the wine glass down on the side table. "The best is yet to come."

He smiled, nodded.

Somewhere in the house, a clock chimed twelve times.

*****

"The war's done over."

Samuel held the paint can over the shelf and stopped. "What's that?"

Luther stepped in from the back. "The radio said the Germans quit. Hitler offed himself. Whole army's quitting."

He sighed and set the can down. "Thank, God."

Shouts echoed down the streets of the small community. Children raced by on bikes with baseball cards in the spokes, shouting down the sidewalk. A couple of adults wandered out into the sunny morning.

"Mr. Luther, reckon we should buy a paper?"

"Thought you'd never ask." He pulled off his work gloves. "I'll finish this truck in a bit." Samuel watched him hurry out into the street.

Across the street, Annie Ruth peeked out from the door of the post office. She shielded her eyes with her hand as she watched the two children race by on their bikes. He waved through the window and returned the grin.

Patrons came in the rest of the afternoon to talk about the latest.

"The boys'll be coming home soon."

"Never thought this would end."

"Now we need to finish things with the Japs."

He listened to it all, saying little or nothing. He kept the conversation to business until Mrs. Burns walked through the front door. She wore a dark wide brimmed hat and smelled of flowers. It was the first time Samuel had seen her downtown since he had returned home last fall, the first time he'd seen her since he knew about her son's death in the war.

His mouth was suddenly dry. His tongue felt like a cotton ball as it dragged across the roof of his mouth.

"Afternoon, Mrs. Burns."

She nodded, clutching at her pearl necklace. "Candles, please?"

Samuel pointed to the second aisle. The woman slowly moved through the aisles, picking up different items. When she returned to the cash register, Samuel waited with a bag. A box of candles, some rubbing alcohol and napkins. "Is that all, ma'am?"

"Yes, Samuel."

Samuel blinked at the sound of his name. He wasn't sure Mrs. Burns would even know who he was. He bit his lip, bagging the items. Before he handed over the change, he hesitated. "Ma'am, if I may...I was sorry to hear about Gary."

The woman's eyes darted outside to the street. "Yes," she said after a pause.

Samuel swallowed. "I always thought he was a pleasant guy. The town will miss him."

She sighed. "Are you saying all this because it's almost over?"

He shook his head and realized he didn't know why he had said it. "No, ma'am."

Their eyes met. "You were over there, too."

It wasn't a question. Her voice remained level, unemotional.

He nodded. "Yes, ma'am."

"Then you know, don't you? You know."

The air seemed to hang still. He wanted to turn away but stayed behind the counter. Looking at her for a moment, he paused before speaking.

"I don't know…"

"You know this will never be over for me." She grabbed her change and the brown bag, which crumpled so loudly he jumped. "My boy is dead."

And with that, she stormed out into the street.

He stared out the window and watched Mrs. Burns hurry away from the building. He shook his head and thought of her son, Gary. The thought of his classmate's death stayed with him until closing time. His hands felt numb like they did when he first woke up in the hospital in England.

The fact is that Mrs. Burns was right: It would never be over for her and it would never be over for any of the soldiers coming back. He knew the effect. He felt it. He tried to suppress it, but it was there lingering in his mind and body.

"Got the paper right here!" Luther yelled.

Samuel spun around and dropped the broom. He snorted. "You really scared me, Mr. Luther."

"Sorry." He walked forward with the paper rolled up between his hands. "You doing okay, sir?"

He wiped his mouth. "I told you not to call me that."

Luther stepped forward as if Samuel would bite him. He held out the newspaper. "Sorry about that."

He grabbed the paper and sat down on the stool behind the counter. "Thanks for getting the paper, Mr. Luther. Have you read it, yet?"

"No."

Samuel handed it back. "I can read it later. You go ahead."

"Really? You sure?" Luther grinned. "Well, thank you, Sam. That's real nice. Real nice of you."

He turned back and went into the stock room and left Samuel alone in the front.

"I don't want to read about it," he said softly while he stared out the front door.

Closing time rolled around. The rest of the town seemed quiet as Bloomsdale slowed down for the day. The occasional cars and trucks driving through from the county to Bloomsdale had stopped. Luther left a little while later while Samuel swept the floor. Someone tapped on the front door. He turned.

Annie leaned against the front door. "Is the owner here? I need to speak with Mr. Wrightman."

Samuel set the broom against the wall and walked toward the door. "What took you so long?"

"Things got a little busy," she said as he opened the door. They kissed, and she walked into the store. "Seems word got around pretty fast. You've heard?"

"About twenty times."

Annie laughed.

"I'm just finishing up, and I'll give you a ride home."

She frowned. "I thought you'd be happier. The war's almost over."

"I know. I am."

Ten minutes later they were riding in his truck on the way to Annie's house. The light had finally started to fade late in the night, and cool air swirled into the cab of the truck.

"What's wrong, Sam?" she asked.

"Had a strange day, that's all."

"Want to talk about it?"

He reached over and grabbed her hand. "Not right now." He pulled in front of her aunt and uncle's home. "You want me to pick you up tomorrow? I think Max is going to start getting jealous if you don't walk him to work anymore."

She laughed. "I'll give him extra scratches behind the ear and let him know he has nothing to worry about." She looked down at her hands after the car had stopped.

"Something wrong?" he asked.

"Have you thought about what we're going to do?"

Samuel frowned. "What do you mean?"

"We're getting married in June."

"Really?" he joked.

She rolled her eyes. "Seriously."

"I know."

She turned away. "It's not that it matters to me. Where do you want to live?"

He shook his head. "I thought we could move in closer to town and the store. Closer to work. I never liked the drive." He laughed. "Pa never said much about it. He seemed to like it. We'd talk the whole way home about this and that. A lot of the time we talked about the future. Where I'd be. That sort of thing." He stopped, the memories flooding back to him. "Never really thought about what that drive might have meant to him."

Annie sighed as she leaned back in the seat. "That sounds great. Have you thought about any specific place?"

He looked over at her. "You seem really happy. Do you like this idea?"

"Yes. I just thought, well, I thought you were going to live back on the farm."

"Well, my family hasn't been farming full time since I can remember. Mama can make enough money renting out the land. I'll be out there every now and then to check on things. It'll all be fine."

She nodded. "I'm happy."

"You're happy?"

"Yes. I love you." Her bright eyes flashed in the dimming light. "I can't wait to marry you."

He leaned closer. "I love you, too."

They kissed and embraced. Her hands squeezed the back of his neck.

"Tell me something, will you?" she asked when they pulled apart.

"Sure."

She licked her lips and faced out the front window, a frown on her face. "Where were you?"

He blinked. "When? Today?"

"No." Annie buried her face in her hands for a moment, and then wiped her mouth. "It was just so long."

"Hey." He held her hands, rubbing them with his thumbs. "Whatever you want to talk about, we have all the time in the world. Just tell me what you want to know."

"I don't want to seem out of line or impatient, Sammy. I want you to talk to me about whatever you can. It was so hard here, waiting, thinking something happened. I thought I'd never see you again. I had to keep it from everyone, pretend to be strong when I thought you were in the ground somewhere. "

His jaw dropped. "You are strong. You're the strongest person I know."

She stared at him with her dark eyes. A thin layer of tears covered them as she looked at him. "Where were you? What happened to you?"

He covered his mouth. He put one hand on the wheel and peered out the window. Something in her voice sounded different, uncertain for the first time since he had known her.

"Were you in prison? In a hospital?" She leaned forward. "Why can't you tell me where you were?" She turned away. "The telegram said you were missing in action. I've told you we all thought we had lost you. I didn't think I'd ever see you again. And then, you were here. People came into the post office telling me you were back. I thought it wasn't true. I thought it was just a rumor or a cruel prank." She touched his cheek. "And here you were. Where have you been?"

"It's not important."

"Not important?" she asked. "How can you say that?"

How could he tell her he lived another life for two years? It would crush her. Even though Samuel kept his distance from Maria, he still provided and cared and lived as part of her family. How could he tell her of his guilt for not finding Maria and Charles before the left. How could he tell her he had a second father figure while his real Pa was dead. He would tell her, he just had to think about how he would tell her.

"I love you. Can't that be enough?" He sighed, the thoughts of the bleeding soldiers and Maria screaming filling his mind. "I just…I'm just not ready to talk about it."

She grabbed his hand. "I promise you. I won't ask you again. When you want to tell me, I'm ready. You know I love you."

He nodded, and she left the truck. He lingered for a moment after she disappeared inside the front door.

Some days, his time in France didn't seem real. The night before, he dreamt in French, speaking with Gerard and Maria, and leading Charles through the woods. Somewhere inside his mind, the language lay dormant. But it still felt like the entire experience had been a dream. It was a dream that changed his home.

As he had done every day since he'd been back, he pushed the memories of "over there" far into the back of his mind. He wasn't ready to go back there. No, not yet.

The truck rumbled to life, and he drove toward his family's home. The engine held so many memories of his father. Late night chats. The drive to the train station before he left for the war.

God, how he wished his father were here.

18

He wiped a tear from his cheek. Wiping his forehead, he leaned forward and slipped off the flannel shirt.

*****

It was hot.

The June sun seared down with all the force a Georgia summer could muster. The heat seemed to make even the insects cease their incessant buzzing. The breeze felt like sitting in front of a running muffler. Taking a breath was like trying to breathe underwater.

Yes, it was a typical summer day in McGovern County. Only this was the day Samuel would marry Annie.

The church in Bloomsdale packed with people. Some came from Terrytown and Ericsson, others from the north end of the county near Hawkridge Mountain. Cars and even a few horses lined the grass under the ancient oak outside the church. Old ladies fanned themselves in the pews as Samuel stood at the alter, Mr. Luther by his side.

Joe would have been his best man, without a doubt. But Joe was still fighting the Japanese in the Pacific. Lord knows when he'd be back. Samuel wondered if they would ever visit McPherson's Pond again. If they did, would it even be the same? Would they talk about what they had seen? Or worse, would Joe make it home?

He turned to his coworker and friend. Mr. Luther grinned. Samuel nodded, tapping the older man's shoulder.

The crowd inhaled sharply. The fans ceased moving. With a groan, the audience stood and turned toward the door at the back of the church. The doors swung open. Samuel swallowed, and bit his lip.

Annie Ruth stood in the doorway, her white dress flowing around her like she stood in a cloud. Mr. Taylor tapped her hand wrapped around his arm. The man smiled at her. Samuel knew she would have liked to have her father there, but her uncle stared at Annie with pride.

Samuel grinned as they made their way down the center of the church. Whispers spread through the church as the piano played.

"She's so beautiful."

"Oh, my word."

"My, oh my."

As she reached halfway down the aisle, a few women sniffled lightly. They wiped at noses and passed around handkerchiefs. Annie never took her eyes off him. Their eyes locked, and he somehow felt they were alone. He thought of the first time they met, the first time she came to school. She was a mystery, the first of Samuel's life, a person who didn't have their life story told in sewing circles, salons, and underhanded whispers. Annie Ruth, the first and only true love of his life. He thought of their first kiss and how all of it led to this moment.

He tried to act solemn, but only smiled at his beautiful bride.

Pastor Daniel's hair had grayed in the past few years. It had been a long time since Samuel went to church.

Daniel went through his speech, sounding like a sermon Samuel had once heard. He didn't listen. He only stared into Annie's eyes. As Mr. Taylor gave Annie over to him, he took in a deep breath. He couldn't believe how beautiful she was. He thought he would be nervous, get cold feet, but he felt only happiness and peace. They exchanged vows and held hands as they placed rings on each other's fingers. After they had kissed, they strolled down the aisle. He couldn't wait to leave. He recognized all the faces in the pews as he passed them

Samuel smiled at all of them.

The reception took place under the pavilion near the church. It seemed like every other social event in Bloomsdale. People brought food in from around the community. Desserts made in kitchens by little old ladies he'd know his entire life. He held on to Annie's hand tightly throughout the event.

After everyone had nibbled on the food from kitchens around the community, Samuel leaned over toward Annie's ear. "You ready to go?"

She nodded and Samuel waved toward the nearby woods. A horse emerged from the leaves followed by a buggy. Annie's eyes widened and her mouth dropped open as she covered it with one hand. Tears formed and then spilled over onto her cheeks. The hot breeze tossed the brown wisps of hair around her ears. Samuel exhaled. She hadn't noticed Luther had disappeared from the reception. He turned and saw the man, wearing a black top hat complete with a bow tie and smiling as he led the buggy over to the pavilion.

Annie turned to him, her watery eyes twinkling in the sunlight. "What did you do?" she whispered.

"You'll see." He smiled.

Luther tipped his hat as he helped Annie onto the buggy. "Afternoon, ma'am."

Annie nodded and smiled as she boarded the buggy. Luther winked as Samuel stepped up after Annie. Those in attendance tossed rice at them, clapping and cheering. He held her hand as she waved to the crowd. The buggy slowly made its way toward Main Street in Bloomsdale. They passed the homes they had grown up around. The community was empty except for dogs running around vacant yards. The horse whinnied as it trotted down the street, its hooves clattering throughout the town. She leaned against him as she watched homes go by. She ran her thumb up and down the top of his hand.

The buggy stopped a few hundred yards from the family general store.

Luther turned around. "Here you are, Mr. and Mrs. Wrightman."

Annie Ruth sat up. "Where are we?"

Samuel tapped her on the shoulder. She turned to look at him. Grinning, he pointed across the street to a one-story brick home, his father's truck parked out front. She spun around, a huge smile on her face.

"Welcome home," he said. The word was barely out of his mouth when she kissed him, pushing him back against the seat. "How did you do this?"

"Don't worry about that right now." He nodded toward the house. "Go inside, Mrs. Wrightman."

She ran to the front door, holding her wedding dress high with both hands. He watched his happy bride, swallowing back a lump in his throat. Placing a hand over his mouth and leaning his elbow against the side of the buggy, he gazed at the simple house, thinking of what it meant to his family. The house symbolized more than brick and mortar. All the hours his father worked…the vacations he missed. A life full of labor, creating a world for Samuel from the ground up.

He patted Luther on the shoulder. "Thanks, my friend."

Luther tipped his cap, his eyes brimming.

Slipping off the buggy, Samuel strolled down the sidewalk leading to the front of the home. His footsteps in the fancy shoes cracked against the concrete. He took a deep breath, watching as Annie opened the note left by his mother on the front door. He knew it informed his new bride of how this home had become theirs. His father had left Samuel enough money for a down payment, money his mother hadn't spent in hopes her boy would come home.

He gazed up into the tall trees surrounding the home within walking distance of his father's—no—*his* store.

"Thanks, Pa," he whispered, his jaw trembling.

Annie turned around, the note still in her hand. "It's ours?"

"Yes, dear," he breathed, nodding slowly. "It is ours."

19

The young man finished the letter and now reread it.

He stood to walk to the bathroom. Partly because he had to, partly to allow the young man his privacy.

The bathroom was occupied. He leaned against the wall, nodding at the young brunette attendant as she passed. He turned to look out a different window on the opposite side of the train. Sunlight flickered into his eyes, reflecting off the traffic.

*****

The fireworks flashed across Main Street, bathing the storefronts in a wash of blues, greens, and bright yellows. A brown and white dog scattered down the alley across from the Wrightman General Store, whimpering away with its tail tucked between its legs.

Carvy Henderson laughed as he flipped fat burgers with one hand, cradling a bottle of beer with the other. The man had asked Samuel if he could grill out on the sidewalk in front of the store. Of course, he had obliged and kept the store open until dark to help celebrate the New Year. Some of the residents had thought it would be good to celebrate the New Year since it would be the first without war in years. Who was Samuel to spoil the town's happiness?

So he stayed open the extra hours and simply kept an eye on the things. Annie Ruth sat with his mother on the sidewalk. Children laughed at the fireworks shot from the old Wilson place at the far end of town. The volunteer firefighters gathered at the end of Main Street.

"Sammy?" Henderson called from the sidewalk. "Bring out some of that salt, will you?"

He nodded and went inside the store. The sky flashed again, reminding him of the skies over Europe when flak exploded around his bomber. The air seemed to catch fire around his plane, and men on the bombers lost their lives. When more bombers failed to return from the European skies, he started to lose faith his superiors knew what they were doing. It was all a game, and he was a pawn.

He shook his head and grabbed some more salt.

"Thanks, buddy," Henderson said with a grin. The chef hat he wore shook as he moved. "These burgers are gonna be great."

Samuel nodded. Mr. Henderson had always been a lover of food. Since he could remember, Mr. Henderson had started two different restaurants in McGovern County. One had been a diner of sorts in Bloomsdale. He made good money from the work going on at Hawkridge Mountain. Loggers would come in after a hard day of work and eat heartily. When Henderson thought it would be a good idea to start serving liquor, things changed.

First there were the fights; horrible engagements where men would beat the life out of each other with bottles, chairs, and their bare hands. Word had it the police would be there nightly. When the first ladies of the evening were hanging around the restaurant, the place became a taboo subject around Bloomsdale. If anyone local was ill thought of, some of the church ladies would even say they belonged at Carvy's place.

Henderson was run out of Bloomsdale by the time Samuel had entered high school. He wasn't the first to be run out of a small southern town. People were often figuratively tarred and feathered for different reasons. Sometimes they were criminals. Others were simply part of a love triangle or other embarrassing scandal. The difference with Henderson was that he didn't go far.

The man showed up once again on the outskirts of Bloomsdale soon after Samuel's graduation. He opened a small barbecue stand in a grassy field at the end of Main Street near the Wilson place. At first, no one stopped by the shack with a few concrete tables out front. Henderson had been trying since to endear himself to the community by attending church, hosting the cookouts for the McGovern County football games and offering to cater any event from graduations to birthday parties to family reunions.

And now Henderson wanted to cook out for the New Year's celebration.

Samuel surveyed the Main Street sidewalk. It seemed like most of Bloomsdale had turned out for the event. A few had even come inside the general store to buy last minute items for the celebration. Annie tapped his mother on the shoulder and strolled over to Samuel. She wrapped her arms around him.

"You having fun?" she asked.

Samuel nodded. "Just thinking. Maybe we should extend the store hours?"

"What?"

He gestured around. "Seems the people have enjoyed having a place to shop later. Might be something to think about."

Annie smiled. "Always thinking, aren't you?"

He kissed her forehead.

Henderson turned around holding a fresh, steaming burger with cheese dripping off the bun. "First one's for the M-R-S."

Annie brought her burger back toward Samuel's mother. Henderson offered Samuel a burger. It was good, he admitted. Henderson knew his business. He leaned against the doorway of his store and enjoyed the burger. The fireworks flashed and spun around the sky like fireflies. The crowd erupted in "ahhs" and children laughed. He watched a particularly large cinder spin out of the dark sky toward the ground.

Henderson took off the hat and moved next to him. The grill smoked as the heat died.

"You heard from Joe, yet?" Henderson asked.

Samuel frowned. He knew the man meant well, but he had wanted to enjoy the night. "No."

Henderson wiped his brow. "Word has it he had come back to the States. Just hadn't come home, yet. Everyone's saying if he were to contact anyone, it would be you."

"Well, you can tell everyone he hasn't."

Some of Bloomsdale's boys that had survived had come home. One was still in Europe. Joe had apparently been wounded on Okinawa and discharged, but that's all Samuel knew.

Henderson shrugged, apparently annoyed at the lack of conversation, and meandered off into the crowd to find another victim of worthless conversation. Samuel was glad to see him go.

He crumpled the paper plate and tossed it into the trashcan in front of the store.

Soon, the fireworks ended, and the crowds dwindled. Henderson wheeled his grill down the sidewalk, the wheels squeaking so loudly it prompted a chorus of barking dogs. Someone told the canines to "shut up," and Samuel laughed as he locked up the store.

Samuel, Annie, and his mother piled into the cab of the truck. They drove her home in near silence. He asked his mother if she would be okay, and she said everything was fine. Samuel knew she wasn't, but he didn't want to push her.

*****

"We'll stay open until eight p.m.," Samuel said as he cut into his steak. "It's a twelve-hour shift, so I might need to get some help."

Annie sipped her tea. "What about Luther?"

"Well, Luther'll always be a great help. You know, he is getting older. He will want to retire eventually. We can just plan ahead."

She swallowed her food and shook her head. "You don't think that'll offend him?"

"Don't think so." He shook his head. "Got to start attracting some of that traffic heading to Atlanta. Might even rent a couple billboards on these new roads they're building around."

"What's the hurry?"

He frowned. "I keep hearing about this Hearn Store moving to Bloomsdale. They've spread to a couple towns around the area. They just built an extra storage area to store dry goods and have been shipping them around the area. Just got to make sure we can compete."

"Compete?" She smiled. "Since when has that been a problem? Everyone in Bloomsdale shops here."

He shook his head. "Not everyone. Heard a couple people talking about shopping in Terrytown. Where there's one, there's more. Need to make sure it doesn't spread. That means more hours, more employees. Need to make sure they want to stay around here. What's wrong with that?"

"Nothing at all." She took another drink of tea. "Any ideas who to hire?"

"I'll figure out the money. Maybe put an ad in the paper later this month. I'd like to try and get this settled soon."

"I understand. I know you know what you're doing."

For a few moments, the only sound in the kitchen was the silverware scraping on their plates. Annie cleared her throat, saying something he couldn't hear.

He leaned forward, still chewing his food. "How's that?"

"I said, 'I heard a rumor today.'"

"Yeah, what's that?"

"It's probably not true, anyway."

He snorted. "I know you better than that. Every time you hear something good you think it might not be true."

"You're probably right." She smiled. "Post Master Trapnell said the government's talking about building a lake in these parts."

"Did you say a lake?"

"Yes. A lake for drinking water."

Samuel set down his silverware. "Where?"

"Some say Springfield."

He frowned. "What do others say?"

"The talk says it might be around here. Parts of McGovern and other counties."

Samuel shook his head. "You're serious."

"Well, you know how rumors are."

"How far along is this talk?"

Annie shrugged. "I don't know. Mr. Trapnell said they'd have to build a dam somewhere. Something about water for the city. It doesn't matter anyway."

"Yeah."

Annie stood and cleared the table. He sat and finished his tea, watching the night fall around his home. The lights on Main Street blinked on one at a time. Walking over to the front window, he checked out his family's store.

Annie cleaned the dishes in the kitchen. He turned back and watched her. He lingered at the window for a moment, and then walked to their second bedroom, currently the family office, to start checking the bankbooks.

*****

The spring rains had provided a healthy green across McGovern County. The cows fattened up on clumps of thick grass covering the rolling land pockmarked by fire ant hills. Cool air fresh with the scent of a morning rain rushed into Samuel's truck as he drove back from his mother's house.

He snorted.

His mother's house. It seemed like his father had been gone for years. In reality, it would be three years this Fall. Some traditions, like this Saturday's breakfast, remained. His mother's pancakes made him wonder if he would fit back into the truck. Annie opened the store every Saturday so he could visit his mother.

He sighed and leaned back in the truck. The road winded through the eastern part of the county leading toward Bloomsdale. He passed the fields and chicken coops. Two miles outside of the city, a man carrying a large bag over his shoulder walked on the side of the road. Wearing a leather jacket and blue jeans, the man looked like something out of the movies. Samuel accelerated past the drifter, turning into the other lane as he passed the man.

Samuel glanced over his shoulder.

He froze.

The breaks squeaked as the truck slowed to a stop. He took off his father's hat and stared back down the road into a familiar face. Lines creased the corners near the man's eyes, and heavy stubble covered his cheeks, but it was Joe, strolling down the road toward Bloomsdale. He shut off the truck and opened the door.

Joe stopped and stared at the truck. He said something, but Samuel couldn't hear him, his bad ear still failing him.

He walked toward his friend. "Joe."

Joe tilted his head. "You gotta problem, mister?"

He shook his head and frowned. "Joe, it's me."

"Who?" Joe's eyes widened. He swallowed and blinked. "Oh, Sammy! You look just like your Pa with that hat on."

"And you look like shit."

Standing a few feet apart, they stared at one another on the road they had traveled countless times driving from the Wrightman place to Bloomsdale to the pond to wherever else life decided to take them.

Samuel squinted as he looked at his friend, a smile forming at the edge of his mouth. He extended a hand. Joe accepted, gripping tightly.

Following a laugh, they embraced on the side of the road. "You need a ride?"

Joe shrugged and stared off into the distance. "I don't know." He seemed to be elsewhere. When he looked back to Samuel, his eyes seemed glazed over. "I'm not really sure I'm ready for this, Sammy."

Samuel stared back toward the city. "To hell with it." He turned around with a grin. "Fishing?"

"Absolutely."

*****

McPherson's Pond rippled as they tossed the old metal boat into its waters. Samuel had cut back the weeds growing over their old boat they had bought years ago, and the fishing poles were waiting for them. It was as if they had just left it the fall before. The two friends climbed in and paddled out into the center of the water. They didn't speak for a while, content on sitting in silence. For a good half hour, they didn't even get out fishing poles. The boat rocked, the gentle breeze moving across the water. They finally cast, ignoring the fact they had no bait and fished the murky waters without saying a word.

When they finally spoke, it was Joe asking about the recent weather. The small talk continued as if they had nothing new to share as if three years and two different theaters of war had not separated them. They spoke of business, women, baseball and beer. The sun dipped low on the horizon. Samuel paddled to shore, and Joe leaned back with a smile. The boat hit the soft bottom. Joe dropped into the water with a splash.

"I'm married," Samuel said as they yanked the boat up on shore.

"Annie?"

Samuel nodded, felt a boyish smile coming across his face.

Joe turned the boat over and put his hands behind his head. "That's good." He nodded, staring into the water. "That's real good, Sammy."

They lingered on the pond's edge for a moment before heading back to the truck. Samuel drove them back toward town.

"You staying with your parents?" Samuel asked when they reached downtown Bloomsdale.

"Guess so. They don't know I'm coming."

Samuel nodded, knowing his friend had been back in the states for a while now. He didn't want to ask where he'd been, didn't want to let him know about the gossip mill conjuring up stories about his absence. He would find out soon enough.

"No, wait," Joe grabbed his shoulder when they passed the liquor store. "Stop here. I need a drink."

He stopped the truck. "Should I wait for you?"

Joe shrugged. "No. I can walk from here. Besides, your wife's waiting."

He froze, studying his friend. "Yeah. I better get home." He smiled. "Glad you're home, Joe."

"Yeah." He jumped out of the truck and slammed the door, rushing into the store without saying another word.

Samuel continued driving home, planning what he would tell Annie Ruth to explain why he disappeared for the day.

*****

"Where have you been?" Annie's eyes flashed wide, her shaking spatula pointed outward like a sword.

"You won't believe me." Samuel stormed through the kitchen, tossing the keys down on the counter. "I wish you'd give me the chance to explain before you give me that look."

"What, Sammy? Huh? What could possibly explain leaving me at the store all day without a phone call?" Her eyes softened. She licked her lips. "Is something wrong with your mother?"

He shook his head and stared out at the front yard. "Joe's back."

"Joe?" A pause. "He's back in town? When?"

He nodded. "Just today."

"How is he?" Annie placed the spatula down, the cooking dinner forgotten behind her. She stepped over and handed him a glass of water.

"I don't know, Annie."

"Where has he been?"

"Not sure."

"You spent all day with him and didn't ask any of these questions?" She placed a hand on his shoulder. "Is he hurt?"

"I don't think so."

She sighed. "Well, you were gone all day. What did you talk about?"

He shook his head slightly. "Not much."

"All day?"

"Yeah."

"Where did you go?"

He exhaled. "I don't mean anything by this, but I don't really have anything to say about today." He turned, placing his hands on her shoulder. "You understand, right?"

She nodded and glanced down at the floor. He cupped her face in his hands.

"I'm sorry I left you today. You're right I should have called. I didn't expect to see him. I gave him a ride back to town. We stopped at the pond. I didn't plan it."

She shrugged and allowed a smile. "Sorry for lashing out. I was worried." She grinned and then spun around. "Dinner'll be ready soon."

He nodded. He dragged his feet across the kitchen floor to look out the back yard. Max chewed on a bone in his doghouse, suddenly raising his head with the bone still between his teeth, and then went back to his chew. "You checked Max's water today?"

"Sure did. Hey, honey? Your mother called here this afternoon?"

"Yeah?" he asked, watching Max devour the bone.

He halfway listened as Annie filled him in on the family gossip. His cousins from Macon had returned home from the Pacific. Second came the city gossip. Most of the boys still alive in his class had returned home from the war. Finally, came the general gossip of happenings around the country.

*****

The street outside Wrightman General Store flashed with lightning. Waves of rain pounded the pavement, forming tiny swirling rivers near the streets and gushing waterfalls off roofs. Samuel rested his chin on the end of the broom. The Thursday morning storm had moved in quickly and hit the city with little warning.

A man rushed across the street toward the store, a newspaper over his head shredded into a mess of pulp. Large raindrops slapped the man's gray hat as he jumped over the same pond-sized puddle that had formed in front of the store every rainstorm since Samuel was a child.

The front door flew open, and the man dropped the wet newspaper on the floor. Samuel watched a small pool form around the paper and the man's black boots. With one motion, the man swept off his hat and walked toward him with the squishy sound of wet leather.

Joe.

"What the hell?" Samuel smiled.

He laughed. "Think it's raining, Sammy. Might want to let some people know."

"Yeah." He placed the broom against the wall behind the cash register. "What's going on?"

"I got the day off. Needed to run some errands."

"Still working in chickens?"

Joe shook his head. "I hate when you say it that way."

He squished down the isles. Small water-filled footprints marked his way. When Joe finished winding through the store grumbling about prices and the weather, he brought his goods to the register.

"That it?" Samuel asked as he punched keys into the cash register.

"Guess so."

"You moving out of your parents, yet?"

Joe smiled and tossed items into the brown bags. "I got to do that soon. I got a date tonight with Mary Hartman."

"Another one?"

"Yeah. Someday I'm afraid she'll make me marry her."

Samuel frowned. A familiar smell, something recognizable. "You startin' awful early this morning."

Joe blinked. "What?"

"You smell like a brewery." He glanced at the clock on the wall. "It's nine."

"Says the guy who's known for going to church drunk or hung over."

Samuel shrugged. "Long time ago."

"Jesus Christ, Sam. You ain't my Pa. Besides, I didn't start early today. I never quit from last night." Joe grinned. "It's my day off."

He shrugged. "I guess so."

Joe tossed the money on the counter. "Keep the change with the advice." He grabbed the goods and hobbled out into the storm.

Samuel sighed and watched his friend disappear behind the waterfall of rain.

He walked home alone, long after Luther had left for the day. The man's hair seemed to grow white overnight, a salt and pepper beard covering his once smooth face. His laugh had turned rocky, the rumbling sound of metal scraping together culminating in cough spasms that made him slower in his work. Despite his condition, Luther had accepted Samuel's extension of hours. Samuel had to shake his head as he watched the old man climb into his truck an hour before he, too, left the store for the night. He had called Annie to make sure she knew he was working late.

There was nothing on the streets but the sound of his footsteps, the hum of the streetlights, the whoosh of the fall breeze in the treetops.

Joe's words from earlier, the look in his eye, all flashed in his mind as he walked. There was a harshness to his friend, an unfamiliar edge. He had seen it in some of the veterans in England. It was hollowness to the eyes as if they had lost something. Some called it the "thousand yard stare."

Who was he to lecture someone? Nobody. His friend returns to this town and all Samuel does is make him feel bad for having a wild night. Some friend.

Samuel shook his head, remembering all the times Joe had listened to him over the years, all the times they had backed one another through it all. When Joe's parents fought late at night, Samuel was there to listen to the thoughts of a scared little boy, a boy that wanted to run away. When they had tried, they made it up into little Hawkridge Mountain. They spent the day wandering around, peering into the old mining tunnels, until the sun threatened to leave them up there in the darkness.

He sighed. Joe deserved better than a lecture from him. Better than any judging comments. It wouldn't happen again. Joe had been back a few months, and Samuel remembered it took some time to get back. He had the help of playing the part for Annie Ruth and his mother. Both helped him push the memories of France far into the depths of his mind. Still, the sight of the men who died in front of him followed him everywhere. Sometimes, he saw the dead boys in the faces of customers as they wandered the store. Other times he saw Charles and Maria, even Gerard, burning alive in their farmhouse. Or at times, he simply saw the German soldiers as he shot them, the crackle of the rifle, the snap of light, twitching of the bodies. The house falling around him like hellfire from the sky, the popping hiss of the burning embers.

"Sammy?"

He blinked. Their mailbox stood a few feet in front of him. He shook away the memories. "Annie, sweetheart."

"You okay out there?" she asked, her voice rising in pitch.

He glanced down at the sidewalk. "Sure. Just lost in thought."

Samuel walked toward the house, hands in his pocket. She studied him, smiling slightly after their lips met. She touched his cheek.

"But you're all right?"

He grinned and kissed her again. "Glad I've got you, honey."

He held her gaze for a moment before moving inside.

20

The brunette attendant smiled at him as he made his way back to his seat. The young man still stared at the letter. When he sat down, it appeared the young man had started a new draft. He took a deep breath.

The attendant loaded a drink cart at the front of the train car. He watched a metal tray slip from her hands. It flew in the air and fell toward the floor.

*****

Metal crashed against the floor from the back of the store. Ignoring Mrs. Patterson and her groceries, Samuel leaned over the counter to stare down the aisle.

"Luther?"

He could see the edge of the stock room since the door had propped open. Several boxes had fallen out into the back alley. He held up a finger toward his customer and tried to offer a smile, but hurried toward the back of the store. The entire morning shipment had spilled all over the floor and into the alley.

And then he saw him: Mr. Luther's feet on the ground stretching out from underneath the truck, unmoving.

"Damn it!" He dropped the paper bag onto the floor, heard glass breaking. He turned back into the store. "Call a doctor! Now!"

*****

Samuel sat outside Doctor Galliford's home, rocking slowly in a white chair on the front porch. He stared out at the leaves rustling from the wind. He inhaled and exhaled slowly. His teeth sunk into his bottom lip, and he swallowed. The front door squeaked open followed by soft footsteps.

"Sammy?" When he didn't answer, Annie Ruth stepped over to the front porch railing and leaned against it. She remained silent, staring at him.

Minutes passed as the wind blew. Finally, Doctor Galliford came out of the house.

"There wasn't much we could have done, Samuel," he said.

Nodding, Samuel abruptly stood and walked to the edge of the porch.

"Where are you going?" Annie asked.

"Mama's going to want to know. Luther was family."

He stomped off the stairs and toward the truck. Dimly, he heard Annie apologizing to the doctor as he opened the truck door. He gripped the steering wheel tight, his knuckles turning white with red lines. He placed his forehead on the wheel, fighting back the emotion.

"Sammy? Do you want me to walk home? It's not far."

He shook his head. "No. Come with me."

*****

His mother listened to the news. The grandfather clock chimed in the background twelve times.

She nodded as her chin quivered, forming a series dimples. Tapping him on the hand as she walked by him, she slowly made her way up the stairs toward the bedroom. The door shut. Samuel bit down on his lip again. Annie Ruth sat near him, hand resting on his knee.

"Bound to happen sooner or later, I guess," he said, his head swaying.

She frowned. "Not a very nice way to look at it."

"Only way I can." He stood and walked over to the kitchen sink, his feet scuffing the floor.

The ride home was taken in silence. His mother had not come back out of the room. Somehow, in some recess deep in the back of his mind, his father had died again today.

21

The land was flat. The mountains had long since disappeared. The grasslands stretched into the distance.

An old house stood at the end of a straight dirt driveway wide enough for one car. A moving truck had backed up to the house. A metal ramp extended from the back. A man and woman hoisted an old stained couch into the truck. A teenaged boy wearing a tank top that probably used to be white leaned on the front of the truck, smoking a cigarette. The couple came back from the vehicle, and the man yelled at the slacking teenager.

*****

"Gotta do this faster, Nick," Samuel said as he pulled a stack of crates off the back of the truck. "These trucks don't unload themselves."

"I know, Mr. Wrightman. I know."

The boy had been back behind the store for an hour. Samuel knew he was barely in his teens, but the kid moved like he had all the time in the world. When the kid showed up that morning for his first day, hands deep in his pockets with a baseball cap covering his blonde hair, he had a little life in him and zero pep in his step.

Now, after working in the heat for a few hours, Nick's feet dragged, and his arms moved slowly. His virgin fingers cracked and bled on the crates. Samuel had gone back inside to grab some work gloves.

Carvy Henderson's nephew.

With Carvy being such a town character, Samuel had hesitated to hire the child. But considering Nick's mother had died to leave him all alone up in Terrytown and the fact Carvy was always running around trying to find the next failed business he would start in McGovern, Samuel figured the boy could have something to do during the summer days until school started. Of course, Nick had to stay with Carvy during the nights, despite the man's constant pestering and hinting that Samuel and Annie Ruth had no children at home.

Samuel swept the store floor and stared through the back door to see Nick attempting to finish the truck. The bells on the front door jingled.

"Hey honey," he said when he saw it was Annie Ruth.

"Hi."

She walked over toward the front of the store. Her fingers slid across the counter top as she bit her lip.

When he saw the look on her face, he stopped sweeping and rested his hands on the top of the broom. "What's going on?"

"I'm pregnant," she said without a pause. She stared at him.

"Pregnant?" His voice lowered and glanced back over his shoulder. "Seriously?"

"Just went to the doctor."

"I thought you were working."

She smiled. "I was. I wanted to go without you knowing. I didn't want to get your hopes up."

Samuel nodded and stared out at Main Street.

A child.

He would be a father.

"Well?" she asked.

"This is…great news."

She frowned. "I thought you'd be excited."

He nodded. "I am. I just don't know what to say."

She shook her head and turned around. "This played out completely different in my head. I'm sorry I came into the store. We can just talk about this tonight."

Samuel nodded and watched her walk back across town to the post office.

The day went by as they always did. A few customers spoke about local issues, gossip, and other meaningless chatter. Samuel nodded, smiled, and said little. When Nick dragged himself back in from the alley, sweat causing the white shirt to stick to his skin, Samuel allowed him to go since the truck had finally been finished.

On the way home, Samuel passed what looked like Joe driving. He honked, and they both slowed in the middle of Main Street.

"Hey, buddy," Samuel said as he walked toward Joe's window.

"Where you going?" Joe asked, cigarette dangling out of the corner of his mouth.

"Home." He shrugged. "Closing time."

Joe took a drag off his cigarette. "You wanna come with me?" he asked as he exhaled. "I'm heading over to the *Corner Pocket*."

He shook his head. "Can't. Wife's waiting."

Joe snorted. "Yeah."

"What about you and Mary?"

His friend blinked through the haze of smoke floating around his head. "Mary?"

"Yeah. Aren't you two dating?"

"Guess you could call it that." He flicked the cigarette away, sparks like fireflies twirling around the side of the car. "Listen, man, I got to get going."

He frowned. "Yeah, okay.'"

He shifted his car back into drive, turning back toward the road.

"Hey!"

Joe looked at him.

"Annie says we're having a baby." He stared at Joe. "Thought you'd like to know."

Joe's eyes glazed over, and he stared off toward Hawkridge Mountain for a long moment. "That's great. Boy?"

"Too early. I just found out today."

"Go home to your wife, Sam." Joe nodded.

He smiled. "Stay safe."

Samuel watched Joe's car turn toward the edge of town and disappear around a corner.

*****

Annie Ruth said little when he returned. She stayed in the kitchen, preparing dinner in silence. Samuel placed his keys on the hook near the front door and bit his lip. He hesitated before moving back to their room to change out of his clothes that smelled of gasoline. He shook his head and picked out one of his older shirts from before the war and a pair of blue jeans.

When he returned to the kitchen, it was filled with the spicy smell of chili and buttered toast. He exhaled.

It was his favorite dinner. "Smells great, Annie."

"Yeah?" she asked without turning around. She stirred a large wooden spoon and kept her eyes on the pot.

He pulled the chair back from the table and sat down with a grunt. Sore muscles and feet mixed with old wounds, he thought. Annie said something he couldn't hear. He leaned forward with his good ear. "How's that?"

"How's Carvy's nephew?"

Samuel shrugged. "Guess he's doing okay. Had a rough first day. He ain't no Luther."

"No, I suppose not."

He rapped his fingertips on the table. "Sorry 'bout today, Annie."

She nodded without turning. "Sure."

"No, really. Just caught me off guard, that's all."

Now she turned to look at him with bloodshot eyes. "It's nothing."

His stared at her for a moment. He realized his reaction hurt her more than she was letting on. He leaned forward and stood up from his chair. She looked down at the wooden spoon as chili ran down the sides before turning around again. He walked slowly over to his wife. He placed his hands on her shoulders, brushing the hair away from her neck and pressed his chin gently onto her shoulder.

"Forgive me?"

She nodded and inhaled as he wrapped his hands around her waist.

"I wasn't ready for the news today," he said. "You deserve better than that."

She placed the spoon into the pot and turned. "It wasn't what I expected. Sometimes I feel I don't know you at all."

He backed away. "What's that mean?"

"I thought you'd be happy about the baby. You come and go without saying a word sometimes. What's worse is that I don't even think you notice we haven't spoken in a day unless I tell you of something we need from the store."

He frowned. "Not true."

"It's not? Then tell me why the longest conversation I've had this week was with Carvy Henderson about what happen with his sister's family up in Terrytown."

He turned away toward the window. "I don't know what you want from me."

She tugged at his elbow. "I want you to talk with me. I want you to be happy. Why won't you? Is it me?"

"Of course, it's not you."

"Then what? What?" She dropped the spoon on the stove. "Why won't you let me in?"

Samuel snorted and stomped across the kitchen toward the bedroom. "I don't know what you mean. How do you want me to let you in?"

"Say anything. Say what you want. Tell me what's going on with you."

He slapped his hand on the wall. Annie shrieked, recoiling against the stove.

He sighed and stepped away from the wall. "I'm sorry."

Turning around, he clenched his teeth.

"I don't know what you want me to say. You want me to tell you about what happen over there? It was a hell I don't think I could tell you about. You want me to tell you why I've been quiet? My best friend came home from the war, and I can't even figure out why we have nothing to talk about anymore. I came home to a different life, a different world. None of this place has been the same. All of you people act as if nothing happen. Well, something did happen! The war ruined everything. I haven't felt the same since I got back. I don't know if I can be the man you want me to be. Life is just going on like it has been for you, but for me it's not the same."

"You people?" She frowned, her chin quivering. "You people."

He shook his head. "Not you. You're all that has been good. I came home and had to take over my father's business. You think that's what I wanted? You think I wanted to stay here? To listen to the same old stories, worry about who's going to what church, what marriage is falling apart, who got pregnant, who graduated—I don't care about any of it. Don't you understand? It is all so unimportant. And now, I find my best friend is a drunk. I can't even talk to him about what we went through. Worst part is that I'm not sure I blame him."

"You want to join him at the bar?" Her eyebrows furrowed.

"No. I want to be here with you." He wiped his hand over his face and closed his eyes. She stepped forward and stopped a few feet from him. "And…"

He gasped and stood in silence. When he continued, he spoke in a lower tone, almost in a whisper.

"And my Pa. My Pa is gone. I wasn't even here when..."

Her face relaxed, and she sighed. "Why are you telling me all of this now?"

He wiped his nose, fighting back the memories of his father's face now flurrying around his mind. "I don't really know. I do know that having a baby with you is a wonderful thing, but I'm not sure I want to have a child here with this life. I wanted something more before we had children. I guess life's not giving me the chance, that's all."

"How's that?"

He thrust his hands down into his pockets. "I made poor decisions and I feel like we are living with the consequences. I went to the war for someone else. I took over the business for someone else. It's not that I regret it, Annie. I just thought life would be different. I thought I would have a chance to figure out who I wanted to be. What I wanted to do, you know?" He looked at her. "But I'm so glad I've got you. Marrying you is the only thing I ever did for me."

She nodded. They embraced tightly in the kitchen. "Just try to be happy. That's all I want. That's all I've ever wanted since the first day I met you."

They parted, and he smiled at her. Their lips met, and they kissed for the first time in weeks.

She shut off the stove before they left the room.

*****

The women laughed in unison from his living room, a chorus of giggles mixing with a cackle and a series of coughs. Samuel filled a glass of tea and stared out at the collage of colors painted in the leaves of the trees outside his window. A collection of leaves whisked by in a flutter. Max barked and spun around as he played a game with himself in the backyard.

He smiled and cupped his face in his right hand. He thought of his old dog Henry, who had passed away earlier that summer. His mother had found his first friend in the doghouse, a bone resting between his paws. A lump formed in his throat, but the laughter from the other room forced him to shake it away. Still, the memories of his old friend remained. Henry was the first of his family to welcome him home. He was the first one to be there after his first date with Annie. Henry, his gray face looking at him as if he expected something, was never far from his mind.

He took his plate to the sink after tossing the crust from his sandwich into Max's bowl. The kitchen clock showed it was almost one, nearly time to head back to work after his lunch break. He couldn't leave Nick at the store alone too long, might have some kind of accident.

Laughter erupted from the living room as Lucy Turner burst through the door to the kitchen. "Well, Sam, are you still in here?"

"I guess so."

Lucy grinned to show all her ivory white teeth. "You don't have to work today?"

"I do. Just came home for lunch and was watching the dog play."

"Oh." She stared out the window as if she just realized the Wrightmans had a backyard.

Lucy Turner. Samuel shook his head. Lucy had been Annie Ruth's friend in high school if you could call her that. She moved after the first year because her father took a job in Atlanta.

"You know David's got two dogs that we might breed at the first of the year. They're these big, huntin' dogs. You seen 'em?"

He shook his head. "I really better get back."

"Well, your wife's baby shower is going just fine. It's almost as big as my shower was. I'd say about half that came to her shower, which ain't half bad."

"Goodbye, Lucy."

"I'll keep an eye on things for you while you're gone."

2 2

Mountains loomed in the distance. He squinted and realized they were dark clouds far away. The blackness of the clouds streaked down like a wet painting. He watched the storm in the distance and saw a flash of lighting miles away from the train tracks.

*****

Thunder rumbled in the distance and rattled the windows. The wind howled under the doors and in the unseen cracks of the house. Samuel rolled over in bed. Annie Ruth was on her side, her large stomach visible through the sheets. She said something in her sleep as lightning illuminated the bedroom. He slid his fingers up and down her arm and then put his hand on her belly. She smiled slightly and released a short moan.

Something popped outside the bedroom. He raised his head. The wind?

He slid out of bed and avoided the creaks in the floor as he moved toward the bedroom door. The living room was dark, only the streetlights filtered in like moonbeams across the furniture. He glanced into the kitchen and saw nothing. Rain whipped against the roof in sheets, and shadows of the rain flickered through the windows as if he were underwater.

Something rattled again, louder than everything else in the house.

He tripped over the baby's gifts, kicking a balloon across the floor left over from the shower. His heart pounded, a cold sweat running down his scalp. Someone was in the house or maybe they were trying to break in. Maybe the front of the house?

Someone knocked on the back window.

Samuel turned around, expecting to see a man trying to break through the back door. Instead, he saw a figure leaning down and petting Max as the dog sat inside his doghouse. The figure stood and knocked gently on the back door once again. He swallowed and made his way toward the door. He grabbed a long metal flashlight from the hallway closet, gripping it tightly.

Who the hell would be here at this time of night, he thought. The clock in the kitchen read two in the morning. His fingers locked around the piece of steel. He softly unlocked the back door, took a deep breath, and swung it wide open. Water flickered into the house with the door, and the figure jumped backward.

"What the hell?" a familiar voice asked, recoiling back into the yard.

"Joe?" He blinked. "Joe! You gave me a heart attack."

"You? What about me?"

He grabbed him by the elbow. "Come inside."

After brewing coffee and listening to Joe describe what sounded like a normal night a the billiards' hall, the two friends wandered out into the garage and sat on Samuel's tool bench that had once belonged to his father. His mother had asked him to take it away, and she didn't want it around the house any longer.

"I remember this," Joe said and slid his fingers across the scarred, wooden surface. "We used to pretend to fix your Pa's stuff here."

He nodded and sipped on the coffee. "Yeah."

Joe reeked of alcohol, but stood and spoke fine. The coffee mug hadn't even trembled when he took it. He studied the tools on the shelf, told stories of how he and Samuel had tried to fix this and that, how they thought his Pa was amazing when he repaired things around the farm.

"I'm sorry about your Pa," Joe said after he had just finished laughing about a particular story. "I really am."

"Yeah? Thanks."

"He was a good man."

Samuel nodded, pursing his lips. "The best."

Joe fiddled with a screwdriver as he sloshed the coffee around in his mug. "I wanted to come by to tell you and Annie I was happy for you."

"You could have done that in the morning."

He shrugged. "I guess. Could a done a lot of things, but I didn't."

Samuel watched his friend stare at the ground. Joe's face wrinkled, and he pressed his knuckles into his mouth. He placed his hand back down on the table.

Samuel stood and looked at the steam from the coffee swirling in front of him. Somehow he knew Joe hadn't come over here in the middle of a rainstorm to talk about his father.

"I can't get it out of my head, Sammy. I just can't. I've tried."

He nodded. "I know."

"I see their faces. I see them in everyone at the plant."

"Yeah."

"I hear it in the machinery. I hear it in a car backfiring. The sound of the hunters in the woods … it keeps me up nights."

Samuel peered down at the coffee, watching steam twist into shapes.

"I wake up at night," Joe continued after a moment. "I smell blood, sometimes gunpowder. Willie Hanshaw, some runner from Cincinnati, his head exploded in front of me." He closed his eyes. Tears fell. "Bastard's blood splattered on my face and…God. Oh, God. I couldn't blink it away. It burned."

Samuel took a sip of the coffee and then placed the mug on the hood of his father's truck. As Joe buried his face into his hands, Samuel walked over next to his friend and leaned against the workbench.

"I killed, Sam. I killed so many. Cut their throats. Cut their ears off. I shot a man as he tried to surrender. I watched his face come apart, his teeth shattering to the ground. I didn't care. Not then. No … didn't care then."

Joe glanced around the garage. "I never thought I would get back to a place like this. To all this…normal." He wiped his eyes and turned to Samuel, his eyes unblinking. "Jesus Christ, Sammy, why did we go over there? Why? I wish I was dead. God. I, I wish I was … dead."

Joe pressed his face into Samuel's shoulder. Samuel took a breath and listened to his friend sob.

"I don't know," Samuel said as Joe's sobs lessened. "I don't have any idea."

Joe sat up, wiping his face. "I came over to ask what you were going to name the baby."

He managed a smile, the lump in his throat subsiding. "James for a boy. Malissa for a girl."

Joe nodded. "Good names."

"Yeah?"

"Yeah." He looked at him, a familiar twinkle in his eye. "Joe would be nice, but James'll do." He stood up and stretched. "Not sure if I ever said it, but I promised myself I would when I came back. You're my best friend, Sam. No one else ever came close."

"Same to you."

Joe slapped him on the shoulder. "I should get going. I left Mary at my place."

Samuel frowned. "What?"

"She's stays over from time-to-time. We kind of had one of those nights. Just didn't feel like being there. That and I heard it was your baby's shower."

He snorted. "You sure didn't miss much."

"I didn't?"

They laughed.

After standing in silence and smiling into nothingness, Joe nodded and disappeared out the garage door in the back. Samuel stood in the garage, watching the steam disappear from his coffee. He slid his fingers across the hood of the truck, thinking of the times he and Joe took it out on the town without his father knowing.

23

"I don't like this."

The young man crumpled the second letter in his fist and tossed it to the ground.

He reached down, ignoring the pain in his back, and grabbed the letter. "Smooth this out. Write it again. Don't destroy the next one. You hear?"

The young man nodded. "She's going to forget about me while I'm gone."

"No." He handed over the letter. "Been sittin' here watching you try and write this letter for a hundred miles. Finish it."

He turned back to the landscape, watching people work in the fields alongside the railroad track.

*****

The unusually cool September breeze tossed a color of leaves on the courthouse lawn when Samuel heard the news Annie Ruth had gone into labor. He had left Nick to run the store for a couple of hours, now had to hurry back and close up shop. Post Master Trapnell had taken her to Dr. Galliford's.

Annie gave birth to James Horace Wrightman two hours after Samuel had arrived and three years to the month since he had returned from Europe. Doctor Galliford had been concerned at first because the baby was early, but James appeared healthy. His mother had come by that evening. Annie's aunt and uncle also made an appearance. Guests filed in for the next couple days until Samuel finally brought his new family home.

He held James only twice the first day. The guests seemed to do most of the holding and talking. Joe stopped by with Mary Hartman. The woman had bright red lipstick and powder caked on her face like a frosted cupcake, her low-cut dress revealing most of her chest. She said little, spending most of the time gazing out the window. For ten minutes, Joe stared with bloodshot eyes at James like the baby was a science experiment.

As soon as they had arrived, Joe and Mary left. They never spoke about the night of the baby shower. Samuel didn't mind.

He stood over his son's crib long after Annie had gone to bed. He watched the sun dip behind Hawkridge Mountain in the distance. James sniffled a few times, and he reached down to touch his son's face. Silence covered the house, only his grandfather's clock ticked from the living room. Samuel took a deep breath, smiled.

He hadn't prayed since he returned home from the war. Didn't see the point anymore. He had seen men cry before they took off from England plenty of times. Men cried and spoke beautiful prayers about home, death, and women.

It didn't help.

So many went home in boxes. So many more died in fiery wrecks in Europe. Seeing the men around him die after such lofty prayers led Samuel into numbness. And he concluded prayer did nothing.

He took a sip of water, washing it around his mouth.

It was time to change his thinking.

Dear God, he thought and closed his eyes. I hadn't spoken to you … well, in a long time. I don't know if you'll hear me or if you'll even care. I know you know I would die for my son. Let him have a life without pain. Let him experience none of what I've seen. More than that, give me the strength to be a good father and a good husband.

Amen.

*****

Water lapped the corners of the canoe. Samuel dipped his rod down and exhaled. The water looked like a mirror save a few ripples. Joe had called him the day before to ask if he could fish Friday morning. Not a usual time but Samuel figured it couldn't hurt to take a morning off at the end of the week. He could unload the Thursday truck Friday evening. Right now, he decided to enjoy the day with his friend.

But they had sat in silence once they paddled out to the center of McPherson's Pond. Joe seemed content to sip on his flask and lean back in the sun. Samuel hadn't even had a nibble. The air was too hot, the sun beating down on the water.

A familiar buzzing groaned in the distance. Samuel closed his eyes. A plane. One twin-engine plane soared in the cloudless sky. He leaned back and smiled, thought of pilots barking orders back and forth between themselves and the crew. Of course, this plane wouldn't have machine guns bristling from the corners.

"What was that like?" Joe asked, still leaning against the corner of the steel canoe.

Samuel frowned. "Flying?"

"You haven't talked about it." He kept his eyes closed, his cheeks red from the sun and liquor.

Samuel shrugged. "I don't know. Nice, I guess."

Joe opened one eye to stare at him. "Nice…you guess? Man, that's pathetic."

"Why?"

"How many hours did I spend with you out here talking about flying? All you wanted to do was fly up there."

Samuel pulled his rod in the canoe. "I know. It was nice."

Joe leaned forward, taking a long gulp from his flask. "I might never get the chance to fly, you know. What was it like?"

Samuel thought back to the feeling when he first took off with his crew in training. The wind howling in through the windows, the Lieutenant barking orders, the crew confused. He smiled.

But flying over Europe had been…different.

"I was in the air, flying high." He swallowed. "Like sardines in a tin can. Bullets bouncing around the cockpit. We'd shoot down a fighter. They'd send up two more. I hated it, Joe." He stared at his friend. "I hated every day. Saw guys killed and blasted out of planes like baggage."

Scott Adams' face, the last guy he flew with. The image burned. He remembered the clueless, frightened boy dying, the blood flowing across the floorboard of the bomber. He took a deep breath. "Anyway, I'll never get in a plane again. Not ever."

Joe nodded. "You were shot down, right?"

"Yeah."

"You a prisoner?"

He shrugged. "Something like that."

Joe cocked his head to the side, staring at his friend. "Well, buddy, I'm getting married."

Samuel blinked. "What?"

"Mary finally talked me into it."

"Congratulations! When?"

Joe tilted his head back and laughed. "I'm not doing the whole white wedding crap. Not me. You imagine Mary in a dress like that? Shit. I've never seen her wear something white, come to think of it."

"Where you guys going to live? Have you thought of that?"

He shrugged. "Not really. Just figure it's time. Some of the guys at the mill been asking me about it. Tired of all the questions."

Samuel paused, considering how to ask this question. "I don't know anything about Mary. What does she do?"

"She types."

"She what?"

Joe laughed. "Works in a law office in Fulton County. She types." He moved his fingers around in the air on an imaginary typewriter. "You know, types?"

"I know what a typewriter is." He smiled.

Joe nodded. "We're going to live up in the north end of the county. It's a little place on a couple acres. Mary's got her car, so we'll be fine."

Samuel took a deep breath. "You believe it?"

"What's that?"

"Both of us married. I've got James now growing up nearly three years old. Time goes too fast."

"Yeah."

"Speaking of time, I need to get back to work."

Joe sat up and rocked the boat. "Knew you'd say that. I just wanted you to know. Will you be a witness before the judge?"

Samuel grinned. "Of course."

*****

Nick had been sent home earlier. The boy had a bad habit of allowing his mind to wander. Samuel had caught him on the back porch, staring off into the sky with his chin on the end of the broom. The child could work when he was prodded like a stubborn mule, but Samuel wasn't in the mood for such high maintenance.

Business had been nonstop for the past two weeks. Women came in and cleared out his picnic baskets, blankets, and pitchers. Little boys bought the plastic bags full of green army guys. Men purchased the small amount of bait he had on hand. Springtime in McGovern County had arrived.

Samuel clicked the lock on the front door and glanced up at the dark blue sky. The days had been lasting longer. Soon, the heat would follow, and summer would begin. He smiled and sighed. The passing of winter always brought with it a sense of sadness. For some reason, he thought of France, of Maria, and little Charles. Most of his memories of that place, his second home, were painted in the blankness of a snow-covered landscape. While McGovern brought little in the manner of snow, the cold weather always brought France back into his mind. He stepped across Main Street and meandered down the sidewalk, his toes tripping over some of the weed infested cracks in the concrete.

Nice night for a walk, he thought.

Lights flickered across the sidewalk. A police car took a sharp turn down the street and headed for him. His jaw dropped as the car stopped.

"Samuel?" Robert Hendrix, an old friend of his father's who had been at the Bloomsdale Police Department since he could remember, asked as he opened the car door.

"What is it, Mr. Hendrix?" Samuel asked, fighting back the hard spot forming in his throat.

"We found Joe up at the *Corner Pocket*," Hendrix said and frowned, his gaze lingering on the sidewalk. "He's busted up pretty bad, Sammy."

He sighed. "What happened?"

"Not sure. Someone dumped him near the trashcans out back."

Hendrix stopped and stood with one foot on the road, one still in the car as the lights flickered across the Main Street. Samuel swallowed. Joe's mother had passed away the year before. He had no one else.

He nodded at Hendrix. "Take me there."

*****

Joe's eyes had been swollen shut, two colossal puffs closing the lids. His blood-covered face swelled, revealing two major cuts on his forehead. The odor of alcohol drifted off his friend's body. Samuel used a frayed handkerchief to clean the blood before transferring him into the truck with Hendrix's help.

"Mike said a couple guys from the northern end of the county had been gambling with Joe all night," Hendrix said as he scooped Joe's legs into the truck. "They were fairly regular, come in every now and then. Field hands probably. Looking for work either up on Hawkridge or in the chicken houses. Or they could just be passing through. The largest one worked as a grill man for Carvy. I could check with him in the morning." He stared down at Joe, who moaned as he lay across the back seat of the truck. "You okay taking him home? I don't want it to cause a problem with Annie or your son. It's just our cells are already full, it being Friday night and all."

Samuel nodded and sighed. "I'll take him."

They shook hands, and he drove home in silence.

The lights still beamed out from his home as he pulled up into the garage. Annie Ruth stood at the doorway soon after he shut down the truck.

"What's wrong?" she whispered as he stepped out of the truck.

Great, he thought, James is fast asleep. "What time is it?"

"Nearly midnight. Where have you been?" Her eyes flashed wide.

He glanced back at the truck. "I'm not alone. Hendrix found Joe beaten up out the back of the billiards hall. I told him he could spend the night."

"The night?" She rolled her eyes and leaned against the doorway. "Is he okay?"

"I don't know," Samuel sighed. "Looks pretty bad. Probably doesn't feel nothing, the state he's in."

Annie blinked, her eyes forming a cold stare. "Why couldn't he stay in jail?"

He snorted. "Why would you want to do that? He is our friend."

"Some friend." She shook her head.

"Look, the jail's already full. It's Friday."

She nodded after a long pause. "Bring him to the couch. I'll make sure he's got coffee in the morning."

He touched her neck, pulled her close, and kissed her forehead.

"Thank you," he whispered.

She smiled. "Just don't wake the baby. He really didn't want to go to sleep without you home. Kept asking about the boogerman."

He grinned as he propped open the doorway. "Mama tell him about that?"

"Who else," she said before disappearing into the house.

His father always told stories of the boogerman coming to get children who didn't go to bed on time. Great job, Pa.

Samuel dragged his friend into the house and dumped him onto the couch. He slipped off Joe's boots and placed Annie's small blanket over his legs. Joe snored, licked his chops, said something in gibberish and settled back into a deep snore.

Samuel sighed and stepped toward the backdoor. The stars twinkled over Hawkridge Mountain in the distance. He saw his father's face in the mountain. His father telling the stories of the mountain, how the Indians had used it to pray, how men had once searched for gold in those hills. Funny how two different groups searched for God and gold in the same place.

He exhaled.

"Sure do miss you, Pop," he said aloud.

He closed his eyes and felt his father's hand grip his own at the train station the day he left for the war. The last time they had spoken one on one. And Samuel knew, deep down in places he didn't want to talk about, his father had died believing his son had died in the war. Samuel had first believed his mother, thought Pa had never stopped believing in his return.

But Samuel knew better. A man would lie to his wife to hide the pain. One of them had to keep the hope.

If only I had come home sooner …

A shooting star flickered across the sky, so briefly he wondered for a moment if he had really seen it. He blinked as he stared out the window. He closed his eyes.

Joe's snore brought him back to the moment. Samuel shook his head quickly, and walked back to the bedroom.

When Samuel woke up the next morning to James crying, Joe had disappeared. Only a small dot of blood remained on the arm of the couch, something Samuel tried to cover before Annie saw it. He positioned the blanket Joe had used to cover the spot. She walked by the backyard window, James in tow, his brown eyes wide as he followed a yellow and black butterfly, his hair sprouting at the back of his head like a corn stalk.

He watched them cross the grass. They laughed and spoke about something for a moment before they continued running around the yard.

Something caught his attention from the corner of his eye. He cocked his head to the left to get a better view of what was under the coffee table. He shook his head. Collecting a pool of condensation around its base, a half full beer bottle sat under the table. He stared outside at his family for a long moment. He frowned and grabbed the bottle, hurling it into the trash in the kitchen and shattering the glass.

Annie's eyes darted up from her son, her hair wrapping around her shoulders. She picked up James and started toward the house.

"You okay?" she asked, entering the living room.

"Everything's fine," he said, bitting his lip. "How's my big guy this morning?"

James reached his arms out away from his mother. "Da da."

He spun his son round, watching his eyes glance around the room with a smile bursting from his face. "You wanna come to work with Daddy today?"

Annie plopped down on the couch. She sighed and leaned her head back on the couch. "You feeling all right?"

"Sure." He kissed James on the forehead. "Why?"

"You slept late for you. The store opens in an hour."

"Yeah, I know."

She paused and leaned back to look at him while her head was still upside down. "You did a nice job."

His brow wrinkled. "Nice job?"

She smiled. "I like how you hid Joe's blood stain. Very nice."

He stopped spinning his son. "Never pull one over on you, will I?"

"You remember that," she said, giggling like he hadn't heard in months.

*****

Robert Hendrix paced the front of the store as if he had been on watch for hours. Samuel pulled his truck around back to find the Bloomsdale Police car already parked. Hendrix marched down the side street toward him.

"Sammy? You hear from Joe?"

Samuel sighed and yanked his car keys from the ignition. "Not since last night. Why?"

Hendrix sighed and peered around the parking lot in the early morning light. "Couple guys were found at the other end of town this morning, beaten pretty bad. Some say they have been seen at the billiards hall quite a bit lately." He stared at Samuel as if he expected something before he bit his lip. "I need to know where Joe is."

"You think Joe's out beatin' people up now?" Samuel squinted, staring into Hendrix's steel blue eyes. The man sounded much different than the night before. "I don't know where he is."

"Helping him out's not gonna do you any good."

He put his hands on his hips. "What does that mean?"

Hendrix sighed and crossed his arms, lowering his voice. "You tell me where he is, right now. We can't have men running around downtown beatin' each other. This ain't Duluth. You've heard the

206

stories of men killing each other over money over there." His eyes turned into mere cold slits. "It's not gonna happen here, sonny."

Samuel stepped closer. "I don't think I appreciate this."

"What?"

He nodded. "You gonna come to my store this morning, start making threats? I want you to know I don't appreciate it. You make me take a drunk man into my house in the middle of the night, put my youngin' at risk—not to mention my wife. And now you have the gall to bother me about this the next day? All because this city doesn't have enough jail cells to take care of its own problems?"

He didn't wait for an answer. He stormed off toward the back of his store, unlocked the backdoor and slid back the loading dock with a crash.

Hendrix stood in the parking lot, his arms still crossed. "If only your Mama could hear the way you're talking to me."

Samuel spun round. "You leave my Mama out of this. You're in the wrong, and you know it. You can't come here making threats. Joe's gone. I don't know where the hell he is."

Hendrix walked toward the back of the store slowly. "I believe you, Sam." He pointed a bony finger. "But let me tell you, the only reason I'm not writing you up for disorderly conduct is because I respected your Daddy. You better let me know if you hear from Joe, you hear?"

Samuel stared down, sweeping out the back of the store until Hendrix walked away.

Something boiled deep inside. It was a feeling he hadn't felt since France, a feeling of violation. He didn't owe this town anything. Now, its police officer was trying to nail something on his best friend. Joe had his problems, but Samuel knew how he felt. A part of you stayed overseas, probably would stay there forever. But this town didn't see that. They thumped their chests, spoke of bravery, patriotism, the red, white and blue.

But they hadn't seen the cost. They hadn't seen the boys dying for this flag, dying so these people could sit back here on colorful lawn chairs, sip sugary lemonade and question why or how. The country had made them monsters, taught them to be killers. And they had learned their lessons well. Samuel still thrilled with the memory of a German plane burning on its way to the ground. He only imagined what memories Joe carried tucked away in deep recesses of the mind in places no one entered, no one understood, and no one knew about.

Samuel hurled his broom across the loading dock and went to unlock the store.

No one came into the store until eleven that morning. Two stocky, heavyset men made their way through the front door. They stepped slowly, heads moving around as they appeared to take in the entire room and glance down the aisles. When their vision finally rested on Samuel, the men had stepped up to the front counter, close enough to lean over it.

"We hear you're friends with Joe from the mill," the man said in a voice that reminded Samuel of sand rubbing against small pebbles. "You know where he is?"

"Yeah," he said without hesitation. "He left town as far as I know."

"Really?" The man fiddled with the candy dish on Samuel's counter. "He ever tell you about the time he spent playing billiards?"

"Not much."

The man leaned farther over the counter. "You hiding something from us, Mr. Wrightman?"

Samuel gritted his teeth. "Mr. Wrightman was my Pa. I'm Sam or Samuel or just plain Sammy. What the hell do you two want?"

The larger fella stepped back and folded his arms over his broad chest. The younger one glanced to his partner and grinned. "Joe owes us a bit of money."

Samuel cocked an eyebrow. "Gambling?"

"Let's say ... extensive bar tab."

He nodded. "If I see him, I'll let you fellas know. Of course, how do I get a hold of you? You guys cops?"

They both laughed.

"No," the younger one said. "We're just passing through."

The men left, but their stench of cheap aftershave, raunchy chewing tobacco and body odor remained. Samuel watched them wander down the side of Main Street. Christy Taylor, owner of the dress shop at the opposite end of town, strolled down the street in a bright white dress. The two men stared at her with open mouths. And both disappeared around the corner.

24

¦¦¦¦¦¦¦

The train passed over a rusty bridge. He listened to the clackity-clack of the wheels moving over the large, peaceful lake. Two boats cut through the still water, one pulling a skier.

*****

"A what?" Samuel blinked, unsure what the man in the expensive dark suit had said. "You say the government wants to build a lake?"

The man with closely cropped hair and an expensive blue suit nodded, looking at Samuel through thin glasses. His thin nose cropped forward at the end as if it had been caught in a car door, his skin smooth like he had never shaved a day in his life. The suit man waltzed in through the front of the store, a sly smile on his face like he was in the middle of a poker game and had a hand you didn't want to call.

"That's right," the man said as if he knew the secret of the universe. "My name is Donald Harrell. I represent the U.S. government."

Samuel shrugged. "And?"

The man sighed and placed his briefcase on the counter. In one smooth motion, he produced a stack of official documents from the case and extended them toward Samuel. "The government is going to buy your family's land at a fair price. The reservoir is going to take up a large portion of McGovern County and some other neighboring counties. Your family's farm is going to be underwater in a few years."

Samuel frowned. His father's land, his home, gone. "You're kidding!"

Harrell shook his head. "Nope."

"Did Hendrix put you up to this? I know he's been on my case for a while now, but I'd thought he'd gotten over this."

Harrell's face didn't move. "Sir, this is not a joke, and I have little time."

Samuel nodded. He thought of his mother and the farmhouse, remembered Henry running through the fields on all those summer days of his youth. The image of his father piddling around the house and the barn, working on projects for hours.

"I don't think we want to sell, Mr. Harrell. Not now. Besides, you'll have to speak with my mother. I have no authority over that property."

Harrell snorted. "I think you're misinterpreting my reason for being here. I have already spoken to your mother, and she threw me out of the house with these papers." He gestured down to the stack, and Samuel saw the wrinkles on the surface.

He locked his gaze with Harrell. "Then you already have your answer, sir."

"No," Harrell said as he shook his head. "This is not an offer for you to decide upon. This is the way it is. You have to present these papers to your mother. You will be paid fair market value for the land and will be asked to vacate the premises by the date listed on the papers."

Samuel stared at the documents. "You can't do this," he said softly, reading over the first lines of the paper. "That's my family's land, been so since before I was born. You can't just take it."

"We can. And we will. It's called eminent domain. Look it up." Harrell grinned now, displaying his bright white teeth. "This can't be any surprise. People around these parts of have been discussing a lake for sometime now. There had been talk of doing it down in Roswell—"

"Do it there, then."

Harrell shook his head. "This is the location. This lake will mean drinking water for the area for years to come." He clamped his briefcase shut. "Talk to your mother, Mr. Wrightman. Good day."

Harrell nodded, spinning on his heel and marching out of the store. Samuel watched him leave, clenched his teeth, and read through the documents.

A lake. A lake on his home. Water would rush in and cover everything he ever knew.

He called Annie Ruth, told her what was happening. He left Nick in charge of the store, explaining everything twice before he left for his family's land. The hot August air rushed in through the truck's windows as he followed the two-lane winding road. A pair of horses galloped across the Boggins' land to his left. He chewed on his lip. If what this Harrell said comes to pass, the Boggins' land will be underwater, too.

His mind went blank as he pulled in front of his family's home. Nothing moved, and silence fell over the land when he turned the key to shut off his truck. A warm breeze touched his cheek and sent dust twirling in front of the home. The large oak tree covered the house in shadow as it always had, making the shade cooler.

As he stepped out of the truck, he noticed his mother swinging on the front porch in the chair his father had made. He closed the truck door quietly and stepped toward the house while he tried not to make a sound. She opened her eyes as he walked up onto the porch, the wood popping, and creaking as he did so. Their eyes met, and she allowed a brief smile. He gestured toward the porch swing, and she nodded.

He sat with his mother, swinging on the porch. A car drove by on the main road. Henry would have chased it had he been here. He grinned and exhaled.

"How's my grandson?" his mother asked, folding her arms over her chest.

"Fine. Good. At home playing with Annie right now, I reckon."

"You've got a good boy there," she said softly. "I can tell already."

He smiled. "Thank you, Mama."

"He's just deep down good."

The chain creaked as the chair moved back, forth, back, forth. The wind picked up and tossed pebbles, leaves and sand across the base of the oak tree.

Underwater. All of it.

He looked up at the old oak tree, thought of the water filling up over his head.

"I know why you're here, Sam."

He swallowed. "Mr. Harrell stopped by the store."

"It doesn't matter." She pressed her lips together, her eyes wincing. "I'm not selling…not selling."

He nodded. "I know."

"What would your father think of me? Giving this land to you was his dream. It's all he ever thought about. He wanted to pass it to you to start your own family one day. When you were first walking, he always talked about you having your children out here to play, to walk, to run around … they want to take this away from me."

He wrapped his hand with hers. "I know."

"It's not just land." She buried her face in her free hand, sobbing. He pulled her closer, and she leaned her head onto his shoulder.

The wind blew again, tossing leaves around with a rush of sound like the sea coming in on the sand.

*****

Samuel locked the front doors of the store and sent Nick home. The boy rolled his apron into a ball in one hand and disappeared down the street. Samuel took a deep breath and walked to the back of the store to his truck. He slid the key in the door.

"Boo!"

Samuel spun around, his heart thundering in his ears. "Give me a heart attack, why don't you?"

Joe laughed and stumbled out of the truck bed. "You should have seen your face, Sammy. Priceless. You thought I was going to shoot you or something, didn't you?"

Samuel sighed and rubbed his mouth. "The hell you doing here anyway?"

Joe propped himself up against the back of the truck, producing a silver flask and taking a long gulp. "Came back to see my friend, what do you think?"

Despite the darkness, Samuel saw Joe's mud-stained clothes and the stubble on his face. His torn pants revealed old scabs on his knees. His hair had matted against his head like a dried brown rag.

"You alright?"

Joe grinned. "Hell, yeah. Never better."

"Where's Mary?"

"Oh right, you've just got to go right into my life don't you?"

Samuel exhaled. "I haven't seen you in nearly a year. Heard you got married last year, but you never came to get me to be a witness. And then you left town."

"Yeah. So? You mad I didn't get you to witness the wedding?"

"No." He stepped forward. "What's going on?"

Joe looked at him with wide, bloodshot eyes. "I need money, Sammy. Just a thousand or so."

"Yeah." Samuel laughed, but his friend continued staring at him. "You serious?"

"Yeah. I need a thousand at least. I've got some debts to pay back in Atlanta."

Samuel swallowed. "You've got debts here."

"Here." Joe snorted. "This is just Bloomsdale. Doesn't matter."

"Matters enough for people to come to me looking for it."

"I'm talking about some guys down in Atlanta."

He sighed. "I'm not giving you any money, Joe. I'm sorry."

"Sorry?" Joe tossed his flask down and sent it clanging across the back alley. "You're sorry? You've got this store and your family, and you've got it all laid out real nice and pretty like. Your friend comes asking you for money and you just slam the door on his face."

Samuel stared at him. "Slam the door on your face? I took you in when the cops didn't even want your sorry ass. I took you to my house, didn't even get a thank you, dealt with thugs coming into the store looking for you, and you just left town. And you think I've turned my back on you?" He shook his head. "What the hell are you doing here?"

"Mary locked me out of the house cause I came home late."

"You came home drunk."

"Whatever." He wiped his mouth as he slid against the side of the truck. "She wouldn't let me in, said she was through with me. So I threw myself through the glass door and shattered it." He laughed and fell back off to one knee. "I hitchhiked the rest of the way here."

"Hendrix will be looking for you."

"Screw that old man." Joe sat down next to the truck and stared up into the sky. "You let me stay at your house, Sammy?"

"Yeah."

"I don't remember that."

"I'm not surprised."

Joe covered his face with his hands and stared into the night sky. "Can't believe you won't give me the money now. Bastard."

"What?"

"Just give me the money, Sam. You know you owe me."

"I owe you?" Samuel leaned against the truck door. "How do you figure that?"

"I introduced you to Annie. I took you fishing all the time."

Samuel shook his head. "What do you want from me?"

"I told you already. I want a thousand bucks." Joe balanced himself with one hand and managed to stand, swaying in the parking lot. "Now give it to me."

"I'm not giving you the money, Joe."

"Come on! You don't know what it's like coming back from a *real* war. You flew in your plane above everything. You didn't have to fight. You didn't have to see your buddies die!"

Samuel's eyes widened. "You don't know what I went through, what I've seen. You don't know anything about it."

Joe stepped forward. "I know enough! I know you came back home before me, started a life like nothing happened."

"You don't know what you're talking about." He opened the truck door. "You're drunk. Get the hell out of here!" He slid into the cab. "You're right about one thing, though. I don't know what happened to you. I used to be jealous of you, wonder how everything always fell into place for you. Now, I just feel sorry for you."

Samuel went to shut the door. Joe grabbed his wrist and yanked him out of the car.

"What the hell is wrong with you?" Samuel asked as he turned to face Joe.

The scene exploded, Joe hitting him across the face. He heard the glass breaking. Ringing seared in his good ear, his vision blurring. He fell back into the store's brick wall. He pulled his fingers back from his face to see dark red blood. Samuel turned to face Joe, who stood next to his truck, holding a broken beer bottle in his hand.

"Fine," he breathed. "You wanted this."

Samuel rushed forward, plowing into Joe's midsection like a linebacker making a tackle. The two bodies fell to the parking lot in a series of grunts. Blood flowed in tiny puddles on the pavement. He managed to grab Joe's throat in the struggle. Joe hit him in the face, the wound from the bottle flaring from the contact. He rolled over, hands still around Joe's throat. He slammed Joe's head into the pavement. The grip on Samuel's wrist lessened. He pounded Joe's head against the pavement once more, and the man went still.

Samuel backed off, wincing. He touched his fingers to his forehead and felt the burn. A gash had opened above his eye and forehead. He tried to catch his breath as he gasped. Joe breathed deeply, his face red and swollen. He wondered if the man would even remember what just happened. He crawled over on his knees to look at Joe. Blood trickled from his lips and over his right eye. The smell suddenly hit Samuel. It was the stench of garbage, body odor, vomit and alcohol, all coming from Joe. He pressed a hand over his mouth and nose.

He remembered their fight on graduation night, that time they were on the same side, backing each other as friends do. They had been like brothers. Somewhere inside, Samuel knew he hadn't been fighting his best friend tonight. He wiped the blood out of Joe's eyes and tapped his friend on the shoulder.

"Joe? Hey, Joe?" He nudged his shoulder. "Come on, man, let's get you to a doctor."

Joe shook his head and grunted. "Leave me here, Ryan. Leave me here."

He blinked. "It's Samuel."

"Leave me, Ryan. Let them take me."

"What?" he pulled his friend up from the pavement.

"No," Joe grunted, his eyes still closed. "Leave me here. It's not worth it. Leave me."

"I'm not leaving you." Samuel shook his head. "Come on, get up. Get up now."

Joe shoved him away. "Ryan, leave me!"

"I don't know what you're talking about. I'll not leave you."

Samuel gently set his friend back down. He wiped at his face and stared up at the cloudless night, the stars twinkling. He tried to stand, felt as if he stood on a ship far out at sea. He stumbled over to the back door of the store. Inside, he called the police.

Hendrix drove up in the squad car a few minutes later. "Knew you would do the right thing eventually, Sammy."

"Help him," Samuel said, pointing at Joe as he sat on the back porch.

Hendrix pulled Joe up and over his shoulder. "You going to be all right?" he asked as he tossed Joe in the backseat.

Samuel nodded, pressing the white cloth closer to his face, watching as it turned to a blood red.

"Yeah."

"Can you get home?" Hendrix stepped closer and pulled back Samuel's cloth. "Looks a lot worse than it is. You're gonna have a cut and a nasty lump, but nothing more. Can you drive?"

"I guess."

"You mind telling me what happened?"

Samuel shrugged. "Just a fight between friends."

Hendrix shook his head. "I doubt that."

He looked at Hendrix, his vision blurry. "I really don't know what he's doing back here."

"Why did he hit you?"

"He needs money, I think. Money I don't have."

"Hmmm." Hendrix nodded. "You get on home now. Have your wife look at that cut, okay? I'll swing by tomorrow morning."

"Just take him, Bob." Samuel nodded, tasted the salty blood trickling into his mouth. "I don't want anything to do with him."

25

He sat in silence, interlocked his fingers and cracked his knuckles. He took his index finger and traced the old skin between his knuckles and down the blue vein on the back of his hand. He held up two fingers, remembering how Pa taught him to grip a baseball over the seams ...

*****

"No, not like that." Samuel lifted the baseball high above his head and nodded. "Like this, see? You'll be able to throw it better, I promise."

James caught the ball and tried to throw it back. It bounced across the grass still wet from the morning dew. The boy kicked the ground and folded his arms.

"I'll never be able to do this," he said for the seventh time in the past ten minutes.

Samuel fought back the urge to laugh. I used to say the same thing, he thought. "Don't worry. We'll keep trying, okay?"

James nodded, and they continued playing catch in the backyard. His baby boy was becoming a little man. Samuel shook his head. It seemed like James had taken his first steps a few days ago and now he was about to start playing little league baseball. Unbelievable.

The early spring morning had revealed another cloudless blue sky, the third in a row, following a week of rain and clouds. The city of Bloomsdale seemed to be waking for the morning, cars driving toward the downtown area.

Samuel took in the cool air and tossed the ball to his son, watching as the baseball bounced off the boy's still stiff leather glove and rolled into the neighbor's yard.

"It's okay," he called but knew James would think it was his fault for dropping it.

Annie stood at the backdoor, smiling as she wiped her hands on her apron. "You boys want some lunch?"

Samuel glanced at James, who already sprinted toward the door. He gathered together the baseball and the bat before heading inside.

Lunch was Annie's grilled cheese, something Samuel considered marketing for the store since Carvy Henderson's most recent endeavor had gone out of business, yet again. But selling his wife's delicious sandwiches was something he had decided against, feeling instead it would be better left for home. James took a big bite out of his sandwich, and Samuel tapped him on the back of the head.

"Pray first, and take off your hat."

The boy did as instructed, and the family prayed. When finished, Samuel took a bite out of his sandwich and stared out the back window toward Hawkridge Mountain. The bright sunlight illuminated the mountain's fresh green leaves that seemed to have sprouted overnight.

"You ready for the game today, James?" Annie asked.

"Yes, ma'am."

Annie turned to Samuel. "We are all riding together, right?"

"Yeah. Nick'll take the store for the middle part of the day. I hope the kid can handle it."

She smiled. "He's been working for you for years now. Not really a kid anymore, is he?"

He thought a moment. "I suppose not."

"You ever think about hiring some more help?"

Samuel shrugged. "Not really. Didn't see the point."

"There's plenty of help around town."

"Yeah, but I don't know any of them. Sometimes I feel like I don't know anyone in this town anymore."

"You know me, Daddy," James said and smiled, cheese still clinging to his teeth.

"Sure do." He looked at his son. "I just meant that a lot of the old timers have been going away, that's all. The store regulars."

"Well," Annie said, taking another bite before continuing, "you know that lake has lots of people moving. Kind of turned things upside down lately. Lots of workers in town looking for places to eat and shop. That dam they're building sure is quite the project."

Samuel nodded, thought about his mother and her refusal to move, and wondered if she had been serious. "Yeah, I know. "

"What I'm saying is that you could probably get some more help or pay that poor boy more money."

"I'll think about it."

"If you don't, he'll leave."

"I know." He glanced at his watch. "We've got to go—it's baseball time!"

Someone knocked on the door. Samuel wiped his mouth. "I'll get it." He rustled James's hair as stood.

Samuel opened the door. His jaw dropped when he saw Officer Hendrix. "Bob?"

"Morning, Sam. Sorry to bother you this morning."

"What's going on? Everything alright?"

Hendrix gestured away from the house. "Can we talk a minute?"

"Sure," Samuel walked down the steps as he wiped his hands clean of the grease from the sandwich. His stomach turned a bit when he recalled the last time Hendrix came to his house unannounced. "I hope this isn't bad news, Bob. We've got a game to get ready for in a little bit."

Hendrix glanced back at the house. "Oh, yeah, James is starting baseball … hard to believe." The man seemed to be lost in thought. He blinked and returned to the moment. "I don't know how to say this, Sam. They found Joe in Atlanta last night. He's dead."

The blood rushed out of his face, his mouth suddenly dry. "Dead?"

"Yeah."

Samuel stared at the ground, thinking of the last time he had seen Joe as a bloody mess in the lot behind his store. "Good Lord, Bob. How?"

"He was shot."

"Shot?" He thought of the debts Joe owed and the debts Samuel probably didn't even know about.

"It's not what you think," Hendrix took off his hat and exhaled. "Joe was apparently fooling around on his wife."

"Mary took him back?"

"Guess so. Anyway, Joe was drunk and ran off with this mistress. Crazy drunk gal from way up in North Georgia somewhere looking for work in Atlanta. Well, Sam, they got in some kind of fight, and she shot him. He died right away, so I'm told."

Samuel continued staring at the ground. "So the Atlanta police told you all this?"

"Yeah. Joe still claimed Bloomsdale as his hometown. He'll be buried here, and they thought I should know." Hendrix placed his hat back on. "Joe has no immediate family here anymore. Thought you were the closest thing."

"Thanks," he murmured. "I hadn't seen him in three years. Not since…"

Hendrix tapped him on the shoulder, squeezed lightly. "I know." He turned to go. "I'll let you know when I hear more, Sam. They should be bringing him home soon."

He nodded and gazed off toward downtown. Hendrix's car traveled toward Bloomsdale and turned down a side street. He sat on his front steps, cupping his hands in front of him. Propping his elbows on his knees, he thought of Joe's speech on graduation day for the first time in years.

We are on the cusp of greatness.

It seemed like a different life when Joe stood at the front of the class, overflowing with the life, projecting hope and the cocky nature he had always exuded whether it was on the football field or in the classroom. Samuel had watched his friend end an era of their lives that day.

The world better watch out.

Yeah, Joe, the world better watch out.

The friend who always seemed to have the answer, the one who the world bent over backward for, was now gone forever. Samuel always thought he would have the chance to mend the situation with his friend once he conquered the demons he had carried from far away battlefields. Maybe they should have talked about it more, discussed what they had seen, what they had been through, the friendships they had formed, the men they had killed. Would that have made the difference? Had he done everything he could have done?

It didn't matter now. He pressed his teeth into his fingers, fighting back the constriction in his throat.

They could have spoken about it while they fished McPherson's Pond, but Samuel had thought there would be another day. There's always another day. After everything they had been through, there would always be another day. Wouldn't there?

Not anymore.

He thought of Joe's face on the stage during graduation. The image slowly transformed in his mind to the bloody, broken, drunken man he had seen on the pavement three years ago.

"Samuel?"

He opened his eyes and turned around to see Annie pushing the doorway open enough to speak through it. "Everything okay?"

Samuel reached out a hand, grabbing hers tightly. "Joe died last night."

He told the story as Hendrix had, watched as Annie Ruth's eyes glistened with tears. She wiped at her nose and went back inside to help James prepare for the game. His son had not even known Joe, despite all the promises and talk of getting the families together as they spent their lives in Bloomsdale.

Gone now.

All the dreams and plans of youth, the talk of those who view life as an inexhaustible resource—it all seemed like talk from a different person. He didn't recognize the person he was when they spoke of these plans, and he didn't want to return to the naivety. He ignored Joe's face in his mind, but it remained.

I hope I can come home soon.

Samuel's eyes widened as he remembered Joe's statement before they left for the war.

I hope I can come home soon.

*****

The massive vehicles lumbered along the dirt like steel beasts. They groaned when lifting large quantities of dirt. From the edge of the project, however, they seemed as small as a child's toy. Men worked near the machines like ants scurrying around the dirt. Work on the Bloomsdale Dam was coming along since the groundbreaking several months back.

Samuel remembered the event well. The entire town had vacated to attend the groundbreaking. Of course, most of the town didn't have land the government was taking. Even though some of the seven hundred families were receiving seventy dollars an acre, many were still not happy about it. He sighed.

No, Mama is not happy about it.

Samuel closed his eyes as the wind brushed across his face and tossed his hair about. The sound howled in his good ear, reminding him of flight when the wind rushed inside the B-17. He had tried to get used to the fact his family's land would soon be the home of countless fish. None of this helped with his mother. Work would soon be finished on the Dam, and then she would have to move. She still said there would be no moving.

He tossed a pebble down the hill, watching it roll and bounce like a pinball machine. The river below moved by at a slow pace, nearly invisible from this distance. Some families had gathered near him to watch the work on the dam. One little girl pointed with excitement, told her daddy a crane looked like a toy. She pointed at a lonely farm a few thousand yards from the dam. Samuel noticed a horse surrey outside the house and wondered if the family had already left. The little girl apparently noticed the surrey as well, and asked her father if they could go down to get it.

Samuel smiled, thought of James. I should probably bring him here. The boy did like big machines, sure, but this is also history in the making. He should be able to see it, tell people he could remember when there wasn't a lake in the county.

He stood, brushing off his pants and nodding to the father of the nearby family. The sun had dipped past the tree line, signaling his little outing was over. Nick had been left in charge of the store on account of Joe's funeral. Not much had been said afterward. Only a handful of people attended, some from their class and two others who had known Joe on the high school football team.

After a long ride home in silence, Samuel had dropped off Annie and James at the house. He told Annie he needed to go for a drive. He had thought about stopping in to see his mother, who had decided not to come to the funeral, but ended up driving past on the way to the dam. He didn't really know why until he had arrived. Seeing a giant hole in the world had made him feel small. Knowing this dam was the reason his mother would be swept away from the land she had built a life upon made him feel helpless.

He took one last look at the family pointing as if they watched fireworks in the distance before he stepped down the path toward his truck. Joe would have liked to see this, would have liked even more they would soon be able to fish a lake instead of old McPherson's Pond. He thought of Joe leaning back in the crappy old steel boat, that stupid grin on his face, the sandy blonde hair sticking out the back of his hat, the dirty jokes, the deep thoughts that in hindsight never seemed to be so deep, and his pushing to take things further with Annie.

Yes, he thought, Joe would have liked the lake a great deal.

*****

"You haven't said a word since we've been back," Annie said as she leaned forward to fill up his tea. "You all right?"

"Yeah." Samuel sipped on the tea, nodding. He watched the tea swirl in his glass.

James fiddled with his dinner, moving the food around on his plate and making shapes. Samuel usually scolded the boy for fooling around with his food. Tonight, he simply watched his son, saw an all too familiar expression.

"You not a fan of mashed taters?" he asked, suppressing a smile.

The boy's eyes shot up from the plate. "What's that, sir?"

"The taters. That face you're making reminds me of your Granddaddy."

Samuel took another drink from the tea, saw Annie watching from the sink.

"Grandaddy?" James asked, his eyes wide. "I look like my granddaddy?"

He leaned forward, pretending to squint and take the boy in. He nodded. "Yep. Sure, do. When my Daddy didn't like something, he made a face just like you just did."

James smiled. "What was granddaddy like?"

His gaze fell on the plates. He looked out the back window. "He would have loved you, son," he said, his voice just above a whisper. "Just like I do."

James looked to his mother. "Did you know Granddaddy?"

"Sure did," she said while wiping her hands clean. "One of the best men I ever knew, 'sides your Daddy, of course."

Samuel picked up the plates as he stood. "You go on to bed, son. We'll be back there in a while."

James cleaned his mouth with the napkin and went to his room. Samuel put the plates in the sink and lingered over the dishes, closing his eyes. Annie wrapped her hands around his waist from behind, leaned her head onto his back, and swayed in the kitchen. He tightened his closed eyes, pressing his lips together.

"I'm gonna miss him," he said through clenched teeth.

"I know."

"Don't know why this had to happen. After what he'd been through. The hell he'd seen. Not like this."

"I know." She tightened her grip around his waist.

He took a deep breath, felt it stick in his throat. He fought back the urge. "What's the point of all this?"

The grip lessened. "Of all what?"

"Life. Working. Suffering. All for what."

She turned him around. Starring at him, she held his face in her hands. "Don't you talk like that, you hear? You're not Joe."

Samuel looked back at her before turning his gaze to the ceiling. "I never thought it would end like this. I never thought … I never thought any of this."

She pulled his gaze back to her. "Talk to me, Sam. Just talk."

"I didn't want this. I wanted more for you. I didn't want to stay in this town, work at the same job, put our son through this kind of life."

"There's nothing wrong with our lives."

"It's a waste."

She released his face, her eyes hardening. "Now how am I supposed to take that, Sam? Huh? You say that and you're saying that about me, too."

"I don't mean you."

"What do you mean, then?"

He sighed as he leaned against the sink. "I get up, go to the same job, and come home so I can do it all over again. Six days a week. This is all we'll ever have." He gestured around the house. "This is as good as it's gonna get, sweetheart. You ever think about that? James isn't going to have anything."

"He'll have more than I did. Two parents that love him and that'll stay with him."

"Oh, here we go."

She pointed a shaking finger at him. "Don't you give me that. You had more than you know. You had a family who loved you. You had me. Was I not good enough? There used to be a light about you."

"Bunch of crap," he said as he shrugged.

"No." Annie shook her head. "You were different when I met you. You cared about life. You were happy."

He shook his head, thrusting the rag over the dirty dishes. "That was a long time ago. People change."

"But let me change with you. Give me that chance. I don't understand why you keep me out. I love you more than you have ever loved me."

He turned away, and she grabbed his hand.

"You were happy when I met you. Now, you're not," she said. "Why can't I make you happy?"

He placed his hand on her shoulder, squeezing. "It's not you."

"What is it then?" She stared at him, her wide eyes pleading. "What happened to you over there?"

He thought of France, of Maria, Charles, and Gerard. The farmhouse. The grazing cows in the golden light of the setting sun. The stars twinkling above the land.

"It's nothing I want to talk about. I've told you that."

Annie reached up to place her hand over his. "And I told you I would never ask. I'm sorry."

He pulled her close. "My life hasn't turned out the way I planned, but you are the silver lining. I love you, Annie. Always have. That won't change."

She smiled. "I hope not."

"I just wanted to help my friend," he said, "and I didn't."

"You couldn't have done anything else. Whatever happened to him over there, it took your friend long before he came back."

Samuel frowned, allowing the words to sink in. He kissed her forehead. "Thanks for putting up with me."

"When you're yourself, that's the easy part."

*****

Margaret Wrightman stepped through the backyard grass, her hands over her eyes. James crouched behind a nearby tree and giggled at his grandmother. Max sniffed at Margaret's pant leg and licked James's face. He scurried away to relieve himself in the bushes at the end of the yard.

As his son and mother played, Samuel turned the burgers and adjusted his tall, white chef's hat. The meat sizzled and popped.

His stomach grumbled. "Annie? Can you bring the buns out here, sweetie?"

His mother laughed as she discovered James hiding behind the tree. The boy squealed and tried to get away, but Mama managed to wrap her fingers around his ankles.

"Dinner's almost ready you two," he said and took a sip of his sweet tea.

His mother waved her hand in the air as if she swatted at a gnat. "Oh, all right. Come on, Jimmy. Go get washed up."

James sprinted by his father and disappeared inside.

"He's just like you," his mother said. She sat down with a groan. "Oh, old bones. Old and wore out."

The wind touched her white hat. She tilted her head back, and the sun lit her grinning face.

He smiled as she kept her eyes closed. "You look beautiful, Mama."

She opened her eyes. "You're such a charmer. Thank you." She studied him for a moment. "You remind me of your father so much sometimes."

He blinked, the thought of resembling his father capturing his attention. "Really? How so?"

"You remember how he used to grill out on Sunday afternoons? He'd talk about your games for hours, talk about what you, Joe or some of other guys should have done during a game. He would light up, just light up, when he'd talk about the rides home after the games. He sure loved you, you know."

Samuel licked his lips as he pressed down on the burgers. He remembered the drives home his mother spoke about. Pa used to talk about the other players, the play Gary Burns made at shortstop with two outs, and how Sammy shouldn't pull his head out during his swing. And his father would always end the conversation on the dirt road when they were almost home. He'd lean over, pat Samuel on the stomach and say, "you did good today, son."

"Thanks, Mama."

Her smile faded as she leaned back in the afternoon sunlight. "I'm not leaving that house," she said after a few minutes of silence.

Samuel blinked and turned away from the grill. "How's that?"

She opened her eyes. "That your bad ear, Sam?"

He shrugged. "No. Just thinking I didn't hear you right."

"I don't know how I can leave the house, so I'm staying."

Samuel chuckled. "Didn't know you were part catfish. Explains why Pa liked you so much."

Her expression darkened. "It's not a joke. I can't leave your father, not again."

Samuel frowned and studied the burgers. Juice bubbled out of the meat and sizzled in the fire. James popped back through the back door, a towel between his hands. "I'm hungry, Daddy."

Annie Ruth came out carrying a fresh pitcher of tea. Samuel served the burgers and listened to the ladies speak to James about starting school. Conversation soon shifted to little league. Samuel gazed at his hamburger and watched the juices swirl around on his plate. He looked at his mother as she spoke with James about all things important to a six-year-old.

Samuel sighed. His mother might not be able to accept the fact the government would come take her home, but the waters would soon come. The home would be underwater. No amount of prayer, crying or complaining would change that now.

But Mama didn't seem ready to accept it.

Despite the dark cloud hovering over their day, he sat at the stone table on his patio. His family laughed and enjoyed the hamburgers. A golden sunlight washed over the backyard, bathing everything it touched. A warmth graced his heart as he watched his beautiful wife help James with his lunch. It was a like a photograph, one he didn't want ever to lose.

"Everyone," he said, placing his hamburger on the plate.

"What is it, sweetie?" Annie asked, one hand still on her son's shoulder.

He sighed and smiled. "Let's do this more often."

"What? Eat?" Mama laughed.

He grinned. "Yeah. Eat." He shook his head, unsure why the feelings of quiet gratitude washed over him. He didn't care, deciding not to question it. "I love all of you. Thank you for being here."

*****

"You do what you have to," Samuel said as he leaned on the broomstick.

Nick rumpled his hat between his hands and shifted his weight from one foot to the other. "I'm sorry, Mr. Wrightman."

Samuel shook his head. "Don't you ever be sorry for improving yourself, you hear?"

Nick nodded, and Samuel tapped the boy on the shoulder. When the "boy" went back to sweep the stockroom once more, Samuel frowned. Tiny wrinkles had formed in Nick's face like roads on a map. Had it really been so long? The kid had grown up and wanted to go to school. Who was he to stop him?

Samuel dusted off the countertop and counted change. He peered over the shelves to see no customers shopping. Might be a good day to lock up early. Light flickered across the room. He turned to see one of Bloomsdale's finest rolling in front of the store. Robert Hendrix stepped out of his car, his gray mustache rumpled in what might have been a frown if the hair didn't cover his lips. The man's brow furrowed in concentration as he stepped on the sidewalk.

"Afternoon, Bob," Samuel said with a nod. "Can I get you something?"

"Uh, no." Hendrix slipped off his hat and slid his fingertips on the counter. "I, uh…"

"You know, I'm going to start dreading the sight of you if you only come visit when you have bad news." Samuel swallowed when he saw the man's face. "What's wrong?"

Hendrix looked at him. "It's, it's your Mama. I need your help."

*****

232

Two police cars parked in front of the farmhouse. Fieldhands walked in the fields, some peering toward the house. Two officers stood on the front steps, leaning against the porch railing and smoking cigarettes.

Hendrix pulled the car around the old oak tree. The movement sent a dust cloud over the front yard and the tire swing swayed. The two other officers tossed their cigarettes into the dirt and wiped their hands together. Samuel opened the car door, took a deep breath, and stepped out.

A cool breeze swept away the cloud of dust. The officers came forward, nodded, and Hendrix tapped Samuel on the back. "Guess we'll let you handle this."

Samuel said nothing, marching toward the house as if he had weights tied to his ankles. The boards on the steps creaked as they had since he was a child. A wind chime rattled off a chorus of gentle notes. The breeze increased and rushed through the leaves.

He pulled back the front door, listening to the squeak his father always meant to fix when he "got around to it." He gasped as he stepped into the dimly lit living room. Photos littered the floor near the sofa. A stack of newspapers leaned on the side table as if it would fall at any moment. The grandfather clock ticked away the seconds as it had through countless conversations with his parents.

A glass rattled. He leaned to peer into the kitchen. His mother sat in silence and stared out the back window. The workers moved through the field in the distance.

"Mama?"

He moved through the living room and stepped around the photographs as if it were a minefield. He frowned.

The photos. A collage of memories. Baseball games. The colors of Christmas gifts. His grandparents holding Samuel when he was a baby. His old dog Henry running through the fields.

The kitchen smelled of burnt toast, a smoking candle, and maple syrup. Discarded newspapers littered the corner of the room. Henry's old food bowl still remained beside the back door. Spider webs had formed at the corners of the old windows. His mother did not turn as he stepped into the room, her eyes fixed on the back window next to the kitchen table.

He swallowed and stared at his mother's graying hair. A full cup of tea sat between her fingertips atop today's newspaper.

"They brought you here to force me out." His mother continued facing the window.

"Yes." He slid into the chair next to her. "That's why I'm here."

She inhaled slowly. He studied her face. Dark patches formed under her eyes, deepening the lines on her skin. She wore no makeup. Her red eyes appeared moist, and the skin around her nose was red with irritation.

"I can't leave." She closed her eyes. "How can you ask me?"

He reached for her hand, rubbing his thumb across her skin. He traced his thumb along a blue vein. He opened his mouth to speak, said nothing for a moment. "They aren't asking, Mama."

She opened her eyes and stared out the window. He held her hand. Minutes passed. Following her gaze, he watched the workers outside break for lunch and huddle under the trees on the far side of the field. What would happen to them, he thought, where would they go when this was all under water?

He glanced around the house and thought of the water slowly advancing to take it all. The water would seep into the house, erase the site of all his family's memories, and crystallize everything in time. He sighed and moved his hand to her shoulder.

"What do you think Pa would have said?"

She shook her head. Her chin trembled. "I don't think he would have gone. Not this way."

"Really? Pa was always big on following the rules." Samuel smiled.

"No one ever tried to take his land away." Her brow furrowed, her voice rising. "This would kill him. *Kill him.* He took care of this house." She gestured to the ceiling and the floor. "He and a couple of friends worked on this before you were born. And…now it'll be gone."

"I know."

"I'm not leaving. I'll let the water take me," she hissed lower than a whisper.

He leaned forward, grabbing her elbow. "How can you say that? What about me?"

"You have Annie. I'm all alone." Tears fell down the left side of her face as she stared out the window. "I have nothing."

He snorted. "You don't think James wants to spend time with his Nana?"

She pressed her lips together and closed her eyes. Sniffling, she pushed her face into her hands and wept. He wrapped his arm around her shoulders and pulled her close.

Footsteps creaked on floorboards from behind. "Sam?"

"We're ready, Bob."

His mother shook her head violently, left her face in her hands as she sniffled and sucked for air. "No. No. No."

"Mama?" He tried to pull her from the chair. "Mama? Come on Mama. We've got to go."

"No! No! George? Oh, God, George!"

He flinched at hearing his father's name. He looked to Hendrix, who simply backed to the wall of the kitchen.

"Mama? Mama! Let's go."

"No! I don't want to leave him. I don't. I don't." She fell from the chair to the kitchen floor. "Leave me here. Oh, God, leave me here with him. I can't go. I can't. No." She pushed her face down into her arms as she spread out on the floor. "George…George."

He knelt beside her as she cried. He rubbed her arm, fighting the knot forming in his throat. "It'll be okay," he whispered. "Everything'll be okay."

After time had passed, Samuel led his mother to the truck. She did not speak as she stepped up into the vehicle. He told Hendrix he would be back to walk through the house once more before the land became the government's. As he drove away, his mother stared off into the sky, her head tilting backward against the side window.

Samuel stared at his home in the rearview, watching the dust cloud form from his wheels. He thought of the long walk on the dirt road to the main road. The stretch of land used to be Henry's favorite. He thought of his return to his home after the war, the thoughts of spending time with his mother and father, and how those dreams had been ripped away with news of his father's passing.

The home disappeared in the trees as he drove farther away. His mother's eyes remained closed as the tires rolled onto the paved road.

26

Cars lined up in traffic outside his window of the train car.

"I'm glad I wrote it."

"Me, too." He nodded and leaned back.

The young man still stared at the letter. "I owe you one, mister."

He shook his head. "Not at all, son. Not at all."

*****

His hand cradled the gun's handle, one fingertip on the trigger. With one hard pull, the hammer pulled back and slapped forward. The sound echoed across the afternoon air.

"I got you!"

"No, you didn't!" James came running around the corner of the house, the small rifle in his hands, his oversized army helmet bobbing on top of his head.

Jason Jackson, who lived on the other side of Bloomsdale, jumped up from the front yard. "You were right there—I got you!"

Samuel watched the two boys yell at one another as he remained on his back under the truck, the old oil filter still in his hands. He replaced the new filter and finished changing the oil. The boys continued screaming at one another as he slid out from the truck.

"Hey, boys! Cut it out!"

The two boys stepped away from each other. James, black paint smeared under his eyes, stared at his father. "Dad! Jason said he got me. He couldn't have hit me from that far away. I was still in the bushes!"

Samuel fought back the urge to smile. He and Joe used to have the same fights. They would play war all through the hot summer day until they collapsed at the base of a tree, bodies drenched in sweat and dirt.

"Jason's the guest. If you boys can't get along, maybe we'll just have to take him home."

James stared down at his feet. "No."

"No, what?"

"No, sir. We'll stop it."

The boys ran around the back of the house. Samuel grinned and wiped off his hands. James wouldn't be playing much longer, the magic of the endless summers would disappear. He and Joe had played their last game of war around James's age.

Samuel grimaced. The lake had taken the pond, too. James would grow up in a county with a massive lake within its borders. If he would learn of fishing, it would be on a much different scale than little McPherson's Pond.

Annie Ruth came out into the garage carrying a glass of water. "What's going on?"

"Everything's fine. Boys being boys." He took the glass with a nod and a smile.

"Your Mama called."

He froze. "She okay?"

"Yes. She was wondering if you could come by the apartment to help her with some things."

"What things?"

Annie shook her head. "She didn't really say. I don't think she felt like talking."

He nodded. His mother had moved down to Atlanta shortly after Lake Sinclair had covered the house. He hadn't been back to see the lake, but Carvy Henderson said he had watched the water rise from the base of the Bloomsdale Dam. Many in town had gathered on consecutive Sundays to watch the water rise above the trees and rooftops.

Samuel didn't return to watch, instead staying behind to help his mother through her coping with the fact she was now homeless. He listened to the stories coming into the Wrightman General Store, stories of boaters destroying props on the tops of chimneys and roofs. Others spoke of tearing out the hulls of their fishing boats on tall trees that had refused to succumb to the water. One local girl had drowned last summer after being drawn into an old chimney, pulled underwater by an air bubble. Even though the U.S. Army Corps was now trying to clear out some of the underwater dangers, the stories continued to find their way into the store long after the lake had been declared at full pool.

"What did you tell her?" he asked as he watched James plop down behind a bush in the front yard, obviously hiding from his "enemy."

"I told her you could come after church tomorrow."

"Sounds good. It's not a problem. I thought you were going to tell me she had finally decided to buy a house somewhere."

"Not yet. She seems to be enjoying her new job."

"Yeah."

He had never really liked the idea of her moving away to the city, but she had been insistent on a change of scenery, kept saying something about staying in the same place too long. Her new job had her keeping the books for a regional trucking company and kept her busy.

He stared up at the cloudless sky. The shadows stretched across the front yard.

"Gonna be dark soon," he said. "You ready for the party?"

Annie grinned. "Cake's ready. I'm not ready to celebrate my baby's birthday."

"Where does the time go," he said before turning toward the front yard. "War's over, James! Let's have some dinner and open a present."

*****

"I don't feel like going to church today," Annie said as she placed her hand on her forehead. "I'm tired."

"Tired?" Samuel tossed some cold water on his face. "You know I don't mind skipping. Are you okay?"

She sighed and rested her head back on the bed's pillows. "I woke up last night with a stomach ache. Now I just feel beat."

He dried his face. "Should we see the doc?"

"No. I just want to rest."

He nodded and walked out into the living room, being sure to leave the bedroom door shut.

James sat reading a comic book and sipping a drink. "Morning, Dad."

Samuel shook his head. The boy's voice seemed to be getting deeper every day.

"Morning," he said. "I don't think we're going to church today, son."

His eyes widened. "Really?"

Samuel laughed. "Don't act so disappointed." He poured a glass of water in the kitchen. "Maybe we could grill out back this afternoon after you've trimmed the hedges."

"Oh, Dad."

"Don't give me that. You said you'd do it this weekend, and I know you didn't do it yesterday."

"But Sunday's the day of rest."

"Yeah." Samuel took a sip of the water. "You can rest afterward."

He poured a second glass and walked back to the bedroom. Annie wasn't on the bed anymore, and he heard movement in the bathroom. He pushed back on the door. "Annie?"

Annie sat on the toilet, her head in her hands. She looked up at him, her eyes watering and a string of spit stretching from her mouth to her fingers. "Something's wrong."

*****

Doctor George Heard came out of the backroom with his stethoscope still around his neck. Samuel hadn't met the new doctor in town since Doctor Galliford had passed away last winter. Doctor Heard arrived in Bloomsdale much younger, his light blonde hair turning the heads of ladies across the city—although none would ever admit it. Samuel was always amazed at the things people would say in his store when he was standing behind the front counter. It was as if people thought he couldn't hear once he was in the shop.

Heard allowed a soft grin, his blue eyes darting between Samuel and James as they waited in the sitting area at the front of the house. The Doctor leaned against the doorway and made a clicking sound with his tongue. "James, isn't it?"

James said nothing until Samuel nudged his son with an elbow. "Answer the man."

"Yes, sir?"

Heard took a step forward and knelt down. "We have a tire swing out back I think you'd probably like to try out. Been told it's one of the best around."

"That's okay. I want to stay here."

Heard glanced at Samuel.

"Ah, James? Go ahead outside and try it out."

"But I'm thirteen, Dad—"

"But nothing." He cocked his head toward the door. "Go."

James dragged his feet toward the door. When the door closed, Samuel looked at Doctor Heard.

"He's at that age, I guess," Samuel said and leaned back in his seat, a hard mass settling into his gut as his mind conjured up the possibilities of what the Doctor wanted to say. "He wants to be a part of everything. Guess he won't be sitting at the kids table this Christmas."

Heard smiled. "I see it all the time."

"So what's the problem, Doc. Annie going to be okay?"

"She is. She's resting comfortably now." The doctor smirked.

"What happened?"

"Well, she has morning sickness, Mr. Wrightman."

Samuel froze. "Morning sickness?"

"Yes, sir. Looks like you're going to be a Daddy again."

He felt like the air had been vacuumed out of his chest. "A Daddy? You mean like another child?"

"That's what I mean."

"How did this happen?"

Doctor Heard lowered his gaze, and Samuel wiped at his brow.

"She's about eight weeks along," the doctor said. "Everything's fine. This is completely normal, as you probably know. I think it just scared her a bit when she felt sick in the middle of the night."

"Yeah." He rested his elbow on the windowsill and watched as James kicked the tire swing around the side yard.

Another child. Another baby in the house. His heart sank. More diapers. More food. More money.

"Are you sure, Doc?"

"Sure as my name's George."

Samuel sighed. "So that would mean the baby's coming when?"

"First of next year."

"Unbelievable." He leaned back, thought of Annie being pregnant with James. "Does Annie know?"

"Sure," he said and leaned against the wall. "I usually like to tell the parents at the same time, but she was really worried. She can be a bit persistent."

"I know."

"I didn't want her to worry. Given both of your reactions, I can assume this was not planned."

Samuel shook his head, frowning. "Don't really feel like discussing this, Doc, if it's all the same to you."

Doctor Heard nodded. "Of course. Annie'll be right out."

"Can I see her?"

"Of course. I'll let her know you're coming back."

A few minutes later, Samuel wandered back to the examining room. Annie sat on the edge of the table, her face white as the sheet.

"Hi," he said. "I would have brought flowers, but I didn't…"

She laughed and bit her lip. "Doctor Heard said he was going to tell you…"

"He did." He shook his head and exhaled loud. "A baby?"

"A baby."

"Didn't see this coming." Samuel hugged his wife and lingered as she nestled her face into his chest. "I mean, with James we kind of knew it, but this?"

"I know. I'll be thirty-seven when this baby's born." Her voice cracked with the last part. He put his hands on her shoulders and stared into her eyes. "Nothing will happen to you. You hear? You're going to be fine. I'll take care of everything."

"I know you will," she said. "I know. What about James?"

He looked away. "This will be a little strange for him. I don't think he thought he'd be a big brother any more than we thought we'd have a baby." He shrugged. "At least, I'll have plenty of help around the store."

She pushed at his arm, grinning like she meant it for the first time since he had entered the room. "I knew something was wrong last night," she said. "I thought it was something I had eaten."

"Yeah."

A knock at the door and Doctor Heard poked his head in. "Everything alright?"

"Yes," Samuel said. "Thanks for coming in on a Sunday."

"My pleasure, Mr. Wrightman. And congratulations. Be sure to invite me to the shower."

He left the room, leaving Samuel and Annie Ruth staring at the closed door.

*****

"I like 'John.'" James nodded. "Yep. You know, like John Wayne. He's tough, knows how to fight."

Samuel pulled back on his fishing rod a bit. "John's a good name, son. Real nice choice."

James smiled and cast his line out into the waters of Lake Sinclair as if he had been doing so for years. "Mama's huge right now, you know?"

"Whoa," he looked to his son. "Don't let her hear you say that."

"Right."

A boat rumbled off in the distance and broke the continuous sound of the water lapping against the steel boat Samuel had saved from McPherson's Pond. The two oars still managed to paddle him and James out into the lake, but fast motorboats zipped past them a couple of times in the past hour. Of course, James wondered why they couldn't have a speedy boat like that.

Samuel leaned back as the wind pushed the boat along the edge of the water.

"Yeah," he said with a grunt, "John's a mighty fine name, almost as good as James. You're forgetting something, though."

"What's that?" James squinted under the baseball hat.

"What if it's a girl?"

"Oh, no, that's gross. You really think that'll happen?"

"It could."

"No way."

"Well," Samuel said as he leaned back on his elbows, "you know there's a pretty good chance it'll be a girl."

"Like how good a chance?"

He smiled. "I'd say about fifty percent."

James frowned and stared at the water. "I don't want a sister, Dad."

"Yeah, maybe you won't have one."

Samuel listened to the water hit the sides of the boat. He stared up at the sky and felt the cool breeze wash over him. The cold weather will be here soon, followed by the holidays that would be followed by his second child being born. The Lord works in mysterious ways, his mother had said when they shared the news. It had been the first time she had spoken of God in months.

"There's a plane, Dad."

Samuel opened his eyes. A plane the size of a pinpoint whisked across the sky. "Must be a jet flying out of Atlanta."

"What kind?"

"Probably military. They're out doing maneuvers."

"What's that mean?" James leaned back, his hand over his forehead to block the sun.

"It's just like you practicing your baseball. They have to practice their flying."

James looked to him. "They practicing to fight the Russians?"

Samuel studied his son, saw the excitement in James's face at the mention of war. "Nothing exciting about that, son. Remember that."

"What do you mean? Everyone at school's talking about us kicking the Russians back to Moscow and all that."

"Let's hope that never happens."

James pulled his line in and recast. "Dad?"

"Yes?"

"Didn't you fly in the war?"

He sighed. This question had come more and more the past few months. "I flew in a plane. I didn't do the flying."

His son shifted in his seat. "What was that like?"

"Flying? It was interesting."

"I want to fly someday."

"Maybe you will."

Minutes passed, and James continued casting with no success. Samuel sat up and paddled over to another cove.

"Did you ever shoot anyone, Dad?" James suddenly asked.

"I don't think we need to talk about that."

"What did you do on the plane?"

He sighed. "I was a waist gunner."

"A what?"

"I shot a gun at German planes."

"Wow! What was that like?"

"Loud. Very loud. And cold."

"Cold?"

He stared up into the sky. "You see that plane way up there? It's freezing when you get up that high. If you touched your fingers to the gun, they could freeze."

"Really?"

"Yep. Real cold up high."

"Wow." James bit down on his bottom lip. "Did you ever shoot any Germans down?"

Samuel paused. "We all did the best we could. Now, catch a fish."

Father and son fished together until the sun had disappeared into the waters of the lake. The crisp air reminded Samuel it would be the last day of fishing for a while.

27

The children at the front of the car squealed. The mother scolded and threatened. He shook his head.

The young man craned his neck to see the spectacle. "What do you think's going on up there?"

"Kids being kids." He stared back out the window.

The young man turned to him. "Do you have any?"

"I…"

He stared down at his hands, pressed his fingers together …

*****

James interlocked his fingers together, bowed his head. "Dear God, please help Mama be okay."

Samuel nodded and closed his eyes. Annie Ruth had been in the back room for several hours.

He had opted to stay with James, per Annie's instructions, as soon as they arrived at Doctor Heard's. The baby was already a few weeks late. The February air had left a light frost on the grass in the morning. James had thought it would be snow, the first time he had ever seen it, and he was disappointed when he discovered it to be simply frost.

Annie Ruth had told Samuel it was time to leave sometime after five that morning. The sun had not even started to light the sky. The family had gathered their belongings, called his mother in Atlanta, and arrived at Doctor Heard's at just before six.

Samuel's stomach grumbled. He glanced at the clock in the waiting room to see it was nearly noon. He rustled James's hair and stood.

"Should we get something to eat, buddy?" he asked. "This could take a while."

"I know. I want to wait."

"Fine with me." He sat again. "You know you were an early baby. Did I ever tell you that?"

James's jaw dropped. "I was early?"

"Yeah. You came sooner than your Mama and I expected. The doctor was worried at first, but we decided you just couldn't wait to come see us. The doc agreed and said you were healthy."

"Why was I early?"

Samuel shrugged. "Why does the sun come up? It just does. And you just decided to be early. This baby decided it would be late."

Samuel swallowed. He didn't mention the fact to James Doctor Heard had been concerned the baby hadn't come by its mid-January due date. Annie Ruth's feet had swollen to the point she had trouble walking, although she did well to hide it from James and to an extent, Samuel. But he knew Annie better than that. He saw the pain in her eyes, heard the brevity of her laughter. She wasn't the same.

The sound of Annie waking him in the middle of the night had been a welcome one. Now, as he sat waiting, he fought back thoughts of concern for his wife and new baby.

"Let's wait outside," he said. "Why don't we try out that tire swing?"

James shrugged. "I'm too old for that."

"I know. You told me. Well, I'm not."

*****

Doctor Heard's wife, Marcy, stepped out on the front porch. "Mr. Wrightman?"

James and Samuel had tried to nap under the shade of a thick hardwood tree. He jumped up at the sound of Marcy's voice. James ran ahead and nearly fell over running up the steps. Their footsteps on the hardwood floor echoed down the hall. Samuel reined in his son by placing both hands on his shoulders.

And then he heard it.

A baby cried, and then screamed. James giggled and tried to pull away from Samuel's grip. The boy had indeed grown stronger in the past year, but Samuel held him back.

Marcy pushed open the door and poked her head through. "Everything okay? We have some visitors."

Annie Ruth held the baby across her breast, her fingers sliding across the infant's forehead. Samuel tried to present a neutral expression, but Annie looked like she had been through a battle. Her hair matted against her head like it had been painted on her skull. The sweat still formed beads on her forehead and cheeks, the bed sheets sticking to the mattress.

"There's my boys," Annie breathed, her voice weak.

"Hey." Samuel led James into the room.

"Meet Malissa Ann Wrightman."

Samuel watched the baby, her eyes closed tight and her lips moving softly. Malissa let out a soft cry.

Doctor Heard nodded to Marcy, then turned to Samuel. "Congratulations, Mr. Wrightman." He turned to James. "You have a new sister."

James nodded before allowing an unenthusiastic "yeah." Samuel tapped him on the back of the head, and James said, "yes, sir."

Samuel reached out to hold his daughter for the first time. "Well, hey there little girl. You've had a big day."

28

The mother held the little girl and bounced her. She spoke softly as the little girl sucked on her thumb. The mother pressed her forehead against the child, closing her eyes.

He turned away …

*****

"Come on, Annie! You guys are going to be late!"

Annie Ruth held Malissa's tiny hand and led her through the garage toward the truck. Both wore bright flowery dresses.

"What takes them so long, Dad?" James asked in a deep voice.

"Be nice," Samuel said. He looked at his son, noticing the stubble forming like splotches of pepper on his cheeks. "You forget your razor?"

James appeared shocked, his hand covering his mouth. "I shaved. Besides, Dad, we're going to church. Does it really matter?"

"You check that attitude in front of your Mother, you hear?"

Annie licked her fingers and wiped at Malissa's cheeks. The little girl's brown hair curled at the ends with tiny ribbons for her big day, her first day of Sunday school. Annie suddenly sighed. "The phone's ringing." She turned to Malissa. "Go to your Daddy. I'll be right there."

Samuel leaned over and opened the door. "Come on in, sweetie."

Malissa hoisted herself into the truck cab with a small grunt, her large brown eyes growing wide with excitement. "We're not going to be late, are we?"

"Yep," James said in the tone only a big brother could muster. "In fact, church has already closed."

"No, it hasn't," she cried and turned to Samuel. "Has it, Daddy?"

"No," he said and glared back at James. "You're brother's being a smart … he's being a jerk."

"Yeah!" Malissa smiled. "You're being a jerk!"

Samuel put his hand on her knee. "Don't you say that—especially around your Mother. You'd get me in trouble."

Annie stepped back through the garage door, her eyes wide as she wet her lips. She motioned for him to get out of the truck.

"What's wrong with Mama?" Malissa asked.

"James, take care of your sister."

James sighed. "Why do I—"

"Just do it."

Samuel stepped out of the truck. "What is it, Annie?"

"It's the phone."

He grimaced, wondering what's so important. "If you're trying to get out of going to church today, remember, God's eyes are always watching." He laughed at his joke, but Annie said nothing. She stepped aside as he walked into the kitchen.

The phone remained on the small side table in the living room. He placed it to his ear.

"Mr. Wrightman? This is Philip Sanders with the Atlanta Police Department. I regret to inform you that I have some difficult news …"

*****

Samuel said goodbye to the final person leaving the graveyard after Margaret Wrightman had been placed into the ground. Annie Ruth kept the children at the edge of the property near the road as various local residents offered their condolences. He had asked to be left alone.

He walked through the rows of gravestones, passing a few names from high school. He remembered strolling through the grounds with his Mother the day he returned home. She had been so happy that day, so full of life. It had been the first time Samuel truly felt he had returned from France. The smile he had seen his entire life, from birthday parties to his graduation day, had never seemed so bright.

She was gone. He would never see her face again.

He thought of her body lowering into the ground and grimaced. He placed his hand over his mouth and stared back toward Hawkridge Mountain. He looked at the courthouse to his left. The remaining cars started and drove away from the graveyard. A short line waited to speak to Annie. His children watched him in silence, ignoring the line of people all waiting to repeat the same statements he had heard for the past two days.

"We're sorry for your loss."

"She was a wonderful woman."

"I remember your Mama ..."

Samuel hated it all, wishing he could have foregone the entire funeral. His Mother was gone. Not anything these people could say would make him feel any better about it.

Malissa wore a black dress with a white ribbon in her hair. The black ribbon had disappeared somewhere in the house earlier that morning, much to her disappointment. The wind tossed her curls around, one falling before her face and dangling. Her hand rose slowly, and she waved. Samuel swallowed, his face contorting, and he returned the wave. Malissa's brow wrinkled, her mouth opening to reveal her tiny teeth. His daughter convulsed as she fought back tears.

Samuel mouthed the words, "Daddy's okay," blinking a tear down his face. James pulled his sister closer to him, and Malissa hugged her brother's leg. Samuel turned away and plunged his hands deep into his pockets.

The spring had always been his mother's favorite, and the March wind still blew with the cold of winter. Samuel took a deep breath and watched as the final group of onlookers disappeared into their car.

His family watched him. Samuel gazed up into the sky, gave a silent farewell to his Mama, and returned to his family.

2 9

The dirt had turned red. The landscape had changed.

The young man closed his eyes after leaning back in his seat. He watched the young man cradle the letter to his love.

He stared out the window as the landscape revealed a familiar look. He thought of the young man sitting next to him, wondering of the transition of going away from his home and attending college …

*****

"I'm thinking about it," James said as he lifted a box from the truck. "I just graduated. I don't want to go to college."

Samuel fought the urge to swear, grabbing another box instead. He winced as the noise blasted from the radio. "Turn that off. Giving me a headache."

"That's the Beatles, Dad."

"I don't care what it is." He shook his head. "Sounds like a bunch of noise."

James sighed and slapped the radio off so hard it nearly fell off the shelf. "So, are you saying I can't volunteer?"

"Yes," he said without hesitating.

James tossed another crate to the ground. "Oh, so you want me to stay here and work in your store forever? I'm not slave labor."

"Slave labor? I pay you, don't I?"

"Yeah. I don't want to do this forever. You think I want to stay here and work in this store the rest of my life? I'm not you!" James put his hands on his hips. "Why won't you let me fight like you did?"

Samuel nodded and lifted another crate into the stock room. "Vietnam's a different thing. Don't go pretending it's the same as what I did, cause it ain't."

"Why?" he asked, still holding a crate. "I've always been proud of you, Dad, even though you've never talked about it. You're able to stand up at church when they thank the veterans."

"And I hate every minute of it."

"You shouldn't. I've always been proud. I've wanted the same thing." He placed the crate down. "Listen, I want to do something with my life. I want to serve my country like you did."

"No." Samuel sighed. "I can't let you do it."

"Why?" James spun around and slapped the wall. He hung his head low. "Why are you like this? Some of the other guys are—"

"The other guys aren't my son!" He turned away. "I will not let you throw your life away."

James backed away, his eyes wide. "You can't stop me if I want to do this. It's my life! I'm not a child anymore!"

"You're my child!"

James stepped forward. "You think I'm going to stay here working in this store forever, go fishing on the weekends till I'm old and gray. I'm not! You can't stop me from leaving! I hate this place! I hate this town and this stupid store!"

James ripped off his gloves and hurled them across the room. He stormed past his father.

Samuel grabbed his shoulder. James paused.

"Is it really so bad here?" Samuel asked softly. "Do you really want to see this?"

James stopped, breathing for a moment. "See what?"

He faced his son, locking eyes with him. "War."

James nodded, and Samuel lowered his gaze. "Very well. Think about it for six months."

"I don't need six months."

"Yes, you do. The things you'll see there … can't be unseen."

"You just want me to wait?" James sighed. "The war could be over in six months."

Samuel sighed, a weariness falling over him. "This war will still be going on. You still want to join up then? Go ahead."

James blew air through his lips. "What if I miss out on it?"

"God willing."

James shook his head. "If that's the way it has to be, fine." He looked into the sky, counted silently. "Summer of 67, then. I can join up."

"If you still want to."

"Oh, I will."

"Why?"

"Because I don't want to be the only guy in town that doesn't. Other guys have gone to college or got married. I don't even have a girlfriend. I don't want to be the only one left here doing nothing."

Samuel sat down on a crate, heard the crackling of the wood fighting his weight. "I once thought the same thing."

James blinked. "You did?"

"Yes." Samuel thought for a moment, chose his words carefully. "You will come back changed. Forever. You will see things you can't forget, things that will come back to you in dreams. I know you won't listen, but you will regret this for the rest of your life."

James bit his lip, staring at his feet. "Like what, Dad?"

Samuel shook his head. "Doesn't matter."

"Mom always says you don't talk about the war, that something happened to you over there."

He stared at the wall. "It's not worth talking about. You won't listen, anyway."

"Fine." James walked off the loading dock and disappeared down the alley.

*****

Annie Ruth tossed the towel into the sink. "No, he's not going."

"He's made up his mind," Samuel said as he motioned for Malissa to take her plate. "It's his decision."

"Where is he? I'm talking to him."

He finished chewing his food. "He left work close to quitting time. Probably out with the fellas."

"You're going to tell him when he gets home that he's not doing it, and that's final."

He looked at his wife and daughter. He stood and wiped his mouth off with a napkin.

"Malissa, honey, go play outside. See if you can catch Daddy a frog."

Her eyes moving between both of them, Malissa nodded and walked through the back door. Samuel watched her leave and stepped closer to Annie. "How can I prevent him from joining up?"

"You just do. He's your son."

"And he's nineteen. I can't stop him." He touched her cheek. "I did make a deal that he waits six months, think it over before doing this. I did my best. Maybe he'll change his mind."

Annie rolled her eyes. "He's like you. He won't. I tried to get you to stay, tried everything I could think of. And you never came back."

He frowned. "What's that?"

She sighed. "The man I fell in love with never got off that train. He was left somewhere between here and France." She glared at him. "And your son's the same way. He'll *never* come back."

He didn't have the words or the energy to argue. "I know," he said, "that worries me."

*****

James swept the floor in the back of the store. A short girl with long blonde hair leaned against the shelves. She wore a skirt so short Samuel thought, at first, it was underwear. She spoke of movies and music he knew nothing about. Keeping one eye on his son and the half naked girl, he helped the customers that came through the door.

With one hour left until closing time, he started on the register. The girl followed James around like a lost puppy, talking as he swept the floor.

"Miss?" he asked. "We're about to close. Can I help you with anything?"

"No, Mr. Wrightman. I was just leaving." She turned to James. "See you around."

The girl left, her skirt revealing more than Samuel needed to see. He immediately thought of Malissa one day wearing such a dress, and he clenched his teeth.

"That some girlfriend of yours? If so, she needs to put some clothes on."

"No girlfriend of mine. That's Lucy Bell Collins."

Samuel blinked. "That's Mel Collins' girl? God, I thought she was still in grade school."

James shook his head. "High school."

"How old is she?"

"She's sixteen."

Samuel placed change in the money bag. "Need to talk to Mel about getting some clothes on his daughter."

"All the girls are wearing stuff like that now, Dad."

"Lucky for you, I guess." He frowned. "Don't let your sister know about those, okay?"

"She's six, Dad."

"I don't care."

James finished sweeping the floor and placed the broom against the wall. "I need tomorrow off if you don't mind."

He placed the money inside the safe. "Why's that?" he asked without turning.

"I'm going to sign up. It's been six months."

Samuel paused. "You still want to do this? You sure?"

"I am. More so than ever."

"Have you been watching the news lately?"

"Yes. General Westmoreland was saying the end is in sight, that we have nearly won the war." He stepped closer to his father. "Have you seen I could make money to go to college?"

Samuel locked the safe and turned to face his son. "Thought you didn't care anything about that."

"I didn't care about paying for it. Going for free's something else."

He leaned against the counter. "I don't have cause to stop you, son. I gave you my little speech on this whole thing. If you still want to go, you're man enough to make your own decisions. Just don't ask me or your Mother to be happy about it."

James's eyes widened. "I can go then?"

"You're a man, James. You do what you feel is right."

James slapped his hands together. "Far out! This is great, Dad. I've got to go tell the guys!" He reached over the counter to hug Samuel. "Thank you, Dad. Thank you, thank you, thank you. I'll make you proud."

"I'm already proud. Come back in one piece—that'd make me happy."

*****

The day arrived like any other. The sun burst through the curtains in their bedroom. Samuel heard the alarm clock from his son's room. He rose from the bed, his joints popping and the soreness from yesterday's shipment causing his muscles to ache. He raised his hands toward the sky and stretched.

Annie Ruth grunted and rolled over in the bed, took half the covers with her. "Time to get up, Annie."

"God, Sam," she breathed. "I really don't want to."

"Neither do I."

Samuel went out into the living room to see James placing his bag down on the floor. "You want to have breakfast, son?"

James placed his hand over his chest. "You scared me," he said with a grin. "Sure, let's eat."

Samuel made some toast. After a few minutes, Annie joined them and poured orange juice. They sat in silence, chewing their food and sipping juice. Samuel watched the sky turning bright blue above Hawkridge Mountain in the distance as his father's clock ticked off the seconds from the living room.

"Time's your train coming?" Annie asked to break the silence.

"Seven."

He glanced at the clock on the kitchen wall. "We better get going, son."

He stood and grabbed his keys. James burped and stretched as he stood from the table. Annie wiped her mouth and faced her son, avoiding eye contact. They embraced.

"I love you," Annie whispered.

"Love you, too."

Mother and son parted. She touched James's face before hurrying toward the bedroom. The door shut softly, leaving only the ticking of the clock as the sole sound in the house. James surveyed the house, his eyes falling on each item before he looked to his father.

"Well?"

Samuel saw the young boy standing in his kitchen, remembered the days he played war around the house, knowing now he was leaving to do it for real. The light in James's eyes, the hope, the open mouth, the spring in his step as he marched around the kitchen. Despite the peach fuzz replaced by the dark stubble, James appeared just as he did the final time he played in the yard with his friend on his birthday. Would the look still be there? Would he be the same when he returned?

Samuel cleared his throat. He knew the answer.

"Let's go," he said with a crackling, wavering voice.

The old truck rumbled to life, shattering the early morning silence. Nothing moved on the streets except the paperboy, who waved as they passed. James waved back and sighed.

"Your Grandfather brought me to this same station before I left," Samuel said over the wind rushing into the truck. "He was proud of me, same as I am of you."

James turned away from the window to look at his father. "Thanks, Dad."

"These old streets have sure changed in that time," Samuel said, forcing himself to swallow. "Hard to believe."

James nodded and sat in silence.

The truck rumbled to the station, one dim light flickering over two other riders waiting to leave. Samuel killed the engine and faced his son.

"My Pa told me…no matter what else happened over there to just do right. James, you do what you feel is right while you're over there. You hear? No matter what others are doing around you, you do the right thing. Remember…we're proud of…"

James grabbed his father's hand. "I will, Dad. I will."

Samuel watched his son exit the truck and strut over to the station. He had already decided he wouldn't sit and wait with his son, didn't know if he could take it. James walked over the bench and sat down.

Samuel brushed away the memories of James's first baseball game, the first time they fished together, holding James's hand as Malissa was born.

His son was leaving.

James turned toward the truck, and Samuel suddenly saw the boy in the young man's face. His son allowed a grin at the corner of his mouth, nodding proudly. He smiled back and raised one finger from the steering wheel as a wave.

Let him experience a life without pain.

Samuel's smile faded, the memory of the words he prayed the night James was born.

Let him experience a life without pain. Let him never see what I have seen.

Samuel sighed, biting his lip. He never imagined his son would seek out the horrors he had spent so many years trying to forget.

He put the truck in drive and drove away from the station, watching his son in the rearview mirror as he moved farther away.

3 0

He pressed his face into his hands and rubbed at his eyes. The train rocked. He turned his head toward the window.

The train slowed as it passed through a small town. The brick buildings on the main street looked like countless other small towns they had passed on the trip. Traffic stopped at the crossroads.

He watched two young men unloading a truck near a rundown general store with faded and cracked brick in the center of town.

*****

Samuel unloaded the truck full of goods at the back of the store. The sun had not yet crept into the sky, although the bluish sky of dawn provided a soft light to the alley. His muscles ached as he dropped another crate onto the loading dock.

He thought of James. They had received another letter the night before. The letter gave the appearance of everything being fine. Boring marches, boring guard duty, boring and long waits. James wrote about the guys he was with, none of them from Bloomsdale or even somewhere nearby.

Many of James's peers who had said they would join hadn't done so. Samuel saw many of them cruising the streets at all hours with their long hair and bright colored shirts ruffling in the wind.

The letters had become family entertainment, even more so than the television, which Samuel gladly turned off whenever he could. Malissa enjoyed her fair share but enjoyed the letters from her brother even more. Despite their constant fighting, Samuel saw the love she had for her brother now that he was gone. Her eyes flashed as she read over James's letter long before anyone else had a chance. With Annie Ruth returning to work at the post office, Malissa arrived home long before they had the opportunity to grab the mail.

Still, when the letter was finished, and they had discussed all of their favorite aspects of James's writing, Samuel felt a cloud fall over his spirits. While Annie and Malissa worked on her homework, he would retreat to the living room and watch the nightly news or sit back to read the paper. Regular scans of the images from Vietnam never produced one of James, but Annie swore the backs of soldiers climbing hills could have been James. Samuel and Malissa squinted, holding the newspaper up to the light, trying to catch any clue that the photographed soldier was James. When they found none, Annie would say they were not mothers and couldn't understand.

Samuel placed the last crate on the loading dock and wiped the sweat pouring from his face. He worked the store alone, refusing to ask for help from any of the long hairs polluting the city's streets with their marijuana and their stupid looking cars with bright colors. He was better off alone.

No. He shook his head.

He was better off with James.

Stocking the shelves full took the rest of the morning until the store opened. By the time eight o'clock rolled around, Samuel's clothing had been drenched with sweat. He turned the door's sign to "open" just in time to see Annie and Malissa walking hand-in-hand down the sidewalk. He smiled, happy they could walk to school and work together.

A delivery van pulled up in front of the store and blocked his view. A bright blue logo Samuel didn't recognize illuminated the side of the van. The van door opened. A tall man with receding blonde hair closely cropped stepped out of the vehicle, his eyes surveying the streets and stopping at the "Wrightman General Store" sign. The lanky man wearing the blue coveralls lowered his shoulders and smiled. He watched as the man rustled through papers in the back of the van.

The phone rang, and Samuel jumped, startled. He answered the first call of the day and kept an eye on the stranger outside. Carvy Henderson's wife had called. She always called on Thursdays to make sure Samuel had some normal item so they could cook a particular meal, throw a specific kind of party or do whatever else they planned to do that weekend. The same phone call, every Thursday. If she didn't call, Samuel knew they were either out on the lake, or something was wrong. Usually, he would get the call Friday to find out they had, in fact, been on the lake.

This call was no different. She needed lighter fluid. Carvy still smoked liked a chimney, even though the man topped three-hundred pounds and ate an entire cow's worth of meat every time he sat down at the table. The Hendersons planned to grill out that weekend and were inviting the entire town. In Samuel's experience, that means a handful would show up.

The driver finally stepped through the front door, nodded and paced the front of the store while Samuel answered questions on the phone. When he hung up, the man eagerly stepped up to the counter.

"Can I help you, sir?" Samuel asked.

"I sure hope so." He wiped his hand on his coveralls before he extended it. "Name's Chad Murdock."

"Sam Wrightman."

"Really? Oh, thank God."

He frowned. "How's that?"

Chad grinned to show all his bright white teeth. "You must be pretty confused, huh? Let me explain. I'm looking for Joe Davis. I believe you know him."

Samuel hesitated, shaking his head. "Why do you want to know?"

"We fought together in the war. He always spoke of you. I told him I would start this shipping business," he said, pointing to the van. "It's not much, but we're growing. It's doing pretty well. Anyhow, I always told him I would cut him in on the deal if the business took off."

Samuel opened his mouth to speak but paused. He didn't know what to say. "You fought with Joe?"

"Yes, sir. We were on Guadalcanal until I got the shits—excuse me, dysentery so bad I couldn't walk without messing my pants." He shook his head and stared down at the ground. "Anyhow, we got separated for a while after that. I ran into him later before the war was done. We talked about this business, and all he talked about was coming home. He really missed you, talked about fishing some pond I can never remember the—"

"McPherson."

"What?"

"It's McPherson's Pond."

Chad's eyes widened. "That's it. McPherson's Pond. Anyhow, we figured we were going to be invading Japan soon, that is, till they dropped the bomb. We didn't think we would make it if we had to go in, so we made all these grand plans. I wanted to start my business. He'd wait in McGovern County until I came a calling." He grinned. "Well, I'm a calling. I just can't find the bastard anywhere."

Samuel nodded. "I know."

"Well?"

He sighed. "Joe died."

"Died?" The man's good humor darkened, his smile fading and his shoulders lowering. "I had looked for so long until I remembered he said something about your Daddy owning a store." He chomped his teeth a couple of times. "How did he die?"

"He was shot."

"Shot? How?"

He leaned against the counter. "He had a bit of a drinking problem after, got himself into trouble one too many times. Let's leave it at that."

Chad nodded, shaking his head slowly. "Can't believe it. All we'd lived through, all we'd been through with hell raining down on us from all sides, and he gets it back here. Shame."

"Damn shame."

Chad slapped his hand down on the counter. "Listen, Sam? May I call you that? I've got a deal for you."

"Really." Samuel crossed his arms, waiting for the sales pitch.

"A promise is a promise. I've got a good business going here, and we're about to spread nationwide."

"Where you from?"

"Montana. Place called Bozeman."

"I have no idea where that is. What are you doing here?"

Chad smiled. "We're making runs all over the east now. Delivering canned goods mostly. I had the chance to deliver something to Bloomsdale. I took it, you know? Wanted to see if I could find Joe."

For some reason, this man, Chad Murdock, reminded him of Joe. Well, Joe before the war. The man exuded some nervous energy; an excitement layered into each word as he spoke. Samuel nodded and listened to the man speak about his business. He had come back from the Pacific some time after it all ended to start his trucking company out of Bozeman. It had started small, Murdock said, with three trucks, but had grown to nearly one hundred vehicles of different sizes.

"So I guess what I'm asking is if you want to join me?" Chad asked.

Samuel laughed. "I can't leave this place. This store is in my family's blood. Sure would be nice to drive around seeing the country, but I can't. Not right now, anyway."

Chad pointed at him. "That's not a no, not completely."

"I guess not. Leave me your card and I promise I'll make a trip out there with the family. Be great to trade stories about Joe." He laughed. "Speaking of that, can I buy you a beer after I close shop?"

"Love to, but I've got a schedule to keep. I really planned on picking up Joe and bringing him back if he wanted. That's all I have time for this trip." He smiled. "Maybe next time."

They shook hands, and Chad Murdock left the store.

31

The pine trees swept past the train. He stared at the blue sky and watched the power lines pass over. A pair of birds circled high overhead in the fading sunlight. He thought about sleeping to pass the time. He knew the trip was almost over.

*****

Samuel woke before dawn as he always did. Annie Ruth grumbled softly, rolling over and going back to sleep. He stepped out into the warm July morning, wandering around the yard until he found his newspaper—that paperboy seemed to enjoy hiding Samuel's news from him.

His joints popped. He stretched in the front yard, listening to the July flies and their chorus that always began right on time. The sky twinkled like diamonds on black velvet. He placed a hand on the mailbox and watched the stars for a moment. His neck ached. He rolled it until he heard the bones crackle and pop before he went back inside.

The newspaper read more of the same news. Losses in Vietnam, protests across the country, marches, shootings, beatings. He tossed the paper back down on the table and sipped at his coffee. The clock ticked in the other room. He glanced up at the time.

Six. Time to wake the family.

He opened the door to Malissa's room. "Honey, time for another day." She grunted and rolled over. "Come on. Let's get ready for church."

Samuel finished off his coffee as he walked toward his bedroom. He stopped in the doorway. Annie Ruth sat upward in the bed, staring at him.

He blinked. "Annie?"

"Something's wrong, Sam."

He laughed. "Last time you said this you turned up pregnant."

She did not smile. Her eyes bore into his. He moved toward the bathroom, but stopped and looked back at her, expecting a joke of some sort. She reached a hand to her temple, grimaced, staring back at him for help.

"Annie!" He rushed toward her, but her eyes closed, and she fell back. "Annie. No. Oh, God, no. What's wrong?" He shook her and sent her head leaning back off the bed. Her graying brown hair spilled onto the floor. "Annie! Annie! Jesus Christ. Annie!"

Malissa pushed back the door. "Daddy?"

"Malissa, honey. Go call the doctor! Now!" Malissa's mouth fell open. "Now!"

She ran down the hall. Samuel turned back to his wife. "No, baby. Not now. Not now. Wake up. You're just sick. You're just sick, damn it. Annie!"

*****

Samuel heard nothing the pastor said. The funeral took place for the sake of the town. It was...expected. He clenched his teeth as the service concluded. Malissa's hand gripped his, but he did not look to her. Instead, he stared down at the coffin holding his Annie Ruth. Red flowers draped over the top. A ring of residents clad in black stood over the hole in the ground he had been forced to purchase two days ago.

They had not been able to reach James immediately to tell him of the news.

Oh, James should be here, he thought.

Hands touched his shoulder as they walked by. Some spoke words Samuel could not hear, either because of his bad ear or because he did not care to listen.

The crowd dispersed and made idle chat as they walked to their cars. When the last one walked away from Samuel, he knelt down and asked Malissa to go with Marcy Heard.

"Why, Daddy?" she asked between sniffling, her eyes red.

"I need to speak with your Mama." Samuel stood and nodded toward Marcy, who reached out a hand and led Malissa back to their car.

And Samuel stood alone in the graveyard.

The diggers waited at the other end of the property. The cars disappeared down different roads. Samuel watched Malissa peer out the back window of the Heard's car. She waved. Samuel raised his hand. The wind rustled his only dark suit he usually saved for church. He took in a deep breath and slipped off his jacket, allowing it to fall to the ground.

He turned toward Annie Ruth. He stood at the edge of the hole, kicking off his shoes as he sat in the cool grass. "I don't want to leave you."

He leaned back on his hands, staring up at the bright, blue sky. He made small talk with his wife, speaking of the recent letter from James and what Malissa was doing with her summer.

He cleared his throat. "Guess I better get down to business, sweetheart." His face wrinkled. He thrust his hand toward his mouth. "I've owed you this for a long time, haven't I, baby? I always thought I would tell you someday. Just … didn't think it would be like this. Oh, God."

When the tears subsided, he wiped his face. "The plane had been hit, and we were going down. I thought I was going to die. I thought of you the entire time…"

Samuel recounted his experiences in France, told the whole tale of being found by Gerard, Maria, and Charles.

"I thought I'd never see you again. I actually spoke French. Can you believe that? Don't know if I could do it now. Don't know if I'd want to…"

He watched a car drive by the graveyard. "Anyway, they took me in. I tried to adapt. I figured you had moved on. It had been so long. Never thought you would have waited."

He sighed. "I never cheated on you, but I felt like I had a separate family out there at the farmhouse. I had to kill to defend it. I killed men, watched them die in front of me. I should have told you about it. I should have told you about the entire experience. I'm … I'm sorry, Annie. You deserved to know." He pressed his lips together and swallowed down the lump. "I miss you. I can't go on without you. It just won't work."

Samuel stared at the sky, wishing he spoke directly to God. "You do nothing but take. Why her? Why Annie?" He buried his face in his hands. "Bring her back to me. God, bring her back."

*****

He walked home, leaving his jacket and shoes in the graveyard. The streets seemed foreign. People stopped to speak with him, but he kept wandering toward his house. He moved into the home, smelled Annie's cooking lingering. He closed his eyes, imagining he heard the sizzling of bacon and fresh morning coffee. Her glorious voice sounding through the halls calling them all to breakfast with her usual cheer. He slammed the door behind him. A frame fell off the wall.

He glared at it.

A photo of their wedding day. He yanked the frame from the floor and hurled it across the living room.

All for nothing. All of it.

Gone.

He dragged his feet into the living room, moving as if he had weights tied to his ankles. He collapsed on the couch, smelling her perfume in the pillows. He opened his eyes to see her magazine still on the coffee table. He rolled over onto his back and listened to the clock tick away the seconds once more.

What was the point?

He stared at the ceiling. Dared God to strike him dead. He begged for it. End his existence. End it now.

Samuel thought of the bomber as it went down, wishing now he had remained on board as it crashed into the ground. It should have ended that day.

He thought of Annie on their graduation day, the glorious sun lighting her skin. Her hair pulled back under the cap. The perfect day.

He sat up from the couch.

Could it still be there?

Tossing the pillows onto the ground, he rushed through the house to the garage. He pushed boxes out of the way but found nothing but old blankets.

Where would she have kept it?

He hurried back to the bedroom and thrust open their closet. Her smell hit him. All of her dresses hung in the closet in front of him. He ran his fingers across them, feeling their softness. He saw a shoebox on the top shelf and pulled it down.

Inside he found memories of Annie. Photos of James and Malissa. He dug deeper.

And there it was.

The crispness of the photo had faded. How he wished it were color, but there it was, a photo from graduation day. Joe had his arm around Samuel's neck, and Samuel's arm draped Annie's shoulder. They all smiled.

Samuel closed his eyes, remembering the moment. The sea of people offering congratulations, his father snapping the photo as his mother watched, the sun high above his head, and the sense of the real world looming over him. He stared at Annie, tracing his finger down her face again. He kissed the photo and pressed it against his chest.

*****

A dreamless sleep overtook him. When he woke to the phone ringing, the sun had set low. He tossed a pillow toward the door to slam it shut. He kept the photo close to his chest and closed his eyes. He dreamed of Annie, dreamed of paying bills with her, grilling out in the backyard, and playing with Max at the park long before he, too, had died.

Samuel woke to the sound of a knocking at the door. The light outside had faded to a dull blue. He stood and saw the photo on his bed, a wrinkle across the top. He pressed it flat and set it on the bedside table.

He opened the door to see Chief Robert Hendrix. "Morning, Sam."

"Morning?" He glanced at his father's clock. "So it is. What do you want, Bob?"

"I wanted to come by to see if you were okay. Lot of people are concerned about you."

"I don't care." He started to shut the door, but Hendrix blocked the door with his foot. "Just leave me alone."

"What about the store? You've been in here for days. What about Malissa?"

"I. Don't. Care."

He slammed the door and walked back to the bedroom, burying himself in the pillows.

*****

The phone rang, sounding as if he heard it at a long distance. He rose from the bed and stretched. He reached over to touch Annie's hair, felt the pillow, and made a fist.

Still groggy from sleep, he wandered into the kitchen. The sky outside had grown dark again. He didn't know what day it was as he picked up the phone.

"Sam?"

"Yeah?"

"It's Marcy."

He frowned and sat down at the kitchen table. "Marcy."

"Everything's fine. Malissa's missing her Daddy. She keeps asking to come home. It's fine if she stays here as long as you need. She's been a blessing."

Samuel thought of his daughter running through the house, her hair bouncing this way and that. "She is that, isn't she?" He cleared his throat. "Let me clean up here. I'll be by in the morning to pick her up, okay?"

"That sounds fine." She paused. "Is there anything we can do?"

"Nothing. You've done enough. Thank you."

Samuel gripped the phone hard enough to turn his knuckles white. He stood up and felt sadness wrap around him like a cold blanket. He wanted to call out for Annie. He sighed and walked over to the wedding frame. Carefully, he picked up the broken glass and stared at the photo. Annie was looking at him as Mr. Luther led the carriage away from the reception, Samuel's attention on the crowd. How excited he had been to show her their new house. He recalled the months of planning, how he tried to hide the purchase.

"Fooled you didn't I?" he asked with a laugh. He touched her face on the photograph. He tossed the glass into the trash can and placed the photo with the frame on the counter top. Annie's face flashed through his mind, and he shook his head.

He grabbed the keys; the sound seemed to echo in the empty house.

"I'll be right back," he whispered.

He drove through the nighttime streets of Bloomsdale. The Hendersons walked along the sidewalk as he rumbled by. He extended a hand as he turned to pull up in front of his store. He smiled.

A white sign, painted with a black brush, read, "Store temporarily closed due to family emergency."

He leaned back in the truck and surveyed the storefront. Flowers and cards lay at the base of the front door. He left the truck running as he scooped up the cards and flowers. He noticed most were from her co-workers at the post office.

He placed them in the truck and headed home.

3 2

■■■■■■■

He opened his eyes to see the little girl standing on her seat, staring at him. She sipped on a juice cup in her one hand and twirled her hair with a free hand. He yawned and covered his mouth. He waved at the little girl, who smiled and returned the gesture. She smiled so sweetly, so ... familiar ...

*****

Malissa played just outside the back door. Her pink plastic tea party table set for stuffed animals. Samuel finished the grilled cheese and did the best he could for his daughter's first day back home. He tried to allow the cheese to melt just so, the same way Annie would have.

He opened the door with one hand, balanced the sandwiches with the other. "Is it lunch time sweetie?"

"Okay. Mr. Bear said he was hungry."

"He did? Well, maybe you could share with him." Samuel sat down on the ground, knowing the tiny pink chairs wouldn't hold him. "Here you go, sweetie."

"Thank you, Daddy."

They ate their sandwiches in peace. Malissa told a soap opera story about Mr. Bear and how he had lost his honey. Samuel smiled and listened intently.

"Are you glad to be home?" he asked when the story had ended.

"I miss, Mama."

He nodded. "Yeah? Me, too." He rubbed her shoulder and finished his sandwich.

"Hello, you two."

Samuel turned around to see Pastor Daniel, his white hair glistening in the sun. Samuel brushed off his hands and stood. He approached the pastor and noticed the deepening wrinkles in the man's face.

"Pastor Daniel," Samuel said, extending his hand. "I thought you had retired to North Georgia or something like that."

"I have." He laughed gently and took Samuel's hand into both of his. "I thought I would come by to say hello, son."

"Oh." He turned to his daughter. "Well, this is Malissa as I'm sure you'll remember."

"Goodness, she's grown," he said and turned to Malissa. "Hello, child."

"Hello," she said with a full smile that showed cheese on her front teeth. "Want some grilled cheese?"

"No, thank you." Daniel turned to Samuel. "May we walk a bit?"

"Sure."

They walked toward the back of the yard and kept Malissa within sight. Samuel listened to the birds singing as they walked.

"I thought it important to stop by to see how you were doing, Sam. I was in town visiting some friends. Carvy Henderson's wife is not doing well."

He nodded. "I heard it's cancer."

"Yes," he said with a frown. "Terrible thing. I knew of the hardships your family has faced as of late, and I felt called to come by to speak with you. Carvy said he hasn't seen you at church lately."

He snorted. "Telling on me, eh?"

"No, not that." Daniel smiled. "He said he's seen you at work and around your house, just not out very much."

Samuel sighed. "I didn't handle this well at first. The first couple days I forgot my duties as a father—I know that. I'm handling this as well as I possibly can, Daniel."

"Perhaps the congregation could provide the support you need."

"No. I'm not going down that road."

Daniel frowned. "You've always been part of the church before, both you and your mother and father."

"Listen," Samuel said and stopped walking to face Daniel. "Don't take this the wrong way, but I really would rather be alone during this time. I've spent most of my life doing what was expected, dealing with a community of people. I don't need a lot of people pretending to care just to get the latest gossip. I'm getting too old for that stuff now or for caring what people think." He pointed at Malissa. "You see that angel over there? That's what I care about. That's who I'm living for now."

"The church could be a great place for your child."

"Why? So children can ask about her Mama every day? So people can come to her and say they are praying for her and her Daddy?" He shook his head. "No. I was this close to going down a path I could have lost everything. I was so angry at God and everyone else." He paused, thinking of Joe and his downward spiral. "Now, I've decided to live for Malissa and James. They are all I have left."

Daniel nodded slowly, placing his hand on Samuel's shoulder. "Believe me, son, I am praying for you and your family. And I mean it."

"Thank you for stopping by. I appreciate it. My Mama and Daddy would have appreciated it. Annie would … have appreciated it, too."

Daniel turned and waved to Malissa, who was deep in the middle of a conversation with Mr. Bear.

33

⬛⬛⬛⬛⬛⬛⬛

"I've really enjoyed sitting with you." The young man smiled and glanced down at the letter he had written for his love.

"Been a pleasure." He cleared his throat.

"Well, sir, I don't think I would have written this letter. Who knows, maybe I'll see you when I head back for Thanksgiving?"

He turned toward the window, swallowing hard. "That'd be nice, son…"

*****

Samuel waited in the car, gripping the truck's steering wheel. Any minute, his son's train would arrive, and he would be home.

Home.

Since James had left, his mother had passed away, and his little sister had grown. His stomach twisted into a knot. He worried about James coping with the problems at home. But it was more than that. He was concerned about James coping with whatever he had experienced in Vietnam.

In the first letter James had sent home following his mother's death, he wrote he didn't want to come home for leave. The army would have allowed it; Samuel knew that. Instead, James had declined. Gone was the flowery language he had provided in the letters when

James knew his mother read them. Now that she was gone, the letters were colder, more to the point.

His tour of duty had ended, and James said he would be coming home. As Samuel waited, he wondered if the wide-eyed boy would be exiting the train station. Somehow, he knew he was dreaming.

A crowd filed out of the station. Civilians embraced on the steps, hugging in the afternoon light. A man picked up a boy, held him high over his head. Samuel rested his elbow on the window of the truck, staring at the reunion.

The group of people clustered at the stairs, but gradually dispersed into the parking lot. He nodded at the people as they passed his truck, wondering if they had been on the same train as James.

He stared back to the station. A man emerged from the station, his eyes wide with caution and hesitation. He wore an army uniform and carried a simple, green duffle bag. The grim face looked at the other people moving around him. He squinted as he stepped into the sunlight. His face was leaner. His body seemed more angular, but it was James.

Samuel inhaled slowly, studying his boy who had become a man. Resisting the urge to jump out of the truck and run toward his son, he slid out of the cab. He rested his arm on the truck, allowing James to acclimate to the sunlight. Samuel lifted his hand over his hand.

James looked at him, his dark expression softening. His eyes fixed on him, his chin quivering. Samuel would never know what his son had been through over there, would never ask him. All that mattered was that he was home.

Dropping his duffle bag, James jogged toward him. Samuel immediately noticed the limp in his step, the difficulty his son had sprinting down the stairs.

"Dad!"

"Jimmy." Samuel hugged his son, squeezing him tight as if he could prevent the world from ever taking him again. If he could have shut out the rest of the world by capturing this moment for himself and no one else, he would have done it. "Thank God you're home."

James hesitated. He nestled his face into his father's shoulder. When they parted, his face was damp and red. "I missed you, Daddy."

*****

"You coming in with me today?" Samuel asked, pouring them both a cup of coffee.

James collapsed into the chair at the breakfast table, the same way he had for the past two weeks after Malissa had gone to school. He accepted the cup of coffee with a nod and smile, turning his attention to the newspaper.

Samuel slid into the chair when his question wasn't answered. "I would love to have you back at work, son."

"I know, Dad." James shook his head. "I don't know if I...can deal with the town. I guess that doesn't make much sense, does it?"

He tapped his son's mug with his index finger. "It makes more sense than you know."

"Really?"

"Sure, son. I couldn't deal when I got back, either." He smiled, remembering being forced to work in the store. "I don't want you to do anything you don't want to do. I want you to be happy. You deserve that."

James slid his finger around the mug, the movement sending steam into the air. "You never had that choice though, Dad."

He shrugged. "Doesn't matter."

James gazed off toward the living room. "Place seems strange without Mom."

Samuel sighed. The third day James was back, they traveled to the cemetery to visit Annie Ruth. It never got easier. Visiting with their son and daughter made it feel like he had lost her all over again. Despite his son's homecoming, he felt the fog of depression falling over him.

"Yeah." He cleared his throat. "Have you thought about what you'd like to do?"

James turned around. "You were right, Dad."

"'Bout what?"

His son rubbed his mouth, his eyes unfocused as they gazed at the table. "You can't unsee these things."

Samuel waited for more, but his son lost himself in thought. "I know."

"I see it all the time. It's in my dreams. Sometimes, I see it when I'm awake." His eyes filled, unmoving. "I hear things, voices in the dark. Memories, I guess."

Samuel opened his mouth to make everything better, realized a father can't always, no matter how hard he tried. He couldn't make it better, knew he shouldn't try or lie that he could make it go away. Staring at the kitchen, he thought of the past.

"Your Mother used to try and get me to talk about things," he said. His son stared at him, silent. "Talking about it didn't help. Some guys feel better after they open up, but I never did. What I can tell you is that you will learn to cope with it. It'll never completely disappear. You'll carry it with you the rest of your days."

"Oh."

Samuel looked at him, saw the pain in his glazed eyes. "You must learn to keep your eyes forward. It's the only way to live. Keep your eyes on the path ahead, make each moment the best it can be."

"That how you do it, Dad?"

He nodded. "I've been living for you and your sister for a long time, James. I want the very best for you." He took a sip of the coffee. "So, what are we going to do with you?"

For the first time since he returned, James smiled. "I think I'll finish this coffee, take a shower and come to work with you."

Samuel grinned. "Sounds like a plan."

*****

James dropped the last crate into the store room and pulled off his work gloves. Samuel made a note on his clipboard and smiled.

"Well done, son," he said, glancing at his watch. "I never thought we'd finish unloading this tonight. We best get home to your sister."

"Dad?"

"Yes?" He stared at James, saw something in his eyes. "You okay?"

"I've decided what I want to do, Dad."

Samuel sighed, knowing this was what he had been waiting for since James got home two months ago. He hadn't pressured his son once about deciding what to do, happily allowing him to sleep in his old room until he figured things out. James had never confessed anything to his father about the war, deciding instead to focus on the tasks at the store. That was fine by him.

James pulled a pamphlet from his back pocket. "Here."

Samuel took the paper, saw the contents. "University of Missouri-Saint Louis?"

"It's pretty new, Dad." He stepped forward, pointing toward the pamphlet. "I could go out there and learn business, use the money I got from the Army. You know? Maybe I could come back here and—"

"I think it's great."

James blinked. "You do?"

"I do." Samuel gestured at the store, closing his eyes. "It'll be good for a fresh start, son. Your sister'll be leaving here soon enough. I think you should go out there, make your life and never look back."

James nodded, his face crumpling. "You won't get rid of me that easily, old man."

"You think I'm getting rid of you?" He wiped at his eyes. "I'm excited to have an excuse to visit Saint Louis!"

They embraced.

"I'm proud of you, son. You'll be great at whatever you do. Keep those eyes forward. You go out there and show 'em what you're made of, ya hear?"

"Yes, sir." James patted his father's back. "Thank you."

"I'll always be here for you."

34

A man across the aisle flipped through the pages of a newspaper. The front page told of disasters, wars, and murders.

He shook his head and stared outside at the ever-changing landscape. Never had much use for newspapers. Well, not anymore.

*****

The young man burst through the front doors of the store. He carried a notepad and had a pencil behind his ear. His curly brown hair nearly covered his ears and his eyes widened when he saw Samuel.

"You are Mr. Samuel Wrightman, right?"

Samuel grumbled as he wiped off the shelves. "Who wants to know?"

"I'm Adam Getts with the local paper."

He turned away to face the shelf. "Got nothing to say to no paper, ya hear? Go ahead and walk yourself back up to the newsroom and find another source to pick at."

Getts walked toward Samuel. "You don't understand. I just want to tell your story, Mister. I think you've got a great one to tell, and the community would like to read about it."

"Who put you up to this?" Samuel wiped off the bottom shelf. "I got nothing to say."

Getts wiped his mouth and frowned. "What about the war?"

"What war?"

Getts stepped forward and moved in for the kill. "You fought in Europe. Your son's fought in Vietnam. Father and son fighting for our country. Veteran's Day is next month. Imagine what a story that would make."

"Not interested."

Getts put his hands on his hips. "Oh, come on Mr. Wrightman. We could even run a photo of you and your son on the front page."

Samuel pretended to stare at the ceiling and think then looked at Getts. "No."

"All right," Getts said as he moved slowly toward the door like a dog that had just been smacked with a newspaper. "Just remember this was your chance to be front page news."

"I'll try to get over it."

With one hand on the front door, Getts turned back. "Call me if you change your mind."

Samuel shook his head. "Just go."

The young reporter stayed in his mind long after he left the store.

*****

"So what happened then?" Getts asked, leaning over the shop counter.

For reasons Samuel couldn't explain, the idea of the newspaper article wouldn't leave his mind. Although he would never willingly discuss his war experience, he thought a newspaper article might be a nice way for this gossiping town to hear about *his* hero, James Wrightman. His son had left for school in August, excited about starting a new life for himself. Samuel had wished he could have gone with him, but he had other plans. He didn't plan on staying around Bloomsdale much longer.

"The Allies moved into France while I was living with the Durant family. I was able to leave with the soldiers as they arrived."

Getts stopped writing. "Did you see any combat?"

"Yeah."

The reporter's mouth opened. "And?"

"It was bad."

"Can you go into some details?"

"It was *real* bad."

Getts sighed, rolling his eyes. "Did you see the Germans?"

Samuel stared out the window. "I saw a lot of Germans, son. Lot of them. So did you get what you wanted about my boy, too?"

Getts stood straight and nodded. "I sure did. The photos you gave me will work out fine. I'm supposed to talk with your son on the phone day after tomorrow. We'll make our deadline in time for Veterans Day. Should be quite the spread. Might even get picked up by the wire. Anything you'd like to add?"

Samuel thought a moment, his memories drifting onto Maria and Charles screaming as the Germans violated their home. He thought of their disappearance the day after the house had burned to the ground. He thought of the men dying on the bomber, the explosions and screaming filling his mind. He wondered what his son had seen, the horrors of jungle fighting on the other side of the world to achieve an uncertain objective. He knew it was something James would never share, deciding to hold it within the same way he had done for two decades.

"No," he whispered, his eyes locking with the young reporter. "I can't think of a thing."

*****

Samuel brought the small Christmas tree in from the sidewalk in front of the store. A frigid wind had scared away any potential last minute Christmas shoppers. Downtown looked like a ghost town. Besides, it was two days until Christmas and Malissa was waiting for him at home.

He started fiddling with the register, shaking off the cold from outside. A figure moved in from the outside, the bells on front door jingling.

"Closing in a few minutes," he said, not looking up from counting the money. "Let me know if I can help."

"I certainly hope you can help."

"Let me know," he said, his eyes still on the register.

"Are you the man in the article?" the man asked, a slight accent to his voice.

Samuel looked at the stranger, his back toward the counter as he stared at the framed Veterans Day article the ladies from the Post Office had given him. He and James dominated the front page. The article had appeared in newspapers across the country. Or at least, that's what everyone in Bloomsdale said. James received a little recognition for being the only volunteer to go to Vietnam from his class.

"That's my son, yes."

"No, Monsieur. The other man in the article."

Samuel dropped the money. The man turned in slow motion. His mouth opened as he took off the black wool hat. He saw the dark eyes, the round face.

"*Charles?*" Samuel breathed. "Is it you?"

Somehow, the boy he knew in France had become a man. And he was standing in Samuel's store.

"Oui." He smiled, his grin filling his face. "It is me. Charles Durant."

Samuel stepped around the counter, studying the man. "It's really you? I don't believe it."

"Oui." He nodded, his eyes filling with tears. "We thought you were dead. The house had exploded. Soldiers were everywhere. We went into the woods."

"My, God! Charles!" Samuel rushed forward, embracing the young man. "You're alive. Thank, God! You're alive. Where's Maria?"

Charles frowned. "It is a little cold to fish like we once did, but let us have a talk."

"Can you come to my home? Do you have time?"

"No." He shook his head. "Can we talk here?"

*****

Samuel brought out an old card table and two metal folding chairs from the stock room. They sat in front of the counter and Samuel listened to Charles's story.

Maria Durant had taken her brother Charles toward the Allied lines and lived out the rest of the war in a refugee camp. When the war ended, she found work in the city while Charles went back to school. When Charles saw the Veterans Day article in the paper, he knew he had to find Samuel.

"We never forgot you, Sam," Charles said, looking at the table. "After Maria married, we didn't talk about you anymore for fear of embarrassing Jonathan. But I know you were Maria's first, true love."

Samuel blinked. "Her husband?"

"Oui."

"I would like to write her if you don't mind."

Charles sighed. "My sister passed away three years ago. She had the cancer. It, fortunately, was quick. I miss her so."

Samuel's eyes welled up as he remembered the frightened young girl in the farmhouse. "I am so sorry to hear that."

"Thank you. She would have loved to have heard from you. We both thought you were dead. I am so happy you were not." He sighed. "We never talked to anyone about what happened on the farm. Some things are better left in the past."

Samuel cleared his throat. "What about you?"

"In New York for business," he said with a smile. "I work in banking."

He smiled, looking at the young man. "I am proud of you."

"Thank you." He leaned forward on the table. "I spent all these years thinking you had died to protect us, thinking I could never have the chance to tell you in person how much you meant to me. I looked up and told the heavens so many times. Now, I am here because I wanted to express my gratitude, Sam. I wanted to thank you for my life and the life of my sister. We would not be here if it weren't for you. My children would not be here."

Samuel smiled, the reason for Charles's journey becoming clear. He hadn't wanted to become reacquainted—he had wanted to thank him.

"I didn't do anything you wouldn't have done," Samuel said.

"Yes." Charles smiled. "You did so much. God bless you. You are a good man, Samuel Wrightman. A good man." He abruptly stood. "I came here to tell you that. I did not want to spend my life regretting this chance. Oh, and of course, Merry Christmas."

Samuel stood and shook his hand. "Merry Christmas to you, Charles."

35

The train stopped. The passengers stood and stretched. The summer heat of Georgia swept into the train car.

The younger man stood and slung his pack on his back. "You need any help, sir?"

He grabbed his small bag from under the seat and wiped his eyes. "I think I've got it, son."

The young man nodded. "Never did catch your name, sir."

He extended his hand. "Name's Sam."

Their hands clasped. "Sam, I'm Ryan."

Ryan smiled, nodding and walking down the aisle behind the other passengers. Samuel watched him go.

"Hey," he said, his voice cracking. He cleared his throat. "Hey, Ryan?"

Ryan turned.

"Good luck at school, son."

Ryan gave a thumb's up before he got swept down the aisle with the rest of the exiting passengers. Samuel turned back to the window and watched the hectic traffic around the train station.

The oppressive heat took him by surprise when he stepped off the train. The crowds zipped around him. He tried to stay out of their way.

People moved so fast. He went to grab his luggage and check for a taxi.

He pulled out the letter from Malissa, checking the time and date for the big day.

The train station reminded him of the last time he'd been there. It hadn't changed much since …

*****

The crowds surged across the grass, students embraced, laughed, cheered and tossed their caps around. The overcast day still brought the heat of summer.

The crowd of the Class of Seventy-Eight parted. Samuel watched his daughter from a distance, observed the other girls in caps and gowns speaking with her. They all seemed to light up as they spoke to her as everyone did. Malissa's smile was returned—it had always been contagious. Some of the boys walked by to wish her luck at the University of Georgia in the fall. Samuel leaned against a tree at the edge of the field, watching his daughter enjoy the moment.

He snapped a photo from a distance, wondering if it would come out. He would have to send one to James in Saint Louis, who had been wrapping up finals and unable to attend the graduation. He thought of Joe and Annie on their graduation day. Joe's wild, enthusiastic speech, and Annie Ruth looking so wonderful. Had it really been so long ago?

Malissa stood on the tips of her toes and searched the crowd. Samuel held his hand high, and she waved. She ran toward him. He opened his arms and embraced his daughter.

"I did it, Daddy," she said into his ear.

God, she sounds like her Mother.

"I always knew you would, darling. Always."

They parted. Her eyes appeared glassy, and the grin seemed to fade slightly.

"What's wrong, honey?" he asked.

She shook her head. "Nothing, Daddy."

"You know me better than that." He reached out to touch her cheek, brushing a rebellious strand of hair back behind her ear. He managed a smile. "I wish she was here, too."

Malissa nodded and stared down at her feet.

Maybe she felt the same way I did today, he thought.

He remembered faking the smiles, the greetings and the farewells from people he knew he would never speak to again, clenching his teeth through all the pretended promises of getting together that summer. Besides Joe, he had seen a handful of those he had graduated with but never spent any time with them.

He touched Malissa's chin and tilted her head toward him. "You want to go home?"

"Please," she said, her chin quivering.

Samuel opened the old truck's door. The door creaked in protest. He helped Malissa into the truck, and the springs on the seat made little noises as she sat down. She waved toward a few of her classmates. Samuel did the same to parents as he climbed into the truck. He sighed as he gripped the steering wheel and enjoyed the relative peace.

Some idiot honked nearby, and a Ford Mustang full of rowdy boys screeched out of the nearby parking lot. Samuel shook his head. "You know them?"

"Kind of." Malissa stared down at her hands.

He grabbed her knee and smiled. "You know I'm so proud of you, don't you?"

"Yes."

"Your Mama would have been proud, too."

Malissa stared at him, her eyes full. "Thank you for everything, Daddy." She leaped over the cab and grabbed him by the neck. "I love you."

Father and daughter embraced in the parking lot as the world swirled by them. The sun beat down on the truck, but neither of them noticed the heat.

*****

Samuel signed the final paper.

"It's done," Attorney David Drake said as he swept all the papers into a blue folder. "How does it feel?"

Samuel stared at the law books around the room, the shiny wood table, and the window with the view of downtown Bloomsdale. "Feels fine."

"Fine?" Drake blew air out his nose and crumpled his face behind his thick glasses. "You just made a heap of money by selling your house and business in the same week. You sold that beat up truck. I thought you'd be dancing or crying … or something."

Samuel stood and took his checks. "I never really wanted the store to begin with. And the house, that was for Annie."

He nodded and left the room.

He walked toward the train station, thought of Malissa about to finish her first year of school at UGA. She had been able to secure a summer job there in Athens helping young children with their reading. Once Samuel realized James and Malissa weren't coming home for the summer, he suddenly didn't understand why he was staying. Malissa seemed to understand and said she wanted her father to be happy. Samuel knew Malissa was starting her own life in Athens. James had written all about his new life and love, Lori, in Saint Louis. Neither of them had any reason to return to Bloomsdale.

And he no longer had any reason to stay.

He passed the store, standing for a long moment in front of the doors. The empty shelves remained as did the small "closed sign" on the door. The rest of the building was empty except for the memories. He thought he could see Pa standing at the counter. Young James sweeping the floor. Annie coming by for lunch with an excited Max on a leash.

Gone now, forever in the past.

And those days would never come again.

He turned away and didn't look back as he walked.

Sweat glistened from his forehead as he strolled toward the train station. He took off his father's old farming hat, wiping his face on the sleeve of his shirt. He thrust his hand into his pocket to grab some change and deposited coins into the pay phone. He dialed the number, turning as a group of boys sped by in a Camaro. He listened as the phone rang.

"Chad Murdock, can I help you?" the phone crackled.

"Yes, Chad. Hey, it's Sam. I'm at the train station and going to board in a little while. Should be on my way."

Murdock laughed, and the phone line crackled. "You sure you don't want to fly out here? Montana's a long ways."

"Oh, yeah, I'm sure."

"All right, we'll see you when you get out here. Travel safe. We're looking forward to having you here."

Samuel hung up and sat on the bench, the same bench he had last seen James awaiting his train that would eventually lead him to Vietnam. His son never truly returned from that place.

Samuel ran his weathered fingers across the wooden bench, thinking of his son shaking his leg. He sighed and turned away. In the distance, Hawkridge Mountain loomed in the morning light. He stared at the mountain's shape as it seemed to watch over Bloomsdale. It had changed over the years. Radio towers popped up on the peak.

Samuel leaned back on his hands and watched the traffic, saw the people rushing to their jobs, to the lake or just plain hurrying. The traffic swept by at a steady pace, the streets busier than they had been when he dropped off James.

The train rumbled up, brakes snapping and hissing. The train squeaked to a stop. Samuel took one last look at Hawkridge Mountain, and climbed on the train, his muscles already aching from the walk to the station.

3 6

■■■■■■

Samuel watched the wind move the leaves in the tall hardwoods outside the church. People spoke around him in soft voices, only one he cared about.

"Daddy?"

Samuel turned, and his jaw dropped. Malissa stood in the doorway of his room. The white dress flowed around her.

"You look beautiful, sweetheart."

"Thank you, Daddy." She held her arm out.

Samuel nodded and stood. He straightened the tie on his tuxedo, brushing his arms and looking questioningly at Malissa.

She laughed. "You look very handsome, Daddy."

"I haven't been in a tux since...well, in a long time."

She nodded. "The ladies are going to be going ga-ga over you."

"Oh?" Samuel yanked a black plastic comb from his pocket and ran it through the sides of his hair. He slipped the comb back into his pocket and wrapped her arm into his own.

"Now," he said as he tapped the top of her hand, "you sure you want to do this?"

"Yes, Daddy. Why?"

"Just doing my job." Samuel stared at the white doors of the back of the church and nodded to the attendants.

Malissa gripped his arm tightly, and Samuel thought of the countless times she had done that very same thing. At Annie Ruth's funeral, her first day of school, when they had lunch with Mr. Bear in the backyard. He looked at her, noticing the perfect skin and gorgeous hair she received from her mother.

What would my life have been without you?

She turned to him, smiling. Samuel turned back to the doors as they opened to reveal a room full of faces he didn't recognize except for James, who stood smiling with the other groomsmen. The wedding march played, and they stepped forward. The crowd stood and whispered of her beauty.

Nothing would be the same after this.

He would no longer be the only man in her life. It would be up to Patrick to take care of her, to make bad days better. Samuel's life, as he knew it, would never be the same again. Tomorrow, he would return to Bozeman alone. He fought the lump in his throat.

When they reached the end of this aisle, she would no longer be his.

But for now, for these last few steps, they walked as father and daughter, as they had so many times before.

He relished each step, rubbing the top of her hand with his own.

Samuel smiled at Patrick as they walked toward him. He thought about how thankful he was for the life he had with Annie. He had regrets, but wouldn't change one mistake. He thought about how pleased he was his children both found someone to share their lives with. He thought about how proud Annie Ruth would be at this moment if she were here.

"Who gives this woman to be married to this man?" The preacher asked Samuel.

"Her mother and I."

Malissa turned to her father and gave him a gentle kiss on the cheek.

THE END